"Dreams are highly overrated," Nick said.

"We only say that when we've lost them," Melissa quietly countered.

Listening to her quiet voice, absorbing her quiet understanding, he felt none of the burning in his gut that usually accompanied thoughts of the simultaneous dissolution of his marriage and business. Touching her seemed to relieve that effect.

"What would you do if we *couldn't* get back?"

His unexpected question made her go still. She frowned into the darkness.

"I'm not even going to consider such a possibility. You promised you'd get me home."

Curious, she couldn't help but ask, "What would *you* do?"

For a moment he said nothing. Then she felt his hands slip from her leg. An instant of disappointment collided with the feel of his hands cupping her face.

Her utter trust in him was balm for his bitter soul.

"This," he murmured, and lowered his mouth to hers.

Dear Reader,

Breeze into fall with six rejuvenating romances from Silhouette Special Edition! We are happy to feature our READERS' RING selection, *Hard Choices* (SE#1561), by favorite author Allison Leigh, who writes, "I wondered about the masks people wear, such as the 'good' girl/boy vs. the 'bad' girl/boy, and what ultimately hardens or loosens those masks. Annie and Logan have worn masks that don't fit, and their past actions wouldn't be considered ideal behavior. I hope readers agree this is a thought-provoking scenario!"

We can't get enough of Pamela Toth's WINCHESTER BRIDES miniseries as she delivers the next book, *A Winchester Homecoming* (SE#1562). Here, a world-weary heroine comes home only to find her former flame ready to reignite their passion. MONTANA MAVERICKS: THE KINGSLEYS returns with Judy Duarte's latest, *Big Sky Baby* (SE#1563). In this tale, a Kingsley cousin comes home to find that his best friend is pregnant. All of a sudden, he can't stop thinking of starting a family…with her!

Victoria Pade brings us an engagement of convenience and a passion of *in*convenience, in *His Pretend Fiancée* (SE#1564), the next book in the MANHATTAN MULTIPLES miniseries. Don't miss *The Bride Wore Blue Jeans* (SE#1565), the last in veteran Marie Ferrarella's miniseries, THE ALASKANS. In this heartwarming love story, a confirmed bachelor flies to Alaska and immediately falls for the woman least likely to marry! In *Four Days, Five Nights* (SE#1566) by Christine Flynn, two strangers are forced to face a growing attraction when their small plane crashes in the wilds.

These moving romances will foster discussion, escape and lots of daydreaming. Watch for more heart-thumping stories that show the joys and complexities of a woman's world.

Happy reading!

Karen Taylor Richman,
Senior Editor

Please address questions and book requests to:
Silhouette Reader Service
U.S.: 3010 Walden Ave., P.O. Box 1325, Buffalo, NY 14269
Canadian: P.O. Box 609, Fort Erie, Ont. L2A 5X3

Four Days, Five Nights

CHRISTINE FLYNN

SPECIAL EDITION™

Published by Silhouette Books

America's Publisher of Contemporary Romance

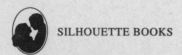

SILHOUETTE BOOKS

ISBN 0-373-24566-1

FOUR DAYS, FIVE NIGHTS

Copyright © 2003 by Christine Flynn

Printed in U.S.A.

Books by Christine Flynn

CHRISTINE FLYNN

admits to being interested in just about everything, which is why she considers herself fortunate to have turned her interest in writing into a career. She feels that a writer gets to explore it all and, to her, exploring relationships—especially the intense, bittersweet or even lighthearted relationships between men and women—is fascinating.

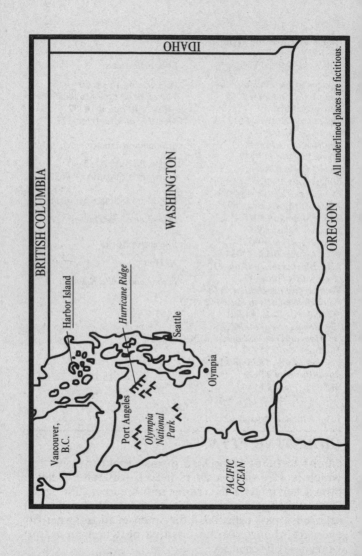

All underlined places are fictitious.

Chapter One

It was time to go home. Past time. He had put it off long enough.

Nick Magruder ignored the knot the thought put in his gut as he strode across the tarmac of the tiny Harbor Island airport. The crisp sea air filled his lungs. The cool October breeze ruffled his dark hair. He had been seeking escape when he'd headed for the relative seclusion of the San Juan Islands in northwest Washington, but he'd never intended to stay. Certainly not as long as he had.

It had already been six months.

Reaching the tail of the plane, he dropped his bag by the boxes he'd carried there earlier and opened the aft cargo door.

He was going to miss this place. The people. The freedom. But things were beginning to get complicated. He had found the escape he'd sought when he'd looked up Sam Edwards, an old buddy from flight school, and learned that the guy was short a pilot. The charter airline Sam co-owned with his partner, Zack McKendrick, had them working day and night to keep up their schedules. With nothing else he wanted to do, Nick had stuck around to help them out—which had worked out fine until Sam asked if he would be interested in staying on and buying into the business himself.

Nick had told him that he really loved the flying. He liked working with both men, too. But he'd never intended to remain. Sam knew that. Nick had left a lot unfinished when he'd headed there, and he had his own business to resurrect.

Sam hadn't pressed. But Nick had the feeling he'd been about to. That was why he'd told them a few days ago that he was leaving now that their busy season was over. He had no business letting his roots grow any deeper there. Especially since it wasn't only Sam hinting that he should stay.

Just yesterday, Maddy, the local café's loquacious owner, had suggested that he pay a call on the new woman on the island. The lady had arrived three days ago, a veterinarian from Los Angeles who had apparently tended the pets of the rich and famous in Beverly Hills.

Maddy—a redheaded busybody with a huge heart—had been possessed of some ''feeling'' that he and Dr. Melissa Porter would hit it off well. Mrs. Sykes, the mayor's wife, had walked into the café and into their conversation just then and immediately informed him that Maddy had ''feelings'' about anyone single and breathing and insisted that he'd be wasting his time going after the newcomer. What he needed to do was find himself a nice local girl because the woman who'd taken over the old vet's practice wasn't going to last out the winter. Not only was she terribly young, she had never practiced on her own and had no experience at all tending the injured wildlife Doc Jackson had always included in his practice. The mayor's wife had also been suspicious of the new vet's reasons for taking the job. It was her contention that a woman didn't move that far from everything familiar unless she was running away from a man. Or looking for one.

Nick's only thought on the subject was that there were other reasons a person might seek such distance. But he'd kept that observation to himself. Dr. Melissa Porter wasn't his problem. And, since the mayor's wife wanted to introduce him to her niece, and Maddy wanted to match him up with the good doctor, it was definitely time to move on.

The only thing he had to do before he could do just that was deliver the plane he was loading to the aviation mechanic in Seattle who did Sam's yearly maintenance inspections.

Edgy, hating the feeling, he picked up a box containing parts of the plane's fuel pump that had been changed out and lifted it into the open cargo hold. He truly didn't care about anything other than getting the leaving part over with. Now that he'd decided that was what he was going to do, all he wanted was to get back to Denver, deal with everything he'd walked away from and get on with his life. He'd put it on hold long enough.

He reached for the box containing the farewell gifts of island memorabilia his friends had given him last night, then turned when a flash of crimson on the narrow airport road snagged his attention. A red truck with a cargo top pulled to a stop by the hangar an instant before a petite blonde wearing a baseball cap, jeans and a quilted vest darted into the office.

He knew the office was empty. Sam had taken off at dawn on a mail run that took him to a dozen of Washington state's more remote islands. Zack had left shortly after him on a charter to Anchorage. The secretary that the men had finally broken down and hired was on a long lunch break. The fifty-something former police dispatcher from Tacoma had left a note on the pilot's bulletin board saying she had an appointment to dye her roots that she'd forgotten about. Since she knew Nick was flying out about now, he suspected she just didn't want to have to say goodbye again.

He actually appreciated that she hadn't been there. He was going to miss the tough old gal, but he was lousy at goodbyes, too.

The woman who had bounced into the office, bounced right back out—and headed straight toward him since he was the only person around.

"Excuse me?" he heard her call as he lifted in the box and climbed in after it.

"Hi," she said, flashing a smile when he glanced from his crouch inside the hold. "I'm Melissa Porter. Mel," she amended. Her glance skimmed the side of the six-passenger plane, taking in the E&M Air Carriers logo emblazoned in blue below the two side windows. Except for two private planes parked farther away, there was no other aircraft in sight. "I have a flight to the Olympic Peninsula at one forty-five. Is this my plane?"

She hadn't had to identify herself. Even if he hadn't seen her name on the day's flight schedule, he would have known who she was by the long ponytail swinging out the back of her cap. That sun-streaked hair screamed California blonde.

His eyes distractedly swept her face. Beneath the brim of her khaki-colored cap, her features were as delicate as a cameo, her skin as fine as porcelain. With her eyes obscured by blue-tinted sunglasses, he couldn't tell what color they were, but her lips were lush and a shade of ripe peach that practically begged to be tasted. The rumors were right. She was cute. Very cute. And young.

"Sorry. This plane is going to Seattle."

"Not the peninsula?"

"Sorry," he repeated, and turned to snap security straps into place to keep the little load from shifting. "Sam's your pilot. I'm sure he'll be here soon."

He double-checked the clips, gave the load a shove to make sure it wasn't going anywhere. After he delivered the plane, he would grab a ride to the main terminal at SeaTac. The maintenance facility was on the airport property. Since his flight wasn't until six o'clock, he had plenty of time to catch a shuttle.

"How soon?"

"Pardon?"

"How soon will Sam be here?"

He plucked a number out of the air. "Within the hour, I'd imagine. Make yourself comfortable in the office."

Figuring that should appease her, he turned to the cargo door, braced his hands on its threshold and moved from a crouch to standing upright on the asphalt.

She hadn't budged. She was also smaller than he'd first thought.

The top of her head barely reached his shoulders.

"Do you think it will be that long? I'm meeting a forest ranger to take him some animals. They're being relocated," she explained, pulling off her sunglasses so she could see him better. "I don't know how long he'll wait if I'm not there on time, and if he doesn't wait, I'll have to bring the animals back and reschedule."

"Give Sam a while." This was not his problem, but even as restive as he felt, she was doing a fair job of intruding on his preoccupation. Her eyes were blue, a soft azure blue that reminded him of the forget-me-nots that had grown by his grandmother's back porch. It was the directness of her gaze that threw him, though. And the concern in it. Both made her look older than she had first appeared with that carefree swath of golden silk swaying behind her head. ''He'll be here.''

Small gold studs gleamed from her ears as she tipped her head toward the sky. With one hand holding the brim of her cap, she glanced from east to west. Seeing nothing but ocean on one side and distant treetops on the other, she checked out north and south and everywhere in between.

The only things visible were seagulls.

She followed him to where he'd crouched by one of the plane's tires.

''My flight is scheduled to leave in ten minutes.''

''This is a charter service,'' Nick muttered, dislodging a rubber tire stop so he could get his own little show on the road. ''Schedules tend to be a little loose around here.''

''Well, my schedule's a little tight at the moment,'' she countered, her easy smile keeping her tone friendly. ''Really tight, actually.''

''I'm sure he won't keep you waiting long.''

''But we can't leave in ten minutes,'' she concluded, the smile faltering.

Nick didn't even glance up. ''Probably not.''

''When he does get here,'' she prodded, not seeming to note, or care, that he was busy, ''how long will it be before I can leave?''

The narrow edge of the hard rubber block holding the wheel in place was jammed. Jerking hard, Nick finally released it. As he did, he scraped his knuckles on the rough tarmac and swore under his breath. He really wished she would go away. Her presence was distracting. ''That depends on whether or not he has to refuel.''

Melissa wasn't sure what it was that made her not ask how long that particular process might take—the man's succinct responses, or the tension she could feel radiating like heat from his big body.

There was a sense of brooding about him. Or impatience. She wasn't sure which because he was actually being quite cooperative with his answers, distressing as they were. There was no denying that he was attractive, though. His dark hair was clipped stylishly close, and the angular lines of his cheekbones and jaw gave him a lean, hungry look that would have had the female population of Beverly Hills going Pavlovian at the sight of him. From the way his denim shirt fit his broad shoulders and his khakis hugged his lean hips, she would be willing to bet her new hiking boots that he spent some serious time in a gym or chopping wood or doing whatever it was men did in this out-of-the-way little community to keep in such excellent shape.

She didn't quite know what to make of him, though. The tension surrounding him was unnerving, and that made her even more uneasy than she already felt. Obviously, she thought, the airline hired him for his flying ability. Not his public relations skills.

She took a peek at her watch, looked back to the air and thought about pacing. She really needed her pilot to be here. The last thing she needed was another complication right now. Arranging for relocation on such short notice had practically required an act of Congress, but she'd learned in a hurry where the red tape could be cut. Because she'd managed the relocation so soon, she'd had to postpone lunch with the mayor's wife, something she'd hated to do because she wanted badly not to make any wrong impressions on her new neighbors. More trouble-some was that, less than an hour ago, her nineteen-year-old half sister had called begging to see her. Cameron had sounded frantic. That actually wasn't unusual at all for Cameron. With her, everything was a crisis. But Cam had decided that this particular crisis absolutely could not wait until tomorrow and was arriving today on the five o'clock ferry.

It was now 1:37.

She was to meet Ranger Wyckowski at 2:15.

The knot of anxiety in her stomach grew another layer. She'd never met the ranger before, only spoken with him on the phone. But she would have to work with him in the future. After the way he'd rushed to get her the tiny tracking chips the Department of Wildlife Management wanted implanted in her furry patients, the least she could do was not make him wait for her.

Then, there was the welfare of the animals themselves.

The hunk with the less-than-approachable manner walked around the high tail of the little aircraft. Following him, she watched him crouch beside the other front wheel.

"Is there any chance you could take us?" She dutifully disregarded the fact that he was ignoring her. She also made a concerted effort not to think about the irony of what she was doing. She hated to fly. Yet, she was ac-tually trying to hurry something she would have normally avoided like the plague. "I understand it only takes about twenty minutes to get there. And I'll pay extra," she con-ceded, deciding paint for the old office shelving could wait another couple of weeks. "If I have to reschedule, it's going to be bad for the animals. They've already been around humans longer than they should have been."

She thought she saw him sigh. "I'm taking this plane

to Seattle for servicing. Sorry," he repeated, pulling out the other block.

"The peninsula isn't that far from Seattle, is it? It'll only take me a few minutes to turn them over to the ranger."

"The peninsula is hundreds of miles of shoreline and a few thousand square miles of land," he replied, not at all impressed by how quickly she could accomplish her task. "Even if I knew exactly where you needed to go, it's not as if I could take you on the way. I'd have to bring you back."

She hadn't thought of that.

"They're coyote pups," she told him, thinking he might be more cooperative if he were privy to details. "Orphans," she explained, "but they're already half-grown. Which technically makes them juveniles," she conceded, "but they're still without their pack. A woman here has been taking care of them, and she's done a wonderful job of keeping them healthy, but they need to be in the wild. The last thing I want is for them to be shot by someone because they lost their wariness of people and wandered into someone's camp." She ducked her head, trying to see his eyes. "I'm sure you wouldn't want that, either."

She was trying to appeal to his basic sense of humanity. What she received for her effort was a look so piercing that the impact had her taking a cautious step back.

Clamping one hand on his powerful thigh, he rose, towering over her in a way that nearly had her backing up even farther. His eyes were the color of old pewter, a silvery gray that threatened to turn into the dangerous slate of a thundercloud at any given moment. The lines fanning from their corners deepened against the glare of the sun.

Nick's glance hardened her face, displeasure mirrored in his own. He recognized manipulation when he heard it. He resented the hell out of it, too. His ex-wife was a master at that little game.

The thought of his ex tightened his jaw. He didn't know which annoyed him more. This persistent wisp of a woman reminding him of the woman he'd divorced six months ago. Or her blatant attempt to pull his strings.

He'd decided it was a draw when the concern in her wary eyes registered. She wasn't anything like his ex. Ellen hadn't cared about anyone but herself. Melissa Porter was asking for his help for a couple of coyote pups.

He stayed annoyed with her anyway. She'd just put the decision about their welfare into his hands whether he wanted it there or not.

"You said a woman around here had them," he reminded her flatly. "Any chance she's Sam Edwards's wife?"

"T.J." The hesitant way she watched him seemed to ease a little as she identified the woman Sam had married last year. "Yes. She is. She has cages built into her woods for animals she rescues. People even bring injured animals to her." She looked as impressed as she sounded. She also looked as if he probably already knew what T.J. did. He worked with Sam, after all. "She was so worried about these pups becoming too acclimated that she came to me about them the day I arrived." She paused, looking uneasy about pushing again, but doing it anyway. "It really could mean their lives."

Nick appeared unmoved. He already had the picture. The animals needed to be in their own habitat. But what he really cared about at the moment was that Sam's wife had a vested interest in the doctor's cargo.

With all that had gone so wrong in the past year, he'd

learned who his true friends were. And he was nothing if not loyal to his friends.

Without a word, he turned his back on the woman in the ball cap, headed up the wing to open the cockpit door and hoisted himself into the pilot's seat. After slipping on headphones, he flipped the radio's controls to Sam's frequency.

"It's Nick," he said as soon as the crackle gave way to Sam's voice. "How far out are you? I have your 1:45 flight waiting."

"Hey, buddy," came the immediate reply. "I thought you'd already gone. I've been trying to raise the shack," Sam continued, referring to the office. "Where's Ruth?"

"Avoiding me. I'm sure she'll get here as soon as I leave. I'm planning to do that in about five minutes," he added, knowing he didn't need to explain about the secretary's absence. Sam knew how sentimental she was behind her gruff exterior. "What about your one forty-five? What do you want me to tell her?"

It took a little repeating because Sam's voice kept cutting out, but the upshot was that he would be another hour. He'd had to wait for the mail truck in Anacortes so he could complete his mail run and was just leaving his sixth stop. It was his intention to head in, deliver Dr. Porter and her cargo and finish the mail run later.

"Unless you can take her before you drop off the plane," he heard Sam continue over the crackle and hiss on the line. "It would take you about an hour to get there and back. She's going just south of Hurricane Ridge on the peninsula. The North Fork River station. I know you want to get on your way. And I hate to ask," came the deep voice, "but it would really help me out. It's Andy's birthday, and T.J.'s getting a cake…"

Nick had forgotten about the little celebration for Sam's

new stepson. T.J. had even invited him, including him in their family gatherings much as Zack and his wife did theirs.

That was just one more reason to get out of Harbor, he thought. His friends here had good marriages. Families they cared about. Thriving businesses that demanded their attention. He was just hanging on the periphery.

He would rather swim to Seattle than take this little detour. "Consider it done," he said to his friend.

"Thanks, Nick. And thanks for dropping off the plane, too."

"Hey. It's a win-win." He had to go to Seattle anyway to catch his flight. "It saves you having to fly me there."

"Doesn't matter. I appreciate the favor. You take care. Okay?"

Nick said that he would, signed off and looped the headset over the visor. Several long seconds passed before he moved. When he did, he drew a deep breath and ran his hand over his face. He really didn't want to have to deal with anything else right now. He especially didn't want to deal with a type-A from Los Angeles who looked like a cheerleader, was as persistent as a gnat and who already knew which of his buttons to push.

His hand fell as he blew out a long breath of frustration. Sam was one of the few people on the planet that he still trusted. And though Sam and his partner were under the impression that Nick had helped them out by flying for them all these months, Nick knew that the months he'd spent hauling their passengers and cargo had probably saved his sanity.

Levering himself between the seats to the door, he headed back down the wing and motioned toward where she'd parked her truck. He didn't want to have to feel guilty about what might happen to her animals, either.

''They're caged, right?''

He didn't know how much of his conversation she'd heard, but since she hadn't heard at least half of it, she looked a little uncertain about what was going on. ''Of course.''

''How big are they?''

''The pups?''

''And the cages. I need a total weight.''

''It's actually only one cage. It's maybe ten pounds and the pups are right at twenty pounds apiece.''

He eyed her evenly. A twenty-pound coyote was not exactly his idea of a puppy. The fact that she referred to them that way told him more about her nurturing side than he figured he needed to know. His only interest was in weight distribution in the plane. Fifty pounds of canine and cage could easily be stowed behind the passenger seats.

''Let's get them loaded, then. While you're backing up your vehicle to the plane, I'll get some coordinates. What's the North Fork River station?''

''I understand it's just a ranger station with a landing strip.'' Confusion, or maybe it was consternation, shadowed her face. ''You're taking me?''

He supposed he had forgotten to mention that. ''I'm taking you.''

He didn't expect her smile. But it was suddenly there, catching him off guard with its brightness. ''Thank you,'' she murmured, backing away. ''Thank you,'' she repeated, shaking her head as if she didn't quite believe he'd caved in. ''I really appreciate this.''

''No problem,'' he replied, resigned, and headed back into the cockpit to look at his maps and figure out where he was now going.

Sam had said the whole trip would take an hour. Timing would be tight to catch his own flight, but it was doable.

"Very much!" he heard her call just before she turned to jog toward the hangar.

Melissa wasn't sure he had heard her, but she really needed him to know how grateful she was for what he was doing. Obviously, rank had been pulled. Or schedules traded. However it had come about, she wanted him to know how she appreciated his change of heart, voluntary or otherwise. As one of her new neighbors, she didn't want him thinking her rude.

That was why she thanked him again a few minutes later when she jumped out of the ten-year-old truck that had come with the clinic and quickly lifted the back window and lowered the tailgate.

She still sensed a finely tuned tension about him, but it seemed tempered now. Or maybe it was suppressed. His response was simply, "Forget it," before he narrowly eyed the sturdy, molded-plastic animal carrier.

The three-foot-high gray shell taking up the back of her vehicle bore the warning Live Animals on either side. The howl coming from inside it confirmed the claim. She had the feeling it was the howl that had him hesitating.

Through the front grid, one of the buff and brown fur balls could be seen sitting on his haunches, his head thrown back and his little black snout aimed at the ceiling. That one was only getting ready to join in. It was his littermate, darker, slightly smaller and wedged behind him, who was making the forlorn racket.

"I take it they're not tranquilized," her pilot said dryly.

"They need to be alert when they're released." Scooting to the front of the vehicle, she opened her driver's side door and pulled out the folder containing her paperwork. "T.J.'s husband said the flight isn't that long, and the ranger didn't want to have to wait for drugs to wear off before he could let them go.'' With her head still inside the vehicle, she shoved the file into her oversize shoulder bag. ''Since I had to tranquilize them yesterday to inject the tracking implants, I didn't want to subject them to more drugs again, anyway. Just a minute and I'll help you,'' she concluded, but he already had the carrier at the opening behind the wing of the plane.

The floor of the cargo hold was shoulder height, but he hefted the carrier and slid it inside with impressive ease.

Grabbing a strap hanging by the door, he hoisted himself inside. ''Are they going to keep this up the whole time?''

''They're agitated.''

The look he gave her said that wasn't what he'd asked.

''They could,'' she admitted, grabbing her water bottle off her console. ''They're in new territory and that's always hard for animals who aren't accustomed to roaming.'' Remembering the bottle of herbal pills she'd bought in case she got airsick, she grabbed those, too, then promptly hesitated. ''The flight is only about half an hour, isn't it?''

He didn't seem to notice the quick unease in her voice.

''Twenty-five minutes, by my calculations.'' Metal clips snapped into place as he secured the carrier behind the back passenger seats. ''If we get a tailwind, I might be able to get you there sooner. Give me your bag,'' he said, sticking his arm out the opening to take it. ''I'll stow it under your seat while you park your truck.''

The man clearly wasn't interested in wasting time—which was fine with her, considering how little of it she had herself before she needed to be back. By the time she returned from parking her car by the hangar, he was in the plane, its engine was running, its single propeller a blur. The drone from the engine either drowned out the pups or the sound had them curious enough to simply listen.

Either way, all she could hear when she reached the closed cargo door was the vibrating roar and the sudden nervous pounding of her pulse in her ears.

Nick appeared in the open doorway above the wing, bent at the waist and one hand braced against the four-foot-high ceiling. Sometime in the last few minutes, he'd pulled on a comfortably worn brown leather jacket that made his shoulders look a yard wide.

"Use the steps," he called, nodding to the retractable metal stairs hanging below the wing. "I put your bag under this seat here."

He motioned off to his side, to a place behind the front passenger seat. Melissa nodded back. And stayed right where she was. Since her sister had called, she hadn't had time to dwell on this particular aspect of her new position. She'd understood from the kindly old Dr. Jackson, when she'd spoken with him about his practice, that flying would be necessary if she truly wanted to serve the creatures of Harbor. It wasn't something that would be required often. Only for relocations when they arose and emergencies she couldn't handle alone.

She thought the Fates truly perverse to require it her first week on the job.

"Something wrong?"

"No. No," she insisted. Reluctance battling resignation, she deliberately flattened her hand against the fuselage and climbed the narrow little stairs. The cold white metal felt solid under her palm. Beneath her feet, the long, wide wing seemed sturdy. Both seemed to be good signs. "I was just trying to remember if I forgot anything." Like my sanity, she thought, and reached for the sides of the narrow doorway.

Her pilot angled sideways as she did to let her pass. Preferring to think she was gripping the edges of the wide door for leverage rather than bracing herself, she slipped past him, ducking her head as she did to avoid bumping it.

Her shoulder bumped his solid chest instead.

"Sorry," she mumbled.

"No problem" now seemed to be his response to everything. He murmured it again as he crouched to pull in the stairs, then closed the door with a decisive thud.

The plane wasn't quite as small as the others she'd noticed, but there was little room to maneuver. Since standing upright was out of the question, she'd sat where he had indicated as soon as she'd stepped inside. Pressing her spine into the high-backed seat to give him as much room as possible, she watched him angle his big body between the seats ahead of her and slide into the one on the left. His glance immediately swept the complex array of instruments on the panel in front of him, his concentration clearly on the switches and buttons he flipped and pressed.

"Are you ready back there?"

Her throat felt a little dry when she swallowed. "Whenever you are," she gamely replied, fumbling with her seat belt, clicking it into place.

"Isn't this where you introduce yourself?" Trying desperately to keep her mind off what she was about to do, she tightened the belt as snugly as she could without cutting off circulation to her legs. "You know? I'm so-and-so your captain. Welcome aboard and all that?"

Needing something to do with her hands now that she was belted in, she gripped the armrests. "I'm at a disadvantage here,'' she admitted. With you, especially, she thought, aware that he was now writing something in a log. ''A lot of the people I've already met seem to know who I am, but I haven't been here long enough to know who everyone else is.''

She'd encountered a fair number of the locals in the past three days. People who had kindly welcomed her. A few enthusiastically. Like T.J. Others with curiosity. Or clear reservations. All had dug for information about her. Some casually. Some with the obvious intention of finding skeletons. Most had offered bits and pieces of themselves. Not this guy, though.

All she got out of him was his name when he glanced through the narrow space between the two front seats.

''Nick Magruder,'' he dutifully supplied, checking to see that her seat belt was on. He looked from the buckle by her hip to her grip on the armrest before his unrevealing eyes met hers. ''Welcome aboard, Dr. Porter.''

''It's Melissa.'' She wanted to make friends on this island. Or, at least, to be friendly. ''Or, Mel.''

''Then, welcome aboard…Melissa.''

The faint smile he gave her was the kind dictated by latent sociability. Or, possibly, a nod to customer relations. Whichever it was, her quiet ''Thank you,'' seemed lost on him when he turned back to the confusing array of electronic gadgetry in front of him.

Not wanting to distract him from whatever it was he needed to do, she drew a deep breath and forced herself to release it to the count of ten.

She was on six when he revved the engine and the plane moved.

Relaxation techniques were forgotten. They were nearly to the end of the little runway when she began wondering just how experienced this Nick person was. But she'd no sooner told herself that she should have thought about that before she'd stepped onto the plane than he turned the plane on the proverbial dime, pulled back on the throttle and she felt her back being pressed against the seat.

They were already speeding down the narrow strip of asphalt. Thinking that the least he could have done was warn her that they were taking off now, she dug her nails into the covered arms of her seat.

Her intention to not distract him took a short break. "Don't you need to get instructions from the tower or something?" she asked, noticing the headphones he'd yet to put on.

"We don't have a tower here. We're flying VFR. Visual Flight Rules," he clarified, pulling back on the U-shaped yoke. "Don't worry," he said, sounding totally unconcerned. "The skies are crystal clear. We can see forever up there."

She wasn't sure she was breathing when she felt the plane lift off and the earth drop away below. But she didn't say a word. She wouldn't allow any outward sign to betray how anxious she felt just then. She had no power over anything at that moment except herself, and she was going to hang on to that questionable bit of command if it was the last thing she ever did.

The conclusion of that thought did nothing to ease her fears.

There were only two things that truly frightened her. Two she would let herself admit, anyway. Not being in control of a situation that had the potential to harm something or someone, and heights. She couldn't stand on the edge of anything over the height of a stepladder without feeling as if she would pitch right on over the side. Since pitching over the side wasn't possible with the plane's fuselage in the way, she figured fear of flying fell more into the control-issue category.

Conceding that, she sought distraction in the fact that in less than a minute they were already out over the ocean. Whitecaps formed on the waves, turning everything below her shades of pearl and gray.

"So, how long have you been flying, Nick?" she asked, thinking it best not to look out the window again.

Nick glanced out his window himself, checking for air traffic. He'd been wondering when she was going to breathe again.

"Since before I was old enough to get a driver's license." He saw no need to mention that, except for the past six months, most of the flying he'd done in the last several years had been in the back of a private jet. It had felt good to get behind the controls again, too—and actually do what he made possible for so many others by producing various systems aircraft used.

Had produced, he mentally corrected. His company had been shut down for months.

"So that's what? Twenty years?"

"Right at," he replied, aware of a familiar tightening in his gut. He would turn thirty-seven next month. As hard as he'd worked, he'd never dreamed he would be where he was now. He should have been at the peak of his game—not having to clean up the debris of his business and personal life and starting over again.

"So you'd know if this is normal, then?"

Ruthlessly shaking off his restive thoughts, he automatically noted his rate of climb, checked the altimeter, compass, horizon and turn-rate indicators. "If what is?"

"This bouncing. Are small planes always this bumpy?"

"This is smooth," he replied, only half conscious of the unease she was busily attempting to suppress. She was a nervous flier. Between the way she'd gone pale when she'd boarded, the way she hung on to her seat and the edge of nerves in her chatter, the clues would have been hard to miss. "There's hardly any turbulence at all."

"Oh."

"Everything is normal."

Her momentary silence spoke of doubt.

"Honest."

Preoccupied, he offered the assurance somewhat absently as he glanced toward the flight map he'd left open on the passenger seat.

Seattle lay south and a few degrees to the east. Trying not to think about how he could have been on his way there right now, he banked west, flying out over the densely forested islands dotting the ocean below and aimed for the peninsula somewhere off in the distance.

"I'll just have to get used to this, then," she replied a few moments later. "I knew I'd have to do some flying with this job, but I didn't expect to have to do it so soon. I took the ferry to the island when I first checked it out and when I moved," she confided, making it sound as if she avoided the air whenever possible. "Since this is the only way to get certain animals where they need to be, I guess I really don't have much choice."

The drone of the engine muffled her voice along with the alternating bark and whine of the pups. Still, it was impossible to miss her grudging resignation. He knew the feeling too well not to recognize it.

He also knew that people always had a choice. They may not like the alternatives, but the choice was eventually theirs. Thinking about the speculation he'd heard over whether or not she was up to handling the old doc's practice, he couldn't help wonder himself why she would take a job that involved something that so clearly frightened her.

Part of him was intrigued by the anomaly. Another part told him it was none of his business. Still, he was inclined to agree with the locals who felt she wouldn't last a year. Despite her practical clothes and tenacious manner, the woman looked as fragile as glass. Delicate. Feminine. He'd give her points for adding style to plain old denim and a ball cap, but if he had to bet, he'd give even odds that she wouldn't make it through the winter.

"Maybe I can talk the rangers into coming to me," he heard her muse. "Or do hypnosis."

He wasn't sure if she was talking to him or herself. All he knew for certain was that she was nervous and that she was doing her best to talk herself out of it. For both their sakes, he hoped she was succeeding. Distracted by the low reading on the fuel-pressure gauge, he didn't particularly care to deal with an hysterical passenger.

Listening to his silence, Melissa had the distinct feeling he didn't want to deal with her at all.

She watched him look out his side window, then back at his map and the gauges. She wasn't sure if he was frowning or if his natural expression tended to resemble a scowl, but it was apparent that he wasn't into conversation, idle or otherwise.

Taking a deep breath, she leaned back in her seat, repeated the personal mantra she'd adopted years ago. *There is an upside to everything.*

She had to believe that. It was how she'd learned to survive, though sometimes she'd really had to dig to find what that upside was. In this case, the good news was that the flight was short, which meant she didn't have to spend much more time in Nick Magruder's taciturn company.

Having found that slender silver lining, her thoughts

were immediately snagged by the little coyotes now barking behind her. Her instinct was to soothe them, to turn and assure them that everything was all right whether she believed it or not. It would have given her something to do, something positive and productive to focus on.

For their sakes, she made herself stay silent. She'd never relocated animals before, but she understood how important it was to keep them from bonding or identifying in any way with humans. They would have to seek their reassurance from each other.

As for her, she would simply have to do what she'd always done and find her reassurance inside herself. Once she got through this, she still had her sister to deal with.

She couldn't have imagined anything short of the Second Coming that could have taken her mind off where she was at that moment. But the thought of her sister's arrival did a fair job of trading one set of anxieties for another. There wasn't a shred of doubt in her mind that her half sibling had gotten herself into some kind of trouble again. The only question was how much it was going to cost in terms of time and dollars. The only time she ever heard from Cam was when there was a problem.

She doubted the crisis had anything to do with their mother. As of yesterday, their mom was still off the bottle, regularly attending AA and holding her own with her job as a waitress at the Waffle House. The place didn't serve alcohol, so Mel didn't have to worry about her being exposed to temptation as she had the last job she'd been fired from. Since her mom hadn't mentioned hearing from Cam, it was doubtful Cam had called her at all. Not that she ever did.

One of the pups jolted her with a sharp howl.

Between the high-pitched barking, thoughts of her family and the occasional buck of the plane, Mel could feel her nerves slowly begin to fray. She didn't care what Nick the Mute said about this being a smooth flight. The steady hum of the engine and the plane's little lifts and sways still reminded her that she was a couple thousand feet above sea level and that the sea was directly below her.

Five minutes inched past.

Land appeared in the distance, an immense swath of it that marked the edge of the continent and the eventual site of her destination. She hadn't intended to look out the window, but it was either that or study the profile of her pilot, and neither did much for her nerves.

Five more minutes slipped slowly by.

The view below her changed, ocean giving way to dense forest and mountains that stretched out as far as the eye could see. Nick's expression had remained much the same. It was beginning to worry her, too. The furrows in his brow seemed awfully deep for just a basically brooding disposition.

He kept frowning at the same gauge.

"Is everything all right?"

She expected him to do what he'd done before. To tell her everything was fine and go back to being silent.

Instead the furrows deepened. "I don't know," he said, tapping another gauge with his finger. "We're losing fuel pressure."

Her heart bumped her ribs. "What does that mean?"

He tapped again, then adjusted a switch.

Apparently his adjustment didn't give the desired result. He glanced out the window beside him, then over at the open map. "It means we're heading for the nearest landing strip."

"How far away is that?"

"Ten miles behind us."

The plane tipped as he started to bank. A lurching

heartbeat later, she felt a jerk as the engine sputtered. The sound was immediately drowned out by the screech of an alarm horn that pierced her ears and nearly stopped her heart.

A red light flashed above a plastic plate that read Stall Warn Fail. Nick slapped at a switch that silenced the blare and flipped another on the overhead panel. He hit it again, abruptly leveling out the plane out as he did.

Changing directions was no longer his priority. With his jaw locked, his mind clearly racing, Mel didn't dare distract him by asking what was. Not that she had the chance. She heard him swear just as their forward thrust abruptly slowed.

Her stomach felt as if it were suspended in air when the engine gave a final cough. That short popping sound had no sooner faded than another alarm started screaming and the propeller slowed, jerked and went still.

Chapter Two

Nick's first instinct was to yank back on the stick. Experience immediately overrode impulse. He had no power to correct an uncontrolled move. What he needed to do was keep his head, keep the nose up and not do anything to jeopardize the precious lift beneath the plane's wings.

Pulse pounding, he flipped off the nerve-jarring alarm and kept the plane steady while he tried to restart the engine.

He tried again.

Once more.

It was one thing to practice a stall. Another entirely to be in one.

His mind raced through emergency scenarios as he jerked his head toward the window. Heading back was impossible. Even if he'd had the altitude to glide in a full arc, there was no way he'd make it over the ridge they'd just crossed. Reaching the little airport he'd had in mind was out of the question.

With both hands gripping the yoke, he swept a hurried glance across the landscape. They were too far inland now for the ocean to be visible and nowhere near anything flat. Except for the postage-stamp-size lakes dotting the dense forest, every surface was either rocky mountain wall or equally unforgiving ground.

From behind him came the yowl of his cargo and his passenger's frozen silence. As nervous as she had already been, he fervently hoped she wouldn't go hysterical on him. He needed her right now. "What do you see out your side?"

"Trees," came her immediate, panicked reply. "And some little lakes."

Directly ahead of them lay a forested wall of mountain. He would lose even more altitude with a turn, but he had no desire to meet that mountain head-on.

"What about meadows?" he urged, banking right. "Bogs. Anything flat without trees. Look for brighter green."

"There's lighter green around the lakes," she hurriedly replied, her heartbeat racing, "but not very much."

"How big are they?"

"Not very. From here, the biggest looks about the size of a football field."

She grabbed his shoulder, the urgent feel of it jerking his glance to her face. He'd seen snow with more color. "They're over there," she said, straining forward to point around the front passenger seat.

With the plane banked, the horizon had disappeared and the forest filled the wide window. In the distance, two amoeba-shaped dots shone like liquid silver in the late afternoon sun. The lime-colored land surrounding them was probably algae. Even if it wasn't, the surface was nowhere near long or wide enough to set a plane on. He needed something bigger. Something without boulders or fallen logs. He also needed something a little farther out so he could glide rather than dive.

He checked the slowly descending altimeter. The good news was that planes didn't simply fall from the sky. The bad news was that they couldn't glide forever. Given his gradually slowing airspeed and altitude he figured his glide path was good for a mile or so at best—which gave him all of a minute to pull a miracle out of his hat.

"Keep looking."

"I am. But everything looks the same." There was no mistaking the quaver in her voice as she cupped her hands to the glass. "Why did the engine stop?"

"I'm guessing the problem is with the fuel line. Is your seat belt tight?"

She gave her belt another tug. "Is yours?"

He wasn't sure why her quick concern for him caught him off guard. But there was no time to consider it. There would be no miracle. It was strictly a case of making do with what he had to work with. As quickly as they were losing altitude, all he had to work with seemed to be another sliver of silver that appeared in the distance. It was narrower than the rest, but marginally longer. The land around it was totally obstructed, but the surface of the lake itself was as flat a surface as he was going to get. He'd take out trees on the way, but they were going to take out foliage no matter how they went down.

They also had a better chance of surviving if he crashed them in water. There'd be less chance of going up in a fireball.

The quaver in her voice became more pronounced. "I hate flying."

"I gathered that."

"I really hate heights, too."

"Height won't be a problem in a minute."

"Oh, Lord."

"Prayer is good."

His grip tightened. His tone went dead calm. "We're going in. Get your head down."

"In? In where?"

"There's a lake straight ahead."

"What about the animals?"

There was no time to answer her, much less do anything to make the yapping coyotes more secure. "Stay where you are," he barked, practically putting them into a dive so they wouldn't miss the lake. "Can you swim?" he called over the high-pitched whistle of air.

Swim? Can I swim? Mel thought, frantically reaching behind her with one hand to touch the carrier. It was too far back to reach. There wasn't a thing she could do to help her charges. It didn't seem there was much she could do to help herself, either. Her heart sinking at the thought, she wrapped her arms over her head.

"I never had a chance to learn," she confessed, dropping her forehead to her knees.

Over the rush of wind, she heard Nick swear again. She just didn't know if the terse expletive was for her lack of aquatic ability or because something else was going wrong.

Hoping desperately it was only because he thought her athletically impaired, she considered that there were actually lots of things she'd never had a chance to do. She'd never seen snow. Or been farther from home that the west coast.

She'd never had her own pet.

She'd never had a man love her.

She'd never had a child.

The list could have gone on, but there was no time to lament what might well not matter, anyway. The steep pitch of the plane had her stomach in her throat. Seconds later her stomach fell as the pitch leveled out even and the plane continued to drop. The coyotes must have felt the distressing effects, too. They went quiet moments before the plane jolted hard to the left with a horrific groan of ripping of metal and snapping tree limbs.

The bite of her seat belt had no sooner threatened to crack her hip bones before the plane bounced to the right, continuing forward, taking more limbs with it. It felt as if they were flying sideways, then straight again, jolting with the force of a freight train with every shift in direction.

She felt like a rag doll, being thrown around as she was. Keeping her head down was nearly impossible. As if in slow motion, she glimpsed Nick's handsome profile and his big hands, steady on the controls. The impression of sheer strength meeting grim determination seared in her mind an instant before the thunderous crashing suddenly stopped and water sprayed with the force of a fire hose against the crazed and cracking windows.

They were on the lake, skidding across the surface like a hockey puck on ice. But the scream she felt building in her throat ended as abruptly as the jolt that would have thrown her into the seat back in front of her if her belt hadn't held. She slammed backward with that same stunning force.

A box the size of a small suitcase sailed past her head. The sound of it bouncing off the instrument panel was lost amidst the cacophony of groaning metal and falling glass.

The sudden loss of motion had her arms falling from

her head. She couldn't see much with the box wedged as it was where part of the front window had been. Aware of Nick's incredibly competent hands sliding from the controls, she could tell only that they hadn't gone into the trees on the other side of the lake. Two huge, angular boulders had stopped them. The rumpled nose of the plane was wedged between those unforgiving chunks of basalt. She had no idea where the propeller blades were.

The rest of the plane was definitely floating, though. She could feel it bobbing beneath her as water rushed through the gaps ripped in the floor.

The rustle of leather joined the slosh and lapping of water as Nick ripped off his seat belt and twisted toward her. The sharp angles of his features were taut, his eyes narrowed as his glance hurriedly swept her face.

"Are you all right?"

She searched back, shaken to the core. "I'm…I think so," she said, shaking hard as she fumbled with her own seat belt. "Are you?"

"Everything still moves." Seeing that she was moving herself, Nick turned to open his door. They needed to be out of there. Now.

The door was jammed. Not surprising, he thought, considering there was a chunk of Douglas fir sticking through it. Shoving the limb aside, he rammed his shoulder against the door—and promptly winced when the contact reminded him that the piece of fir had nailed him on its way in. He could almost feel the colorful bruise blooming on his skin.

Pain radiated down his arm. Sweat popped out on his brow. Deciding not to use his shoulder for a battering ram again, he reached past the box wedged in the windshield and tried the passenger side.

He slammed that door open just as the woman in back disappeared behind the seats.

"Get out of here!" he yelled, crawling back after her.

"I have to get the pups!" Her head stayed bent over the carrier, her hands frantically tearing at the strap holding it in place. "How do I open this door?"

The back cargo door was a few feet behind her. So was the bubbling dark water as it edged closer to the carrier. Through the carrier's front grate, he could see the coyotes' remarkably sweet little faces. They had pushed their heads as close together as they could get them to check out the action. Their bright, inquisitive eyes fairly danced with curiosity.

"You can't get them out that way." Insistence sharpened his tone as he shoved down the back of the seat she had occupied. "Go! I'll take them out to the wing."

She totally ignored him. The part about getting herself out anyway. Her only response was to the animals as she freed the strap. Cooing to them that they would be all right, she crouched to muscle their hard plastic shelter through the space between the seats. Had she not been operating in a panic, she would have realized before her first shove that the space was too narrow.

Not feeling terribly calm himself, he shoved the carrier back, grabbed her by the arm and pushed her through the space instead. "Out," he ordered. "The shore is a few feet away. You'll have to jump."

"I'm not leaving them," she insisted, voice trembling. "They're my responsibility."

"And you're mine," he shot back. "Do you want to get sucked down with this thing?"

He didn't wait for a reply. He had no idea how long they had. One minute or five. He just knew he didn't want to stick around any longer than necessary to find out.

The only way to get the carrier out was to lift it over the lowered seat backs. The carrier was awkward and bulky and his shoulder protested as much as the animals did as they slid from one side to the other. Their shifting weight made handling their container that much more difficult with the floor bouncing like so much driftwood beneath his feet. But Nick figured they weren't being jostled nearly as much as they had been when they'd come through the trees, and getting them to land seemed more important than getting them there gently.

The carrier landed with a thud on the wing that hovered a scant foot above the wildly lapping water.

He had no idea why he'd thought his passenger would have listened to him and headed for solid ground. But she was right there, as pale as milk, grabbing the carrier's handle and trying to keep her balance as she pulled the cage toward the tip of the wing.

She clearly intended to get the animals to shore carrier and all.

All Nick cared about was keeping them all from going in the glacial water. It was deep. How deep he didn't know, but the rocky edges of the shore looked sheer, and the water they were floating on was as black as night. In this pristine wilderness that meant it went a very long way down.

Snatching the handle on the other side, he drew her progress to a halt. She jerked upright. "What are you doing?" she demanded, then promptly grabbed for the cage to keep herself steady.

"Making this simple."

Without another word, he turned the carrier so the opening faced the shore, flipped the latch and pulled up the grate.

The coyotes caught on to what he was doing before she

did. The instant they scented freedom, their heads popped out. A split second later, they bolted from their confines, the mottled light one yipping excitedly on the tail of the mottled darker one as they raced down the twenty-one feet of wide white wing and leaped with exuberant grace for a fallen log.

Melissa swung around, horrified. "Why did you do that? I don't have a permit to release them here!"

"What difference does that make?" He stared, incredulous. "You were releasing them anyway!"

Her only response was to throw up her hands as she whirled around. Mindless of the precarious way the wing was bobbing, she darted to the wing tip, arms outstretched to keep her balance, and launched herself with an ease that would have definitely impressed him had he not been so busy hoping he wouldn't have to go into the water after her.

She missed the log, but landed in the thick ferns growing near it. Grabbing a handful of fronds to keep her feet from going out from under her, she scrambled forward, sprinting after the tails rapidly vanishing into the dense woods.

Nick swore, something he'd done more in the past hour with this woman than he had in the past month.

Had Mel been in the habit, she would have sworn, too. She couldn't believe what he had done. She couldn't believe much of anything that was happening at the moment for that matter. She'd survived their landing only to be risking her neck on the uneven, vegetation-choked ground. Traction was nearly hopeless. The impossibly tall trees filtered out much of the sunlight. The dappled bits that did shine through barely allowed her to keep the little coyotes in sight. They were quick, agile with the energy of youth. And they weren't showing any of the curiosity that would have given her a chance to catch them. Any other canines would have slowed enough to nose around the trees and bushes, or at least paused long enough to mark their scent on them. But these two were tasting freedom for the first time and their instinct was simply to enjoy the run.

She was tasting freedom for the first time, too. Her independence had come with her move to Harbor Island. Pity she was making such a mess of it.

Her lungs hurt. Her heart beat hard against her breastbone.

Don't lose them, she silently commanded herself and kept going. Ahead she heard the rush of water, more excited yips. From behind came the crashing of something heavy through the bushes. She kept her focus on the coyotes, oblivious to the branches that snapped back at her when she shoved them out of the way, stinging her face, attacking her knees. She swiped at the sting, afraid to duck her head for fear she'd look up and the animals would be gone.

The pups gained a lead, leaping ahead to race over the tops of mossy rocks and the wide clear creek that cascaded over them. Not caring to slip and paralyze herself on those slippery boulders, she instantly changed her angle to cross a few feet downstream.

She was two steps from plowing right on through when what felt like an iron clamp snapped around her arm. Her feet nearly went out from under her as Nick hauled her back and spun her around.

As he did, she completely lost sight of the pups.

"You moron!" Faced with a wall of broad, unyielding chest, she tried to pull away, twisting as she did to see on the other side of the babbling creek. The man had the strength of an ox. "I can't see where they went!"

"Hold still!"

"Didn't you hear me?" She gulped in air. "I'm losing them! Let me go!"

"Not until you hold still!"

She jerked around. The thunder in his voice was mirrored in his eyes. Furious with him, she overlooked both. "Those animals were supposed to be let go in an area with known food sources. This is not that place!"

"It's going to have to be!"

"This isn't up to you!" She couldn't believe what she was hearing. What he was *doing.* "You're jeopardizing their future by letting them get away. I can't even hear them now!" She snapped her head toward where she'd last seen them, snapped it right back. "You're screwing up my first official release!"

The thought had her pulling back hard. His grip on her upper arms remained as unyielding as his expression. She didn't care that his touch radiated like heat from her fingers to her chest. It didn't even matter that his glance had fallen to her mouth, causing his own to tighten. She cared only that this was not his choice to make.

"This isn't going to do a thing for my reputation with the Forest Service," she seethed, angrier by the instant that he wouldn't let her go. "On top of that, if I don't get them back, I'm going to have to file a report explaining why they aren't where they're supposed to be." Pure worry underscored adrenaline-fed fury. She had no idea if the young coyotes would survive on their own there. "In triplicate," she snapped out, trying again to jerk away.

His fingers didn't budge. "Will you forget the damn paperwork?"

"Will you let me go?"

"No." The word was as sharp as the crack of a whip

as he pulled her closer. He loomed over her, the carved lines of his face inches from hers. "Not until you calm down and listen to me. If you—"

"There's nothing more important than getting those animals—"

"There's nothing more important," he insisted over her, "than staying dry. You're ready to charge into that creek. If you do that, you're going to get soaked. And then you're going to freeze. We're thousands of feet up, with nothing but a few hundred miles of forest around us, and I have no way of getting you dried off before the temperature drops."

Nick watched her open her mouth, then slowly close it again. A dark, narrow streak slashed from her chin to one high cheekbone. She'd obviously done battle with something on her way through the bushes, but in the dim light he couldn't tell if there was any injury beneath the dirt. At the moment all he cared about was that some of the starch dissolved from her muscles.

His own body felt as tight as a trip wire.

He'd noticed her scent before, the freshness of it. Then there was the lushness of her mouth, the inviting fullness that practically begged a man to taste, to savor. Already taunted by her chin-up attitude, the effect of that combination of soft and sultry teased his senses, adding an edge to his nerves that had nothing to do with annoyance and everything to do with how long it had been since he'd had a woman in his bed.

She'd stopped struggling. Though he didn't totally trust her not to bolt, releasing her suddenly seemed essential.

She promptly turned to glance behind her.

"Don't even think about it," he growled. "Those animals are going to fare a whole lot better than we will if we don't get back to the plane and rescue what we can before it sinks.''

He could practically sense her indecision. She had a responsibility and it killed her to abandon it. In a way, he knew that struggle all too well.

''Okay?'' he prodded.

She must have seen the wisdom of seeking their own survival. The sparks of fury in her eyes had disappeared. All that remained was unease as she glanced one last time across the creek, then to the forest behind him.

''They didn't seem to have been injured.'' She spoke quietly, sounding as if she were justifying leaving more to herself than to him. ''Neither one of them showed any sign of a limp or pain or confusion.''

He could practically see her mind racing to recall the animals' movements. Hoping to speed up the process, he said, ''They looked perfectly healthy to me.''

They really had, though he had the feeling his decidedly unprofessional opinion carried about as much weight as the bug she swatted away a moment before she caved in.

''Okay,'' she finally agreed, not looking at all sure of where it was they should go. She seemed to see nothing but bushes and trees.

What Nick noticed were the branches they'd broken.

''Follow me,'' he murmured and, making sure she stayed behind him, plowed back the way they'd come.

It didn't seem to Mel that she had run all that far. Yet it took a couple of minutes to retrace the path she'd more or less taken. With Nick's broad back blocking her view, she couldn't see ahead of him at all. So she simply hurried to keep up with his long-legged stride—and stopped as abruptly as he did when they broke through the trees.

The water of the lake shimmered and danced in the late-afternoon sun. The half that wasn't in shadow, anyway. Golden ripples played over the surface, waves gently lapping against the rocks that formed most of its shore.

The plane itself was nowhere to be seen. The only indication that it had been there at all were the bubbles rising from beneath the surface a few yards out.

The weight of the water filling the tail end had dislodged it from its perch and carried it under.

"The radio," she whispered.

"My tickets," Nick said with a groan.

Melissa stood beside him, her gaze frozen on the lake. "Your tickets?" she repeated, not comprehending his concern.

"They were in my travel bag. I was going to Denver tonight."

Watching the woman beside him straighten the skewed brim of her cap, he decided it best not to think about *why* he wouldn't be there, either. Dealing with fact would be infinitely more productive than dealing with frustration.

The orange survival pack he'd managed to toss off the plane lay a few yards away. His maps lay under it. "I set the transponder when the engine failed," he said, referring to the electronic device planes carried to help others locate them in such circumstances. "But I really wish I could have used the radio, too."

Melissa swore she heard accusation in the deep tones of his voice. Crossing her arms over the nerves still jumping in her stomach, she watched him crouch down by the brightly-colored backpack. If he hadn't taken off after her a few minutes ago, he might have had time to notify someone of their position. If he hadn't agreed to fly her in the first place, he might have made his original destination before the problem with the plane developed.

As she watched him rip open the zipper on the bright

pack, she also considered that, if his tickets had been in his bag, he'd just lost the rest of his luggage.

She was busy appreciating the fact that he didn't feel compelled to point all of that out when the enormity of their situation hit her.

She remembered the landscape as they'd flown over it. The lush, untamed wilderness had stretched as far as the eye could see. There hadn't been a road or a rooftop, not even smoke from a campfire, to indicate that anything on less than four legs existed anywhere near this totally isolated place. She was miles from nowhere with a man she didn't know. A man who hadn't wanted her with him to begin with—and who undoubtedly wasn't crazy about her being with him now.

She shouldn't have called him a moron. Considering where the plane was and how difficult it would have been to get the animals to shore in their crate, his actions hadn't been totally without merit. Still, the decision to let the pups go should have been hers.

The annoyance she felt at him taking over was overshadowed, however, by the realization that she didn't have a snowball's chance in Hades of being back on Harbor by the time her sister arrived.

Forcing a calm she truly didn't feel, she eyed the orange nylon bag he was digging around in. Assuming the pack matched his other luggage, she decided there truly was no accounting for taste. "The transponder," she said, thinking she would have considered him more the tasteful leather valise type. There was something about him that simply didn't fit the utilitarian neon image. "That's the black box they talk about on the news when they're looking for a plane that went down?"

"Right."

"Do you think it's working?"

"I hope so."

She would assume it was. Heaven knew she needed to think positively right now. "So, that's going to help someone find us," she concluded, staring at the back of his dark head.

Intent on what he was doing, he pulled a deck of playing cards and a flashlight from the pack. "It might once Sam figures out that we had trouble," he replied, setting the items on a thick rectangle of silver he'd already removed. "But that's not going to be before dark."

Her arms tightened. "So we're stuck for tonight."

He set aside a handful of granola bars and a small first-aid kit. "At least."

"So they'll find us tomorrow, then?"

"They'll be looking for debris from a crash." He added matches and a small plastic bag of what looked like thick wooden sticks to his pile. "With the plane underwater, about all we left is the path we plowed through the tree-tops. From the air that'll barely be visible. We could be found tomorrow," he said, pulling out packets of soup, "two days from now," he continued, tossing aside a large metal cup, "or never."

He didn't look up. He simply continued unloading the odd assortment of items from the pack, noting each as if he were doing some sort of mental inventory until he reached the item he was apparently looking for. The small round case he held proved to be a compass when he flipped open the top.

"You wouldn't happen to have a cell phone in there, would you?"

"It went down with the plane. It was in my bag."

"Too bad you hadn't put it in that one."

"Yeah," he muttered, sounding as if he wished he'd thought to do that. Sounding as if he wished he'd had the time. "Except this isn't mine. It's the bush pack from the plane."

"Bush pack?"

"Survival kit," he clarified, stuffing everything but the compass and a canteen back in. "Most bush pilots don't fly anywhere without one."

"This happens a lot, then?" she asked over the rasp of the zipper.

"More in the winter. Sam and Zack keep packs in all their planes." He would forever be grateful for that bit of foresight, too. "In this part of the country, it's usually weather that brings a plane down. Especially small ones."

Mel forced herself to take a deep, steadying breath. Veterinary emergencies aside, she was well accustomed to coping in a crisis. Thanks to her dysfunctional little family, she'd dealt with them for years. She'd always had to be the one in control, the one in charge, the one to bail her mom and her sister out of whatever mess they'd managed to create. And she'd always managed. Somehow.

Unfortunately, her current situation didn't involve truant officers, the police, the landlord or an irate boyfriend. Those she'd had practice with. Here she was totally out of her element.

She was also completely open to options.

Swallowing hard, she watched Nick snag the map as he rose. "What do we do now?"

"Figure out which way to go." The annoyance and exasperation she'd seen in him when he'd caught up with her by the creek was gone from his expression. What she saw now was the remoteness she'd first encountered, along with a definite sense of purpose. "Have you ever been camping?"

"No."

"Backpacking?"

She gave her head a negative shake.

"Hiking? Walking in the woods?"

"Neither."

His cool gray eyes narrowed. "Didn't you ever go to camp as a kid?"

"If I had," she replied, uneasily certain she was about to make up for that lack of experience, "I might have learned how to swim. I'm from Los Angeles. We Rollerblade or jog on sidewalks. We don't have woods there."

She wasn't an inch over five foot two. Five-three tops, Nick decided, which meant she had to tip her head back to meet his eyes. He had the feeling it wasn't the difference in their heights that had her pulling up her dainty little chin again. It was pure bravado. From the way she tightened her arms around herself, it was as clear as the flecks of sapphire in her eyes that she was nervous and worried and desperately not wanting either to show.

He was more grateful for her control than he wanted to admit. He knew any number of women—men for that matter—who would have fallen apart long before now. If he'd bothered to consider how close he'd come to overshooting the lake and turning them to toast, he would be inclined to sit down and do a little shaking himself.

He ran an impersonal glance from her quilted forest-green vest and tan turtleneck sweater to the knees of her jeans. He just wished she were a little sturdier. He had the feeling she was nothing but slender curves beneath that denim and down.

Ordinarily he wouldn't regard that as a bad thing. Under the circumstances, however, he didn't want to have to worry about her keeping up with him. He hadn't simply been going for impact when he'd told her they were surrounded by hundreds of miles of forest. The question now was which direction in that forest they should aim themselves.

A glance at the compass indicated that north was behind them. Orienting the map he unfolded over a waisthigh boulder, he traced his finger over the route he'd followed inland. He made it as far as the 5,200-foot ridge they'd flown over before fact gave way to conjecture. He didn't know how far to the west he'd gone after he'd first made the decision to turn around. From the location of the shapes indicating the tiny lakes they'd seen, he had to assume it was several miles. He just wasn't sure which one of those dozens of glacial potholes he'd landed on.

With the dense stand of trees surrounding them, no other physical features of the land were visible to give him any hints, either.

The creek he'd stopped Melissa from going through seemed to be their best bet.

''We'll follow the creek you found.'' He knew now that it was flowing north. Since they were somewhere in the low mountains beyond the ridge, and north was the direction they needed to go, it seemed as good a route as any.

''Shouldn't we stay here for a while? Maybe build a signal fire or send up a flare?''

Nick couldn't help but hear the hopeful note in her voice. She was looking for options. Unfortunately, the only ones they had were all lousy.

He glanced to the brilliant blue sky. ''There aren't any planes up there. A flare will only help if there's someone to see it. Same with smoke. No one's looking for us yet.''

''But they will be looking tomorrow.''

''We could sit here for weeks hoping they'll see us,'' he countered. ''I've heard of too many pilots who've screamed themselves hoarse waving at search planes that kept passing right over their fire. Wind dissipates smoke. We'd have to build a bonfire to get a signal big enough to be seen from the air. As close as we are to the trees here, we'd torch the forest.'' Paper rustled as he folded the map and stuffed it into the backpack. ''In the meantime, we have at least three hours of daylight left. That's good for a few miles.''

She couldn't deny his practicality. They were standing on the widest part of the shoreline. All twenty-by-eight feet of it. Everywhere else, boulders and tree roots edged into the water and thick-trunked firs shot straight to the sky.

Sparks from a bonfire would catch all too easily in those wide branches.

She couldn't deny his thoroughness, either.

''Here,'' he said, handing her the aluminum canteen. ''You can fill this in the creek. We just dumped oil and what was left of our fuel in the lake. We don't need to get sick. And I wouldn't count on them seeing debris or an oil slick on the water, either,'' he added, sounding as if he suspected she was thinking just that. ''We're on our own here.''

She'd no sooner taken the two-quart receptacle than he turned to make sure he had everything else he'd managed to salvage. There was nothing to be seen other than their footprints on the narrow strip of damp earth. The first rain to come along would wash those away as easily as wiping chalk from a board. No one would even know they'd been there.

She ducked her head to catch his glance. ''Has this happened to you before?''

''Can't say that it has. We'll follow the creek,'' he repeated. ''Just don't get your feet wet.''

She had the feeling he expected her to balk at his decision. From the set of his jaw as his glance held hers, she was sure of it. Yet, even though she still wasn't happy with the way he'd taken over on the wing, she didn't mind him doing it now. She was not an unreasonable person. As far as she could tell, they only had two choices. They could stay where they were and hope for a rescue that might not happen before they were old and gray. Or they could do something to help get themselves out of there and take a hike through the endless forest.

There was no denying the trepidation she felt at that thought.

"As long as we're going this way," she said, desperately searching for the bright side as she started past him, "we can look for the coyotes."

"The only thing we're looking for is a way out of here." He caught her arm, then promptly frowned at her cheek. "You couldn't do anything with them if you caught them, anyway."

She frowned right back, partly because he had a point, partly because of the jolt she felt at his touch. His heat seeped into her, radiating even through the thick knit of her sweater. But it was the touch of his fingers to her chin that caught her breath in her throat.

With his thumb he traced the skin beneath the streak on her cheek. "It looks like a scratch under there." Dropping his hand, he reached into his back pocket and pulled out a handkerchief. "Better check and see."

He held out the pristine white square. Taking what he offered, she wiped at the spot he'd so gently touched. Most of the dark streak came off on the cloth.

"It's just dirt," Nick pronounced, then hesitated. He couldn't see any other sign of injury anywhere. The way she'd torn off into the trees seemed to indicate that she hadn't suffered any ill effects from the landing. So did the surprising strength he'd felt in her slender muscles when she'd tried to pull away from him. Still, he needed to be certain. "You're sure you didn't get hurt when we came down? No sprains or bumps? You didn't hit your head or anything?"

His sudden concern seemed to surprise her. "I'm okay," she said, offering back his handkerchief. "Really."

Grateful for the confirmation, his glance fell to what she held. "Keep it," was all he said, and slipped his arms through the straps of the backpack.

He turned as he did, his back to her as he sucked in his breath and winced at the motion. Angling his arm backward hadn't been a good idea. The dull ache in his shoulder brightened with pain.

He did his best to ignore the sudden throbbing as he headed into the trees. He'd just have to put up with the discomfort. He wanted out of there. He also wanted the woman now following him back where she belonged so he didn't have to worry about her.

He shouldn't have touched her, he decided, gingerly rubbing his left shoulder as he ducked to avoid a low-hanging branch. It was one thing to suspect her skin felt like silk. It was another entirely to know for certain that it did.

Chapter Three

Mel was a city girl. Born and bred. She knew freeways, gridlock and graffiti, smog, skyscrapers, strip malls and apartment complexes that housed more people than lived in some rural communities. The concrete jungle was more reality to her than euphemism, and she had considered herself prepared to face just about anything when she'd left it. When she'd boarded the ferry that had taken her from the mainland to the little island she wanted to make her home, she had even anticipated the new experiences her move would bring, the changes, the challenges. She'd even hoped for a little adventure.

She had not, however, anticipated adventure to this degree.

Breathing in the moist, pine-scented air as she followed the orange backpack through the shaded forest, she reminded herself that a person truly did need to be careful what she wished for. In the meantime she would just be grateful that her very decisive, no-nonsense pilot seemed to know what he was doing—and overlook the fact that he tended to be a tad cranky.

Leaves swirled around her knees as she gingerly slipped past something with stickers.

"You said it was ten miles to a landing strip?"

His deep voice drifted back to her. "That was before we flew farther."

"How much farther?"

"I'm not sure."

"Can you give me a ballpark?"

"Maybe another five."

The rustle of bushes gave way to the silence of pine-needle-strewn ground. "So we cover what? A couple of miles an hour? Three if we push?"

"Forget three."

"Two, then."

"If we're lucky."

"So, if we're lucky," she prodded, stepping over a snag she'd nearly tripped over earlier, "it will take us seven or eight hours to get there?"

"It might if we were walking as the crow flies on even terrain."

She bit back a sigh at the terseness of his responses. "But?" she prompted again, dead certain from his phrasing that he'd left something out.

"There's a little obstacle between it and us."

"What kind of an obstacle?"

Ahead of him a vine maple shimmered in the sunlight filtering through the trees. Shoving aside a thick branch of the autumn-gold leaves, he held it until she caught up with him.

"A mountain."

Catching the branch so he could release it, she stopped dead in her tracks.

"How big a mountain?"

"Too big to climb over," he said, his back to her as he continued on. "We have to go around it."

"The whole thing?"

He turned to see her still holding the brilliant foliage. "I hear the creek," he said, patience fairly dripping from his tone. "Why don't you lead? I don't want to leave you behind."

The bright leaves rustled as the limb swayed back into place. "Is that something I need to know about you? That you change the subject when the news isn't good?"

He frowned at the back of her cap as she brushed past him.

"I don't always change the subject."

"You don't offer any more than is asked, either."

"We don't have to go around all of it," he told her.

"That's not bad news."

"We'll climb over part of it."

"Oh," she murmured, and decided to let it go at that.

The thought of more heights put a faintly queasy sensation in her stomach as she followed the sound of burbling water. But apprehension over what lay ahead gave way to another form of worry when she spotted the boulders the pups had leaped across before they'd disappeared.

Nick was right. Even if by some miracle she were to find the little coyotes, it really wouldn't be possible for her to confine them and pack them out. That logic wouldn't stop her from worrying about them, though. Or from hoping that they would somehow take care of each other.

The thought that she and the man behind her needed to do the same thing promptly changed the course of her concerns. She was stuck with someone she knew next to nothing about. Rather than dwelling on how uneasy that made her feel, she allowed another worry to slide into its place.

"Which way?" she asked, glancing with foreboding at her watch.

"North. That way," he said, motioning over her shoulder when her head came up.

There was no clear path to take. The land was just a low jumble of rocks and plants that lined the banks and the trees that shadowed it all. Picking her way around enormous tufts of lush fern, she kept to the pinecone strewn ground and glanced at her watch once more.

"You might as well forget the time. All that matters right now is daylight and dark."

She didn't slow, didn't turn. She just wished he would lose the clipped edge in his tone.

"The time is going to matter to my sister. She's coming in on the five-o'clock ferry." Mel could only imagine Cam's reaction when she didn't eventually show up. At best she would be furious. At worst she would be deeply wounded, then she'd be furious. Either way she couldn't imagine Cameron worrying about why she wasn't there. Only feeling very put-out and inconvenienced by the fact that she wasn't. Somehow her little sister had never figured out that she wasn't the only person in the universe and that donkey dung happened to other people, too.

That was not something she cared to share with the man behind her, however. It wasn't something she cared to share with anyone. Cam was a brat of a sister, but she was *her* brat sister. "I imagine there will be people worried about you, too."

Nylon rustled against leather as Nick readjusted the strap over his left shoulder. The pain there had returned to a dull ache. "Can't imagine who that would be," he replied, his voice tightening more with the movement. The discomfort eased considerably when the pressure shifted. "Except Sam when the mechanic calls wanting to know where the plane is."

And maybe his lawyer, he thought, since he'd made an appointment with him for tomorrow morning. But when he didn't show, his attorney would probably just think he'd bailed again—as he had the day he'd taken off for the San Juans. He'd had an appointment then, too. At least that day he'd been able to call him a few hours later to tell him he was checking out for a while.

There was no way he would reach a phone tonight.

His sense of frustration sharpened at that thought and left him regretting that he'd set the meeting with him so soon. That was the way he operated, though. The way he always had. Once he made a decision, he never hesitated to put the wheels in motion.

"There must be someone," he heard Melissa say. "Certainly you have a wife or girlfriend who will be concerned. What about your family?"

Preoccupied with just how long it would take them to get to a phone, his only interest was in the people he had already made plans to meet. He had an appointment with his accountant, too. Since he wasn't going to make that one, either, the guy would probably figure the same thing as the lawyer.

"There's no one who will worry," he repeated. "Not for a couple of weeks, anyway."

His seeming lack of connections finally had her glancing back toward him. He ignored the careful look she gave him, much as he ignored the view of her curvy little backside and the gentle sway of her ponytail as she continued on. Talking about himself and the people he'd left behind held no appeal for him at all. Thinking about certain of them held even less.

"This sister of yours," he prefaced, wanting to get off the subject. "Is she coming from L.A.?"

As chatty as she tended to be, he figured she'd take the conversational ball and run with it.

All he got was a long pause before she said, "I don't know. I'm not sure where she's living at the moment."

She offered nothing else as she ducked under a low tree limb and glanced around for the clearest path. Finding it, she kept going, her silence all but echoing in the deep stillness.

So much for thinking her predictable.

"Why don't you know where your sister lives?" he asked, thinking now was not the time for her to be quiet.

Her only response was the shrug of her slender shoulders.

Exasperation nudged hard. "We need to keep talking," he insisted, trying to keep the edge from his voice, not sure he succeeded. "If you don't want to talk about your sister, then talk about something else. Noise will keep the bears away."

Her sudden reticence collapsed as she spun on her heel. "Bears?"

"Bears," he repeated, thinking he never would have predicted that reaction, either. Animals were her thing. Or so he'd assumed. "You hadn't thought about them being around here?"

The scope of Mel's unease widened considerably as she watched Nick's brooding features settle in a scowl. She truly hadn't considered what might be lurking in their surroundings. She'd seen a few crawly things that had given her the shivers, but she'd been too busy wondering how concerned she needed to be about being stuck with this stranger to wonder about any other form of wildlife.

"Noise keeps them away," she repeated, conclusion in her voice.

"You didn't know that?"

"I told you, I've never been hiking before."

"This doesn't have anything to do with hiking. You're a veterinarian. You're supposed to have studied animal behavior."

"I did study animal behavior. It's just that the only fieldwork I ever did was in a zoo. I haven't had a chance to think about its more practical applications."

"And you took a job that involves relocating wildlife?"

She didn't particularly appreciate his incredulity. Relocation was only a small part of the job—the part she would have to study and learn because part of what she'd wanted to do was grow beyond the boundaries that had hemmed her in.

With his scowl threatening to become permanent, she wasn't terribly inclined to share that. "Yes," she said flatly, and started walking again.

"Had you ever been to Harbor before you took the job?"

"Not before I met Doctor Jackson to talk about his practice. He'd retired to Seattle and took me over on the ferry to show me the clinic."

A twig snapped beneath Nick's weight, the sharp sound muffled by the mossy forest floor.

"Let me see if I have this straight." Another twig succumbed. "You left everything and everyone you know to go to a place you know nothing about, to take on a job you haven't even come up to speed on."

In a nutshell, she admitted to herself, that was pretty much it. She just didn't care for the way he made it sound.

Especially with that frown in his voice. He wasn't happy with her for any number of reasons. She knew that. And she would admit that he had the right to a little annoyance. She'd even take blame for them being there if that was what he wanted. But he wasn't the only one dealing with the fact that their plane had fallen out of the sky. She was trying to cope with a little worry and apprehension herself, and she absolutely did not need his disapproval of her choices.

"Well?"

At the terse prod, she spun around again. "Look," she said, forcing patience when she wasn't feeling patient at all. "I'm a good veterinarian. Ninety percent of the practice I took on is caring for people's pets. The same domestic kind I've worked with for the past two years." Except for the insanely expensive groomings and pedigrees, she thought, but that wasn't the point.

"I'll be the first to admit that I've hardly seen everything, but I can handle their health care and their encounters with each other, automobiles and their owner's neglect as long as those encounters haven't left them too sick or too hurt to help. I'm sorry about your luggage and your tickets and that I yelled at you before. I don't usually do that," she admitted, hurrying on, "to strangers, anyway. And calling you a moron probably was a little out of line. But I would hope you'd understand that I was just a little stressed. Actually, I still am."

She crossed her arms over her zipped vest, apology and defense melding with caution as she held his narrowed gray eyes. "I know you didn't want to bring me with you," she continued, needing him to be aware of that before he decided to tell her himself. "And I know that nearly everyone in town is somehow under the impression that I'm as spoiled as the pets I took care of in Beverly

Hills. But I wouldn't have a clue what *spoiled* even feels like. I grew up a block from the projects. I've worked since I was sixteen and went to a school run by gangs.

"I'm also not stupid," she informed him. "I don't know a thing about you other than that you're a good pilot and more wilderness savvy than I am, but I'm at least giving you the benefit of the doubt here. I'd appreciate it if you'd reciprocate by telling me what it is I need to know without acting like I'm an idiot because I don't already know it. I generally know how to take care of myself and, if you'd just give me that much, I promise I won't slow you down."

For a moment Nick said nothing. He just watched her draw a deep breath, then hold it as if she were waiting for lightning to strike. It seemed she had apologized. It also seemed she'd told him off. Sandwiched in there somewhere with all she'd unloaded was the intent to diffuse whatever misconceptions he might have had about her and to let him know she was far from helpless.

He watched her slowly turn and trudge on. As he did, he caught a glimpse of the same wariness he'd sensed when she'd said she didn't know anything about him.

That caution gave him pause. It hadn't occurred to him that she might regard him as any sort of threat. Considering it now, thinking of how his sisters would feel stuck with a guy they didn't know, he realized it was entirely possible that she was as uncomfortable with him as she was their situation. Her bravado impressed him. Her vulnerability tugged at his basic sense of decency.

A bit of orange-gold leaf had caught itself in the ponytail swaying between her shoulder blades. He noticed it as he moved behind her, slowing his stride when he caught up.

It didn't matter that she had badgered him until he'd

broken down and called Sam. Nor did it matter that she had put him in a position where he couldn't in good conscience refuse a favor to a friend. He had made the final decision on his own. He always stood by his decisions, too. Bore their consequences. And one of the consequences of the decision he'd made when he'd agreed to fly her was to accept responsibility for her physical welfare.

He'd already told her he was responsible for her. Regardless of her claim that she could take care of herself, at the moment she needed him for her very survival.

She'd undoubtedly realized that, too.

His conscience jerked hard. It was no wonder she'd looked worried.

"You're right," he muttered behind her. "The moron remark was out of line."

She kept right on walking. "I'm sorry I said that."

"And I didn't want to take this flight."

"You made that clear."

"But I never considered you stupid."

A moment's hesitation preceded her quiet "Thank you."

He , to admit that she'd caught him off guard with the bit about the projects and the gangs, though. Even dressed for the outdoors as she was, there was a polish about her that spoke more of pampering and privilege than poverty of any sort. She looked intimately familiar with salons that manicured, pedicured, hot wrapped and highlighted. No one was born with that many shades of blond in their hair.

Yet, there was that odd wisdom he would occasionally see in her eyes.

Suspecting he had just received a healthy hint about why it was there, he let the rest of her little discourse go—only to find himself wondering again why she'd chosen to leave everything she knew behind.

He promptly told himself it was none of his business. With everything else on his mind, his only concern with her should be getting her out of there.

As for her apology about his tickets and luggage and the implication that she was responsible for the two of them being where they were, he saw no point going into whose fault it was that they were there. Fate and a faulty fuel line deserved as much blame as anything else.

All that was important now was easing her concerns about him. He didn't like that she felt so vulnerable.

"I just thought of someone who might get a little anxious if I don't show up."

She glanced over her shoulder, uncertainty in her profile. "You did?"

"Yeah."

"Who?"

"My mom and my sisters. Mom's going to nag me to death for worrying them if I don't check in with them by the end of the month.

"You might want to head a little to the left," he said, before she could decide how to respond to that. "It looks more open through there."

Mel did as he suggested, moving deeper into the dimming light. Now conscious of the local wildlife, she was aware of the sounds around her in ways she hadn't been before—and terribly conscious of the man she could hear walking a few feet behind her.

She didn't know what she'd expected him to say after she'd unloaded on him. But she hadn't thought he would respond with such civil agreement, much less with sensitivity. Not only had he gallantly refrained from placing blame, he had just let her know that he was a man who had family, and a mom who nagged.

He had just let her know she was safe with him.

"How many sisters?"

"Two. Both younger," he replied. "Grab that stick over there."

A yard-long limb lay near a rotting log a few feet away. When she picked it up, he picked up another.

"We can use these to knock against trees we pass. That'll make even more noise than conversation." He arched one dark eyebrow at her. "Are you okay in the lead?"

The frown was gone. So was a hint of the distance she'd sensed in him. Only his indefinable tension remained. It snaked toward her, taunting the nerves in her stomach, making her a little edgy herself. She could live with that, though. He was doing what she'd asked. He was letting her know what she needed to do in this forbidding and beautiful place without editorializing on her lack of more practical knowledge.

"I'm fine as long as I can hear the creek," she replied, feeling safer with him behind. Especially now that she was conscious of bears. "And thank you."

"It's just a stick."

"That's not what I meant, but for that, too."

A hint of gratitude softened her smile as she turned. But her quiet "Thanks" slipped to a whisper when his hand came up and he reached past her ear.

His fingers skimmed halfway down her hair.

"Leaf," he explained, holding out the bit of curled gold. "And you're welcome." Thinking she looked a little uncertain about his casual gesture he let the leaf drift to the ground and motioned her ahead of him. "After you."

* * *

The light faded rapidly. The verdant canopy formed by the trees already blocked much of the light, and dusk came early in the mountains in fall. By four-thirty the shades of green and autumn-gold had muted to gray. By five Mel could barely see the jumble of fallen logs ahead of them. As the light had faded it had taken the temperature with it.

Movement had kept her muscles warm and her mind off the cooling air. Her fingers were freezing, though. Now that they'd stopped, she rubbed her arms to create a little heat.

The creek beside them had widened to a stream. Nick stood beside her, his hands on his hips as he stared across the swath of dark, swiftly flowing water. Since he'd come up with the sticks, conversation had dissolved to only the necessary.

As they stood side by side at the stream, he admitted that they might as well stop. With night falling, going any farther was pointless, and this was the best place to build a fire. Because water flow was down in the fall, they could build it on the wide edge of the gravel-covered stream bed they'd followed for the past hour.

His glance skimmed the vest she'd zipped to her throat. "Do you want to gather some bark and twigs to get a fire started?"

Heat sounded heavenly to her. So did food. But rather than think about the lunch she'd missed and the Lean Cuisine in her freezer, she gave a nod and headed for the shoreline. If she was hungry, she imagined Nick must be starving. It would take a lot of fuel to sustain all that muscle.

"Everything's damp," she called, wondering if he was going to send her off to find berries while he fished them up a salmon or something for dinner. "How will we get this to burn?"

"We have fire starters in the pack."

His claim was followed by the thud of the pack hitting smooth pebbles as Nick dropped it by his feet. She had the feeling it must be heavier than it looked. She knew he was strong. She'd seen him heft the animal carrier, pups and all, into the cargo hold as easily as she might have lifted a pillow. Yet he seemed truly grateful to be relieved of the weight as he rubbed his shoulder and crouched down to open the zipper.

It didn't take long for him to clear an area of tangled debris the spring runoff had left behind and make a yard-wide circle of rocks near the foot-high bank. The canopy of trees had opened up there, not enough for a signal fire, but enough for the modest one he built to stave off the worst of the encroaching chill.

As long as they were occupied, the silence between them didn't seem at all obtrusive to Mel. They had something specific to do, and accomplishing it gave her something to focus on other than the man moving about with such quiet competence.

What she focused on now was the quiet. Every sound seemed muffled as she gathered more twigs to fuel the fire Nick had built and filled the large cup Nick handed her from the stream. Even the constant rush of water and the screech of something feathered flying overhead seemed muted by the dense forest surrounding them. Those wilderness sounds underscored the snap and sizzle of the fire, the clink of metal against rock when he set the cup near the flames, the crunch of rock beneath his boots when he headed off to find something more substantial to burn.

She was in the middle of nowhere. But the thought wasn't nearly as frightening as it could have been.

For the past couple of hours she'd had the sense that Nick was watching everything. The woods. The sky. Her. Even when he had led for a while, finding a way around a thick patch of undergrowth that had taken them far from the stream, he had made sure he always knew where she was, that she never got caught more than a few yards behind.

He was clearly watching out for her. There was enormous relief in that knowledge. In a way he seemed to be taking care of her, too. Whether he realized it or not, that was what he'd been doing when he'd noticed the dirt on her face and when he'd pulled the leaf from her hair—even if he had been decidedly businesslike about it.

The thought of being cared for was seductive in a way. It also felt vaguely threatening. She had always been the one to take care of others.

"You eat the soup," she told him, when the dehydrated-split-pea mix had finally turned thick and steaming. "I'll just have a granola bar."

"You need more than that."

"I'd had my heart set on roasted salmon."

"Sorry. Fresh out. You get peanut butter or oatmeal raisin."

He held up two granola bars from the pack.

She took peanut butter, though what she really wanted was the chocolate bar she'd seen in there. She always craved chocolate in stressful situations.

"And there's cocoa or coffee," he said.

"Cocoa," she immediately replied, opting for the two-birds-with-one-stone approach. Too much caffeine was the last thing she needed. She doubted she'd get any sleep as it was.

They had spread the beach-towel size space blanket on the low and lumpy bank a few feet from the fire. Picking up the big cup by its insulated handle, Nick lowered himself to the swath of waterproof fabric. "Are you sure you don't want some of this?"

He needed it far more than she did. "Positive."

He eyed the granola bar, eyed her and apparently decided not to press the point. With his feet planted wide on the pebbles, he rested his elbows on his powerful thighs and took a sip from the steaming cup.

The fire snapped and glowed a few feet away. Orange sparks flew up, only to wink out by the time they reached the top of his head.

The only place for her to sit and be close to the fire seemed to be beside him. Sticking to her edge of the blanket, she shivered as a wave of heat from the fire drifted toward her.

Wondering if he was aware of how much space his big body occupied, swearing she could feel heat from him, too, she looked from the little twig he'd used to stir the soup. There hadn't been a spoon in the pack.

"Did they give you a course in this in flight school?"

"This?"

"This survival stuff. You said this had never happened to you before, but you seem to know everything to do."

"I camped with my dad."

"When you were a kid?"

"Actually, we went once a year until he died. That was five years ago. Now I take my nephew out. He's really into the backcountry."

Paper crackled as she quietly ripped the wrapper on her dinner. "How old is your nephew?"

"Thirteen."

She lifted her chin, stripped another piece off her wrapper. ''I'm sorry about your dad.''

''Me, too. We all miss him.'' He glanced toward her, frowning at her meager meal, letting it go once more. ''If you set the canteen by the fire, the water can start heating for your cocoa. I'll be finished with this in a minute.''

They had to share the cup. Telling him not to hurry, she scanned the beautifully carved lines of his profile as he took another sip of his soup. His was more than just a pretty face. There was character in the little furrows fanning from the corners of his eyes and the deep lines bracketing his sensual mouth. There was unhappiness, too. Or maybe it was discontent.

She didn't have the feeling that any of it had to do with her, though. Not now. He had seemed just as distracted and dissatisfied when she'd first approached his plane.

''You said you were going to Denver tonight,'' she reminded him, breaking off a bite of her own meal. ''Were you going for a vacation?''

His glance cut to her, then just as quickly pulled away. With his forearms on his thighs, he contemplated the cup he held between his knees.

''Not for vacation.''

''Business?''

''I was going home.''

His cheerless tone put a note of concern in hers. ''Is someone sick?''

The dark slashes of his eyebrows merged. ''No.''

''A funeral, then,'' she concluded, and would have said she was sorry if he hadn't just turned his confused expression on her.

''What makes you think someone's sick or dead?''

''Because that's how you sound.''

Nick opened his mouth, closed it again.

She looked even younger in the flickering firelight, softer, sweeter, almost…tempting.

"Everyone I know is perfectly healthy," he told her, turning his attention to the fire before it could drift to her incredible mouth. "I'm moving back there."

Pitch from the fire snapped and hissed. The hoot of an owl carried on the faint breeze. "Then you lost more than your bags," she quietly concluded. "You had all your possessions in the plane."

He couldn't let her feel any more guilty than she already did. "I didn't have much with me in Harbor. Hardly anything," he admitted, thinking of how little he'd left with. "My stay there was only temporary. And I am looking forward to going home," he insisted, needing to convince himself if not her. "I have a life I need to get back to, and my family lives near there."

"Your mom and your sisters?"

"And their families," he said, because they were important to him, too.

Part of him truly was anxious to return to the mainstream. He needed badly to get back to work, to feel a sense of purpose and accomplishment again. He had always been driven. Always had goals. The goals that had pushed him for years were gone now, but he had new ones. And he wanted badly to put his new plan into effect.

All he needed to do first was finish the paperwork dissolving his association with his business partner. Reed Archer possessed one of the finest engineering minds in the business, along with an ego the size of a 747. The ego he'd learned to live with. Nick wouldn't have gone into business with anyone who hadn't had confidence in his work. But Reed had lost his sense of ethics somewhere along the way, and Nick couldn't be in business with anyone like that, either.

Thinking of what waited for him in Denver threatened to turn the soup to lead in his gut. It almost did when the thought of all that had gone wrong was replaced by an equally disturbing thought.

He wouldn't have to think about reestablishing himself at all if he couldn't get out of this forest. What he hadn't mentioned to the woman keeping a discreet distance from him was that he really didn't know where they were. He had a general idea, but a general idea could get them into as much trouble as no idea at all. He saw no point in mentioning that, though. Not as long as he had a plan. And at this point his plan was to get them to the ridge where he could see far enough to figure out where to go from there.

He made himself finish his dinner, rinsed the cup in the stream and handed it and a packet of cocoa to Melissa.

Mel took what he offered, eagerly anticipating the cocoa's warming effects. The air seemed to be growing cooler by the minute. She could see their breath, feel the chill creeping up her back.

Somewhere in the distance the howl of coyotes pierced the dark surrounding them. The moon had risen above the treetops, bright as a beacon and threaded with tiny wisps of cloud. She prayed the little coyotes were okay.

It was going to be a very long night.

"I'd give you my jacket," Nick said, pitch sizzling as he added more wood to their fire, "but the blanket will be warmer. There's no sense sitting there shivering. Wrap yourself up in it."

The thing wasn't big enough to share without getting intimate. Rather than taking the whole thing just yet, she handed him the cocoa to heat and pulled the part behind her over her shoulders.

Seeing what she'd done, he sat down on the space she'd left him and peeled a granola bar of his own for dessert.

She could practically feel his discontent as he tossed a piece of wrapper into the flames and watched it curl. She hadn't believed him for an instant when he'd said he looked forward to going home. No one knew better than she did that home wasn't always a place of warm feelings and happy memories. But as the forest grew black around them and the hoot of the owl grew more haunting, she didn't care how far into denial he was as long as he got her out of this frigid wilderness.

Chapter Four

Mel awoke to the drone of constantly flowing water and the darkness of the blanket she'd pulled over her head. She swore she could feel every bone in her body—especially those being poked by the exposed rocks between the dirt and grass. Shifting to avoid one that seemed to have grown a point, she edged the blanket down, only to become aware of rustling in the bushes. Whatever was coming through them was of considerable size.

As she had a dozen times in the interminable hours of night, she snapped to full consciousness with her heart beating in her throat. It wasn't dark now, she realized, sitting bolt upright, but the misty gray light of morning hadn't grown strong enough to penetrate the dense woods.

Looking as big as a buck, Nick emerged from the deeply shadowed foliage.

Her shoulders sank as her breath slithered out in a fog. Clutching her blanket over her hammering heart, she drew a lungful of biting cold air that smelled of damp earth and pine and willed her heart to slow.

Her first thought was that she was safe. Her next was that it wasn't a nightmare, after all. She really had lost the coyotes and spent the night in the middle of nowhere.

She had also let down the ranger, she reminded herself. She also wouldn't be there for the two clients who'd made appointments at the clinic for that day—which meant she was spectacularly failing the kindly doctor who'd entrusted her with his practice. In less than a week she'd lost two patients and stood up two others.

Thoughts of how badly she was failing what she'd barely started immediately reminded her of her sister, but the opportunity to review the list of her inadequacies where her sibling was concerned—or to speculate about what Cam had done when she hadn't shown up—was mercifully short-circuited by the man walking toward her.

Nick pushed his fingers through his dark hair, adding more spikes to those he'd acquired in his sleep. In his other hand he carried a length of white cord and the plastic bag containing their meager meal supply. Because bears could easily scent food, he'd hung the bag in a tree so nothing would come after the pack he'd used for a pillow.

He had slept on bare ground. She'd slept a couple of feet away, cocooned in the silicon-coated material that had held in enough of her body heat to keep her from turning into a Popsicle.

"Morning," she murmured, working herself to a standing position with her bed still wrapped around her.

His glance skimmed her face as he moved closer. The carved line of his jaw was shadowed with a night's growth of beard. A sleep crease angled along one cheek. With his hair sticking up and his face rugged from a restless night, she shouldn't have found him attractive at all. Instead he seemed even more...virile.

She didn't bother questioning the faint flutter in her stomach when she started moving in his direction. As she'd found herself thinking a dozen times last night, she was just glad he was there.

His deep voice sounded rusty when he echoed, "Morning," himself and headed past her for the pack.

Melissa kept going, too, heading for the bushes. There was no point asking him how he'd slept. She knew. They'd both been awake half the night; her from hearing noises, and him from answering when she'd asked what he thought those noises were.

Thinking he had to be as grateful for daybreak as she was, she hurried into the trees. Her immediate needs were for a bathroom, a shower and coffee. Though using the bushes was decidedly primitive and a hot, steamy shower was a pipedream, she knew they at least had the coffee. She'd seen the freeze-dried kind in the pack last night.

The promise of hot caffeine practically pulled her back through the dew-drenched plants a minute later. Knowing they would need a fire, she picked up pinecones and twigs along the way. If she focused only on the immediate, she couldn't worry about her sister or think about how she was blowing her new life. Or so she was reminding herself when she stepped from the trees to find Nick standing out by the water.

The orange pack and their sticks lay a few feet behind him.

Confused, she glanced at the indentations in the grass where they'd slept. The fire he'd set on the pebbles below the little bank was out cold and covered with dirt.

Hugging her armful of fuel, she crossed toward him.

"What are we doing?" she called.

He must have combed his fingers through his hair again. Some of the sleep spikes were gone when he glanced from her to what she cradled in the blanket still wrapped around her.

Looking a little uncertain of how she might react to his response, he reached toward her and scooped her little load into his hands.

"We won't need this right now," he said, dropping everything to the rocks. "We have to cross the stream. Might as well get it over with."

She blinked at his shadowed jaw, then at the hill meeting the water on the side where they stood. Wisps of fog hid the tops of the enormous trees, making it impossible to tell how high that rise in the land was. It was easy enough to see the other side, though, and the bend in the stream that carried the water down away from them.

Since he'd said they had to follow that stream, she would concede that they had to cross. She would even allow that they had to cross there. She wasn't ready, however, to do it just then. "Before coffee?"

"We'll have coffee on the other side. We'll have to warm up after we get there, anyway." He nodded beside him. "That water is going to be cold."

He sounded every bit as logical as he had yesterday. Every bit as pragmatic, practical and...focused.

She could have focused better after coffee.

Her eyes narrowed on his. "Do you always wake up like this?"

As rugged as he looked, his expression when his dark eyebrows merged should have appeared rather formidable. Instead, he simply looked curious. "Like what?"

"Ready to take on the day."

"You make it sound like a fault."

"It is when you're not a morning person," she mumbled. She glanced past the sleeve of his leather jacket. "I don't supposed there's a bridge around here anywhere."

"We're fresh out of bridges and telephones." Sounding as if a telephone was very much on his mind, or at least getting to one, he nodded toward the pack. "You might as well sit down and take off your boots and socks. We'll carry them across in the pack. The blanket, too. You don't want to restrict your balance."

His joints protesting from having slept on hard ground, in need of a little caffeine himself, Nick crouched with the crack of his knees to untie his own boots. Beside him, Melissa reluctantly pulled the blanket from her shoulders, folded it and stuffed it into the pack. She didn't start taking off her boots when she sank onto the pack, though. Pulling off her cap, she reached to the back of her head and tugged off the hot-pink band securing her ponytail.

She'd had the hat on all day yesterday. She'd slept in it last night, undoubtedly to keep her head warm. Watching her scrub her fingers over her scalp, he didn't doubt for an instant that it felt good to be free of the confinement. But it was the way her hair spilled over her shoulders that had the bulk of his attention. It gleamed with shades of flax and wheat, and looked so silky when she ruffled it that he couldn't begin to imagine how soft it would feel in his hands.

He was trying to imagine it, anyway, when he realized he was openly staring.

She must have realized it, too. Skimming her fingers through its length, she gave him a quick, faintly self-conscious smile.

"The band was driving me nuts," she said, holding up the bit of hot-pink fabric.

"I imagine," was all he said before he glanced away. He'd already been aware of how petite she was, of the delicacy of her features. With the cap gone, her hair swept back from her face, the bouncy youthfulness she'd first struck him with was gone. Now, there was a loveliness about her that almost made her look fragile. Especially with the worry he could now clearly see in her tired eyes.

He frowned at the thought, along with the vague sense of protectiveness it brought, and saw her stuff the band in her vest pocket. With a few deft twists of her wrists, she swept her hair back again, clapped her cap back on and pulled the less-restricted length through the hole. Only then did she reach to untie her boots.

The protectiveness he dismissed as nothing of consequence. He was responsible for her. That was all. The artlessness of what she'd done, though, stayed with him as he turned his attention back to his own laces. So did the intimacy of it. He knew women who shamelessly used their assets to taunt and tease, but there was nothing at all coy about the woman peeling off her socks to expose her pink-tipped toes. He'd noticed that within moments of meeting her.

He noticed a lot of things about her, he realized, thinking of the fatigue in her eyes this morning. He had the feeling she'd slept even worse than he had. He'd only had the dull ache in his shoulder to contend with, along with a few aches and pains from being tossed around in the plane on the way down. She was undoubtedly contending with a few of those herself. But he had the feeling she'd lain awake most of the night trying to figure out every shift of every leaf.

The times he'd been awake, his only thoughts had been of how important it was they get to the top of that ridge.

Rolling up the legs of his pants, he glanced to the gray sky. The clouds that had come in last night were hanging right on top of them, but he couldn't worry now about how badly they would obscure the view. He just had to get them there.

"Shall we get this over with?" he asked, stuffing everything into the pack.

She didn't answer. Testing the rocks beneath her bare feet when she stood, her only response was a sigh of resignation.

He had honestly expected her to protest a little more. He'd even thought she was going to in the moments before she'd asked about a bridge. Yet, she wasn't balking nearly as much as she could have. Given what she'd had to deal with so far, he had to admit that she hadn't backed away from anything at all. A few brief moments of hesitation was all she seemed willing to allow herself.

More impressed by that than he wanted to be, he watched her study the water rushing past her toes.

The bank on the other side was about thirty feet away. The water wasn't terribly deep. He doubted it would reach her knees. It just looked awfully swift in the main channel.

Mel figured that as long as she didn't slip and get soaked, she would be fine.

The thought didn't provide quite the assurance she was after, but getting this over with sounded like a fine idea to her. With her jeans rolled to her knees, she was getting colder by the minute.

Beside her, Nick picked up the bulging pack.

From his faint frown when he pulled it on, it occurred to her again that the pack must be heavy. It had to be even heavier now with all they'd stuffed into it. But she didn't get a chance to ask if there was some way she could share the load. She'd barely opened her mouth when his right arm settled over her shoulders and the words stuck in her throat.

"Put your arm around my waist," he ordered easily. "I don't want you to slip and get wet."

She didn't want to slip and get wet, either. "I think I can manage." Aware of his hard body pressed against her side, she swallowed. "Really."

"It's not worth taking any chances. It's all of forty degrees out here and those are the only clothes you've got."

She didn't want him to think she was helpless. Despite the fact that the past eighteen hours hadn't gone particularly well, she was perfectly capable of getting herself across one relatively innocent-looking stream.

Or so she was thinking when he nudged her into the ankle-deep water.

The first step shocked her with the icy chill of the glacial runoff. It also proved how slick the rocks were when her foot slid sideways.

Nick's hand tightened on her shoulder.

"It would be easier if you'd lean on me," he muttered. "Neither one of us needs to break anything, either. The current's going to be stronger in the middle."

With his fingers curled around the top of her arm, he hugged her closer as she gingerly took another step. She hadn't had time before to consider how she felt about him being so close. Thinking about it now, she admitted that she had no problem with it at all. With her footing so much more precarious than she'd thought it would be, she welcomed the solid feel of him and the sure and certain grip securing her to his side.

Conceding that leaning on him might not be a bad idea, she tightened her own hold. Doing as he'd instructed before, she put her arm around his waist, shamelessly sliding her fingers under the hem of his jacket to get a better grip. His heat warmed her fingers. His hip felt as hard as the rocks beneath their feet. His thigh where it flexed against hers felt like hammered steel.

An eagle in search of breakfast screamed overhead. Squirrels chattered their way through the trees. The sounds of the waking wilderness normally would have enthralled her, given that she'd spent her life waking to neighbors arguing or the rattle of plumbing. But her focus was on her balance as they moved through water that ran as clear and cold as ice. The speckled stones visible through the wavering surface were rounded and slick, and with every yard they gained, the current increased along with the depth.

The snowmelt cascading around her calves sucked the heat from her skin, her muscles, and went to work on her bones.

Glued to him as she was, he had to feel her shivering. "We're halfway there," he said over the rush of swirling water.

In the middle of taking another cautious step, she simply took his word for it and kept her eyes down.

A yellowed leaf swept by. "My feet are numb."

"Try to think of something else."

Her breath quivered in, then drifted off in a puff. "Like what?"

She wasn't sure if she was the only one shaking or if he was shaking, too. He had to be as cold as she was.

"I'm thinking about the fire we're going to build in about a minute," he confessed. "Think about heat."

"Okay," she murmured, and concentrated on the warmth she could feel radiating along her side.

Even with her feet feeling as if they'd disappeared, she was aware of the solid strength in his body. She was even feeling exceeding grateful for it when her foot slipped again. A few steps later his did. Each time, they stopped, steadied and moved on, slowly making their way to shallower water and a shore littered with rocks, small boulders and tangled bits of driftwood.

She was beginning to think she would never feel her feet again when they finally sloshed from the stream. With his arm still around her, they picked their way toward the bank and a grassy patch that promised relief from the unforgiving rocks.

She'd no sooner set foot on it, than a rock caught her in the arch.

She sucked in a breath. With her free hand, she grabbed the front of his jacket.

"Easy," he murmured, locking both arms around her to keep her from going to her knees. Soft leather brushed her cheek as he shifted to get his own balance. The faint scent of citrus aftershave and warm male clung to it, filling her nostrils, seeping into her lungs. "Are you okay?"

Cold air on her wet skin had added another layer of goose bumps to those already racing over her body. Looking up from the scarred leather covering his broad chest, she suddenly found herself far more conscious of her erratic heartbeat than the icy sensation prickling nearly everywhere else.

She said she was fine, though fine was the last thing she felt.

She could still sense his heat where he'd pressed her to his side. Now, with her arm in a death grip around his waist, his arms around her back, the fronts of his thighs seemed to burn into her, through her. As his glance drifted over her upturned face, something shifted in the quicksilver depths of his eyes.

The dark glint made her heart give an unhealthy jerk. It did it again when his glance slowly drifted to her mouth. Something warm curled low in her stomach. Her breath turned shallow. The heat he caused to shimmer through her was unmistakable, totally unexpected, and nearly made her forget she was freezing—until the predatory light in his eyes disappeared with the blink of his dark lashes.

As if a switch had been thrown, a muscle in his jaw jerked and he slid his hands to her shoulders. It jerked again when he deliberately pulled away.

"We should get that fire going." The vapor of his breath drifted off as he nodded a few feet ahead of them. "How about there?"

Unsettled as much by her reaction as his, the best she could manage was a nod.

She doubted he even saw it. He shrugged off the pack as he moved past her, concentration etched in his face and totally intent on his task.

The fuel around them was drenched with dew. Apparently having anticipated that problem, he'd put some of the drier pinecones they'd collected last night into the pack. Piling those up, he poked in a couple of the kerosene-and-wax-soaked fire starters.

Within a minute, he had a small blaze going. Settling herself beside it, Melissa gave him a cautious glance, wrapped herself in her blanket and propped her feet in front of the flames, shivering.

Without a word, Nick lowered himself to the ground beside her. Water droplets clung to the dark hair scattered over his calves, but she couldn't make out any goose bumps. Either he was accustomed to the cold or his body mass simply provided more insulation, she thought enviously. Whichever it was, his hands were as steady as a surgeon's when he poured water from the canteen into their communal cup and set it as close to the flames as he could get it.

The thought of those hands on her body, on her skin, had her shivering again.

"You'll be warmer in a few minutes," he promised.

Cupping his hands on either side of his leg, he swept the droplets away. He did the same with the other, the movement so practiced she couldn't help but wonder if that was what he did after he got out of a shower.

Realizing that she was thinking of him naked, his magnificent muscles glistening with moisture, she pulled her glance to her own toes. Beneath her Peony Passion polish, she was certain her nails were blue.

"You want to put this in the cup?" He propped his feet not far from hers, since that was where the heat was going, and handed over a packet of coffee and a twig to stir it with.

"Sure," she murmured, grateful for something else to focus on. It wasn't like her to fantasize about much of anything. She kept her dreams simple, practical. It especially wasn't like her to fantasize about a man she'd just met. But, then, the men she'd known hadn't evoked fantasies once she'd gotten to know them, either. They'd killed them too fast. "How's the granola bar selection?"

"Same as last night. Unless you want a candy bar."

The candy bar was chocolate. With nuts.

Just to prove to herself that she was handling the situation, she said, "I'll have oatmeal raisin."

He handed over the granola bar, took one for himself and pulled out the map. He took the compass from his pocket. While she thoughtfully studied the nutrition information on her wrapper, he just as thoughtfully studied the topographical grids.

Melissa shot him a sideways glance. He was acting as if nothing at all had happened in those moments they'd been in each other's arms.

Maybe for him nothing had. Maybe he was accustomed to having strange women cling to him. Maybe she'd only imagined the interest she thought she'd seen.

The possibilities pulled her focus back to her breakfast. She wasn't sure how she felt about what had happened herself. She wouldn't deny that she felt terribly grateful to him for landing them in one piece. Given that she really needed the benefit of his experience right now, she would even admit that she was feeling a certain dependence on him, whether she liked the idea or not. She had just never before had a man simply hold her and make her stomach quiver. Or make her feel as if he'd branded her somehow.

Not that it mattered, she thought. He was leaving the very place she'd just moved to—once he got them out of here.

"You never did tell me how far we have to walk."

Nick glanced to where she flicked bits of wrapper into the faintly crackling fire. Heat radiated toward them, along with drifts of smoke they both ignored in favor of the warmth.

He hadn't told her because he didn't know. "With all the up and down we're going to have to do, it's hard to tell."

"Can you guess?"

"I imagine we're a couple of miles from the ridge we flew over. That's where we're heading now." That ridge was nearly a mile high and miles long. Unless they'd glided farther west than he'd thought, they would have to reach it sooner or later. "Once we get there, we'll have a better idea of how much farther we have to go."

She lifted her eyes to his, concern shadowing her delicate face. "Will we get to the airport you saw before dark?"

There was hope in her question.

He really hated to kill it.

"I wouldn't count on it."

She took a deep breath, lifted her chin.

"The fire feels good," she finally said, and took a bite of her breakfast.

Picking up his bar, Nick did the same, more aware of her than he wanted to be as he waited for their toes to warm and their coffee to heat.

He knew she was cold. He also knew the best way to get warm was shared body heat. Sixty seconds of holding her had proved that easily enough. Skin-to-skin contact was even better. Not that he was about to suggest it.

His wrapper went up in flames. Melissa tossed in the last of hers a minute later and leaned forward to brush off the bottoms of her feet. As she did, the motion drew his glance to the bright polish on her toes. He'd noticed that she kept her fingernails short and unadorned, a nod to practicality he supposed, considering what she did for a living. But everything else about her was frankly feminine, sensual, and now that he knew how incredible her body felt against his fully clothed, he could only imagine how she would feel naked in his arms.

That was pretty much what he'd been imagining a while ago, too. That, and how soft her lips would feel against his.

His thoughts had him shifting uncomfortably as certain parts of his anatomy stirred once more. He wasn't some teenager with raging hormones who got turned on at the sight of any pair of shapely legs—though hers definitely were. He hadn't even been all that interested in sex, considering how his wife had tried to manipulate him with it in the last weeks of their marriage and how deliberately he'd avoided female entanglements since. He had enough problems as it was without adding a relationship to the mess.

Yet, all he'd had to do was breathe in her scent with her clinging to him and he might as well have been sixteen again.

Considering how cold that water was, she shouldn't have affected him at all.

Thinking he'd need to go wading again if he didn't stop thinking about her, he handed over her socks and boots and reached for his own. From the careful way she watched him, he had the feeling she felt a little uncomfortable herself.

"Are you warm yet?" he asked.

Her smile was soft, and faintly self-conscious. "Warmer than I was. You?"

"Better. Here," he said, pulling the heavy cup from the smoking ashes. "This is as close to hot as it's going to get." Their little fire had nearly burned itself out. "Drink what you want and I'll finish it. Then give me the blanket. You can move around more easily if you wear this."

He rose as he spoke, the rasp of a zipper joining the crack of his knees. Looking up the long length of him, Melissa nearly choked on her first sip of the warm, dark brew. "I'm not taking your jacket. You'll freeze."

"I'll warm up once we get moving."

"So will I. Thanks, anyway."

Nick frowned at the top of her head. "Anyone ever tell you you're stubborn?"

"All the time. I take it as a compliment."

"It's not meant that way," he muttered. Ignoring her refusal, he dropped his jacket to the backpack and tugged the hem of his heavy denim shirt from the waistband of his pants. He could be stubborn, too. "If you won't take the jacket, then at least wear this."

Mel held the cup to her mouth, prepared to take another sip. Her sigh caused steam to waver. "You don't have to share your clothes,'' she quietly insisted. Her sweater was knit and her vest was insulated. Both had served her fine before the temperature had dropped last night. They would again, if it ever heated up. ''I really will be warmer once we start moving.''

''Not that much.''

''Yes, I will.''

His hand slipped down the front of his shirt, undoing buttons along the way. ''You know something?'' he asked, his tone deceptively casual. ''Except for when you first showed up at the plane, and when you took off after we landed, you really haven't been all that difficult. I don't know why you find it necessary to start now.''

Her head snapped up. ''I'm not being difficult. I'm just saying that it's not necessary for you to give up any of what you're wearing for me.''

''And I'm saying that it is.'' Unbuttoning his sleeves, his glance slipped over her. He doubted she weighed more than 105, drenched. ''From what I've felt, there's not all that much to you. I have at least twice your body mass. Since I have more muscle, I can generate more heat and won't lose it nearly as fast as you will.''

She wasn't about to comment on his blunt assessment of her shape. She wasn't going to have him be uncomfortable on her account, either. She'd caused him enough misery. She was about to tell him that, too, when he pulled off the heavy denim, and the words stalled in her throat.

The stark white undershirt he wore stretched over his beautifully formed chest. Its short sleeves ended in the middle of incredibly cut biceps. Yet, it wasn't his taut muscles that had her staring. It was the large crimson-colored bruise she could see creeping below the left sleeve.

Her glance moved back to his, her eyes questioning in

the moments before she set the cup on the ground. The blanket fell to her feet as she rose. Without a word she reached for the pack beside him.

She could practically feel his curiosity when she lifted it up.

She had been under the impression there was considerable weight to what he'd carried, but the pack couldn't have weighed more than fifteen pounds, full canteen and the jacket atop it included.

Dropping it with a soft thud, she straightened to meet his puzzled expression.

"You got hurt." Disquiet melded with a healthy dose of accusation. "Why didn't you say something?"

A shrug entered his voice. "No point. Will you take this?" he asked, lifting his shirt. "It's cold out here."

Obliging him, she took what he held and dropped it on his jacket. "Let me see."

He sighed at what she'd done. "There's nothing to see. It's just a bruise."

"How big a bruise?"

"I don't know," he muttered. "I didn't look."

He had been in pain while watching out for her. He had been in pain while trying to sleep on the cold, hard ground.

Guilt piled atop disbelief and concern.

It was her fault that he'd been hurt. If she hadn't been so insistent...

"Come on," Nick said, watching the curious play of emotions over her face. "It's nothing."

"If it were nothing, you wouldn't wince when you move. I thought the pack was just heavy," she started to explain, then cut herself off with the shake of her head. "Your arm should be wrapped if it's swelling."

He really didn't think there was anything drastically

wrong. Certainly not wrong enough to warrant the worry and guilt he could plainly see in her face. Figuring it wouldn't hurt to indulge her, he pulled the fabric to his shoulder.

Mel's glance shot to his, then back to the angry patch of crimson and burgundy. It widened as it rose, angling toward his chest. She wasn't a medical doctor, but she knew damaged tissue when she saw it. She also knew that a blow that severe could bruise more than what she could see on the surface. "Maybe you'd better pull your shirt up ."

"Look—"

"Please," she insisted. "Have you had any shortness of breath? Chest pain?"

He shook his head, totally puzzled. "I'm fine. What are you—"

"Either pull it up, or I will."

He must have believed her, something she would have found rather interesting had she not been so concerned with how badly he might be hurt. Bunching the shirt at the sides of his waist, now looking a little concerned himself, he tugged the hem from his pants and pulled the fabric to the middle of his chest.

The man was built like a Greek statue. Hard, smooth and beautifully sculpted. He could have been built like a turnip for all she cared as she pushed the fabric higher— and breathed an audible sigh of relief. The angry contusion fanned in a short U over his left collarbone and purpled the top of his pectoral, but it didn't go anywhere near the middle of his chest.

"Oh, good," she said on a whisper.

For a moment Nick said nothing. When he did, his tone was heavy with confusion. "What were you afraid of?"

"Heart damage," she admitted, more relieved by the

second. "A severe blow to the chest can cause the same kind of bruising to the heart muscle as you have here." The discoloration over the collarbone now had the bulk of her attention as she traced that hard ridge with the tips of her fingers. "Broken blood vessels and swelling can cause all kinds of problems we'll just be grateful we don't need to worry about."

She could practically hear his frown. "I thought you were a veterinarian."

"Animals have hearts," she said absently. A smile touched her mouth. "Big ones."

"That's not what I meant. I just didn't expect that you'd…"

"Know anything about humans?" she suggested, when he cut himself off.

Gooseflesh had sprung up on his skin. Whether from the cold or the lightness of her touch, she couldn't tell. "Something like that," he murmured.

"I'd never make it as a medical doctor," she confessed, concentrating on the feel of his clavicle, "but I know enough to recognize a problem."

"Did you want to be an M.D.?"

"Never." Beneath her fingers, the bone felt smooth and even. She was more accustomed to feeling for bumps or misalignment in animals, but bone was bone and muscle was muscle. As she skimmed her fingers over the solid contours of his chest, she was just relieved that she didn't feel anything that shouldn't have been there. "I always wanted to be a vet."

"Why?"

"Because Mom would never let me have a pet." With her hand under his shirt, she curved her fingers over the joint of his shoulder. "Can you lift your arm?"

She was too intent on what she was doing to notice his

frown at her casual response. She was aware only of how he hesitated before he lifted his arm as far as his shoulder. He paused again, as if waiting to see how much pain was going to be involved, then gingerly raised it straight up.

Beneath her palm, the movement of joint and muscle felt beautifully fluid.

"How does that feel?" she asked. "Does it hurt?"

He lowered it a little less carefully. "Not as much as it could have," he said, relieved.

Relieved, too, her hand slid to his chest. "Good," she murmured, and met his eyes with a smile.

With her fingers spread over his smooth skin, she could feel his heartbeat, strong and steady. Her own gave an erratic little lurch. Nick hadn't moved. He just stood towering over her, his eyes steady on hers, and making her more aware by the instant that touching him was no longer necessary.

Slowly pulling her hand away, she took a step back.

She'd just wanted to make sure he was all right, the way he had when he'd put his arm around her to help her cross the stream.

"Did you hurt anything else you didn't see any point in mentioning?" she asked, conscious of him pulling down his shirt as he turned away. "You don't have any sprains or bumps? You didn't hit your head?"

The questions were the same as he'd asked her yesterday. Apparently realizing she was only giving as good as she got, he shot her a sideways glance before he tucked in his white undershirt and picked up the shirt she'd dropped.

"There's nothing else." Denim dangled from his index finger. "Will you put this on now?"

Melissa didn't argue.

Taking what he offered with a quiet "Thank you" she

moved away to pull it on. Aside from the fact that the extra layer would feel heavenly, arguing over whether or not he needed to share his clothes didn't seem like a very good idea. Disagreeing made her aware of him in more ways than she cared to consider, and she was aware enough of him as it was.

From the corner of her eye, she saw him stuff his arms into the sleeves of his jacket, left one first, and zip his jacket to the middle of his chest. A moment later he was pulling on his socks and boots.

She did the same, more careful now to gauge his movements than she'd been before. He still moved with an ease that other men would have found nearly impossible to manage, but she knew he was terribly sore.

She'd just unrolled her pants and tucked another roll in her long sleeves when he reached for the pack.

"I'll carry that," she insisted, and snatched it up before he could. "It's my turn, anyway."

Nick said nothing as she handed him his stick, packed up the blanket and waited for him to down his share of the coffee before she rinsed the cup in the stream. She'd said before that she could take care of herself. It seemed she also intended to carry her weight. Since the pack didn't weigh enough to slow her down, he had no problem with that. His only problem was that he couldn't get the feel of her hands out of his head.

He tried, though, as he watched her rise from beside the water.

His shirt practically swallowed her whole. The shoulder seams hung nearly to her elbows and the wrinkled hem hit the back of her knees. He didn't doubt that the heavy fabric would help her stay warm. But there was an advantage for him in her wearing it, too. Since the thing fit like a tent, it did an excellent job of hiding her curves.

Considering how every nerve in his body had tightened at her touch, staring at that cute little backside of hers could make for a very uncomfortable walk.

"Dump some water on the fire, will you?" he asked, kicking dirt over the faint thread of smoke. A smoldering spark was buried somewhere in there, he thought, then found himself frowning at Melissa's back. There was a spark smoldering there, too. "We don't want to leave until it's out."

Melissa turned, full cup in hand and promptly snuffed any potential for flame. Refusing to be responsible for any other mishaps, she dumped on four more cups for good measure, kicked on more dirt and dumped on four more.

"Will that do?"

She'd made mud of the ash. Watching Nick look up from the soggy mess, she caught his droll glance.

"It'll do," he agreed, and turned her around to stow the metal container in the pack on her back. "Are you always so thorough?"

"I try to be," she replied.

She barely caught the odd glance he gave her as they started along the stream in the misty morning light. She was too preoccupied with the way he'd deliberately masked his injury, too busy trying to figure out why he'd felt he needed to keep such a thing from her.

By midday, after two bush breaks, another granola bar and spotting a herd of deer, raccoons, a skunk and an enormous elk that had him explaining that the huge, ant-lered creatures could be dangerous, too, she began to suspect he was simply a man who didn't share anything that worried him personally. By early afternoon she became convinced of it.

They were over halfway up the ridge when he finally bothered to tell her he really didn't know where they were.

Chapter Five

"I know it's getting steeper," Nick said, "but we're almost there. Once we get to the top, we'll be able to figure out where we are."

The incline they had climbed for the past two hours had slowed them considerably. With the forested terrain too steep to climb straight up, Nick had angled them back and forth across the face of the rise Melissa could swear grew more vertical by the second.

She had promised Nick yesterday that she wouldn't slow him down. She'd been good to her word, too, not asking for any break he didn't offer himself. She'd kept up, kept pace. Since he'd seemed every bit as distracted as he had when she'd first met him, she'd even kept quiet.

Until now.

"Wait a minute." With her back bent and her hands planted on her knees, she lifted her head in pure disbelief.

"You don't know where we are? She tried to catch her breath. "Are you serious?"

"It's only a few hundred more feet." Now that his goal was nearly in sight, he apparently didn't see his admission as any sort of problem. "Can you make it?"

"Why didn't you mention this before?"

"No point," he said in the same dismissing way he had when she'd asked why he hadn't told her about his shoulder.

"Of course there's a point. If I'm lost I have the right to know it."

"I never said we were lost."

"You just said you don't know where we are."

"There's a difference."

"Excuse me?"

"I knew how to get us here. And I'm pretty sure I'll be able to get the rest of it figured out once we get to the top. Even if we were lost," he continued, not looking nearly as concerned as she felt, "what good would it have done for you to worry about it? You were awake half the night afraid of what might be in the trees. You wouldn't have slept at all if you'd thought we might not get out of here."

There was no way she could refute his logic. With everything else on her mind, the thought that he had no clue of their location might have been more than she could handle. It had never occurred to her that he didn't know. She had simply accepted that he had everything under control.

The realization that she hadn't hesitated to trust him collided with her offense at being left out of the loop. That offense was immediately compromised by the fact that he had protected her from being any more anxious than she'd already felt.

Part of her appreciated the reprieve. Another part, the part that wasn't accustomed to having anyone else look out for her, needed to know what else he figured there was no point telling her.

"Just how 'not lost' are we?"

Nick stood a few feet ahead of her, one foot planted higher than the other on the uphill ground. From the forbearance carved in his rugged face, he clearly didn't want to waste time convincing her that he'd had a plan all along. He just wanted to get to the top.

"We'll know when we reach the crest. The ceiling has lifted enough for us to see, so once we get there, I should be able to use the map and compass to figure it out." He looked from where she rubbed the tops of her thighs to the gray clouds overhead. "Unless you really need to rest, we should get moving. We don't want to be up here if those clouds decide to let loose."

"I don't need to rest," she replied, lying through her teeth. "But there is something I need for you to do."

Anxious to get moving, he'd already turned to continue on. Her request had him turning right back. "What's that?"

"I need you to tell me if there's anything else I should know about this…situation. I know you don't see any particular point in mentioning things like being injured or not knowing exactly where we are, but that sort of thing has the potential to directly affect me. Since it does, I want the information." She tipped her head. "Okay?"

She didn't need to be sheltered. Heaven knew no one had bothered to do it before.

From the way his gray eyes narrowed, she was pretty sure he felt otherwise. "If that's what you want."

"It is."

"Fine. Can we go now?"

The man was as dense as the rocks beneath his feet. Either that, or he simply didn't get the concept of sharing. "*Is* there anything I need to know?"

"The only thing I can think of is that we don't want to be here if there's any lightning in those clouds. High points are the first places it'll strike. We need to get up and over this."

His mention of high points had her swallowing her frustration as she moved away from the gnarled old pine she'd stopped beside.

"Is that it?" she gamely asked, needing to be sure she had it all.

"That's all I can think of at the moment." He nodded toward her legs. "You okay to go?"

"Anytime you are," she replied, anxious now to get moving herself.

He turned ahead of her, pointing out a snare she could use for a step.

She scrambled after him, loath to fall behind.

The man had the stamina of an ox. And, amazingly, more patience than she would have expected, given how badly he wanted to get to a phone. He had restrained his pace all day so she wouldn't have to run to keep up with him on the flat, or work so hard on their long haul upward. Still, with his legs so much longer, it felt as if she had to take two steps for every one of his.

She had considered herself to be in decent shape, but her thighs burned and her lungs struggled for air. She'd lived at sea level all her life. Her only mountain experience had been the Matterhorn bobsleds at Disneyland. The closest she'd come to the constant uphill climb was a session on a Stairmaster at a gym that had given freebie trial memberships near her old clinic. Her rubbery legs, however, were rapidly becoming the least of her concerns.

The stiffening breeze had a definite chill behind it, but the shiver that shuddered through her had far more to do with the apprehension she was desperately trying to ignore. She hadn't let herself ask Nick how high they were going. Nor had she let herself look. To keep from worrying about it, she'd kept her glance glued pretty much on where she put her feet—and reminded herself that she was still surrounded by trees so even if she fell, she'd bump into something before she went very far.

That was before the trees thinned to short scrub pines. The few trees she could see in the limited view she allowed herself struggled to survive in cracks of rock the wind had nearly scoured clean of soil. She had caught a few inadvertent glimpses of the incline below them, but each time, she had diligently forced her glance to the ground and made herself concentrate only on putting one foot in front of the other.

"Move ahead of me," she heard Nick say from above her, "and give me the pack."

"I can…" *manage,* she'd been about to say, but immediately changed her mind when she looked up. Above his head rose a short slope of boulders. There were no trees here. No bushes. Nothing to hold on to but rocks.

There was also nothing to block her view of what lay beyond—and below—them.

Her palms began to sweat just as they had when she'd stepped on the plane. *Don't look,* she mentally murmured. *Don't look,* she repeated and, taking a deep breath, handed the pack over when she reached him.

She kept her eyes down, her focus on Nick's hands as he took the pack from her.

"Just take it slow," he said, as if sensing her struggle. "I'm right behind you."

Refusing to let herself think about what she was doing,

she leaned forward to balance herself with both hands and crawled up to a wide ledge of stone. Knowing Nick was behind her kept the panic at bay, but her heart still wasn't beating all that evenly. Her breathing, already labored, didn't feel that normal, either.

She ducked her head against the gusting wind, wondering as she did why she couldn't have had some minor little phobia about something innocuous like blue food or fishbowls instead of being afraid of high places. It wasn't even the height of the place itself, she rationalized. It was all that air between her and the bottom.

Deciding that rationalizing wasn't helping, she glanced up, needing to know where to reach next. As she did, the wind caught the brim of her cap and snatched it back from her forehead.

Instinct had her grabbing for it. More urgent instincts had her canceling that motion to grasp her handhold on the rock.

"Put it on backward," she heard Nick call.

Her heart felt as if it were hammering in her throat when she realized that the hair hanging through the hole in the back had kept the cap from falling off completely.

She murmured a shaky, "Okay." Shaking on the outside, too, she carefully tugged the cap from her hair— only to have the wind catch it again.

The gust tore it from the tips of her trembling fingers, tossed it up like an invisible hand. It had barely sailed beyond her reach when Melissa let out gasp that went as deep as her toes. Flattened against the rocks to keep from pitching over herself, she watched the bit of khaki canvas tumble and float toward the treetops below her.

Frozen, she let the wind whip her hair across her colorless features.

Nick was suddenly right next to her.

"Hey," he said, his deep voice heavy with concern. "Are you all right?"

Eyes closed, head bent, she quickly nodded.

"Are you sure?"

She took a deep breath, let it out. "How much farther to the top?"

"Only a few feet."

Her head still down, she gave another nod and pushed the hair from her face.

The wind promptly threw it across her eyes again.

"You've got to get that out of your face. Do you still have that pink thing?"

"Pink thing?"

"For your hair. You took it out this morning."

She was definitely rattled. Nick didn't doubt that for a moment. Her hand was trembling as she reached between the sides of the denim shirt and pulled the bright pink band of fabric from her vest pocket. Shaky as she was, he took the band himself.

"You don't want to lose this, too," he explained, thinking she might object to what he'd done. "I'll hold it while you pull back your hair."

All she did was nod—and remain perfectly still.

She was afraid to let go, he realized. Afraid to straighten.

He reached for her billowing hair himself.

It felt even softer than he'd imagined, like threads of gold and silver silk in his hands. The impression was fleeting. Considering where they were, what the sky was about to do and how uneasy he was growing about her silence, his only concern was how to contain those wildly blowing tresses. His only experience with a woman's hair was messing it up, not smoothing it down.

She had her back to him, her hands flat against the

angled rocks. Battling the breeze, the best he could do was scoop the fluttering strands back from her face and secure them well enough near her nape to keep the bulk of it from blinding her.

There were still a few strands flying when he edged to her side to get a better look at her.

His first thought when he'd seen the color wash from her face was that he'd underestimated her fear. He knew she was afraid of heights. He'd suspected as much even before she'd admitted it on their way down from the sky. He just hadn't realized she was actually terrified of them.

He didn't care what she'd said about wanting to know about their situation. She could get mad at him later. He wasn't about to tell her it was only going to get worse.

"You're almost there. Okay?" he asked, drawing her glance to his. "I know you're not crazy about this," he admitted, understating considerably, "but there are people who climb these things just for fun. And the view really is incredible. Just take it easy and you'll be fine."

He thought she might give him a bit of a glare at the "fun" remark. He was hoping she would. If she would just show him some spark of her spirit, then he would know she'd be all right. The woman had guts. He'd known that when she'd stepped on the plane.

All she did was give another nod, take another deep breath and edge herself higher.

The rise of the land itself had sheltered them from the wind. With that protection gone, the gusts now bit into her, laced as they were with fine mist from the clouds. The sting against her skin went almost unnoticed. Mel was more aware of how slick the rocks felt beneath her feet and hands.

It was only the thought of reaching level ground that kept her inching ahead. That and the steady pressure of

Nick's big hand on her backside. He wasn't pushing. He was just steadying her so she wouldn't slip, and possibly take him down with her. The intimacy of the touch barely registered. She was too busy trying not to hyperventilate when she hoisted herself up to what she had thought would be level land, and found herself looking across ten feet of jumbled rock and windblown grasses to a view of distant lakes, lush forest and one rather majestic, snow-dusted mountain range.

She slid herself over to a flat rock all but buried in the middle and was hugging her knees to her quivering stomach when Nick crouched beside her.

No matter which way she looked, all she could see was down.

His hand settled on her shoulder.

Worried and huge, her eyes caught his. "It's all edge."

He shifted to move in front of her, his big body blocking her view of the vista ahead.

"Melissa—"

"You said we didn't have to go over this." An inch away from panic, her voice went thready with fear. "You said we'd go around most of it."

"I said we didn't have to go over the mountain."

"What do you call this?"

"This is the ridge. The mountain we aren't crossing," he said, using her way of putting things, "is that way."

She hesitantly glanced to where he pointed past her shoulder. Another mountain rose in the distance. She had no idea how far away it was. One mile or five. She just knew that the cloud-shrouded peak was even higher than they were.

Maybe there were some things she was better off not knowing. If she'd had any idea where he was leading her, she would never have left the lake.

The ridge went on for miles. From her brief glimpse, the angle of the side they had to go down was even steeper than what they'd come up.

"Don't think about it," he murmured. "I need you to help me figure out where we are."

With a faint grimace when the left strap slid across his shoulder, Nick slipped off the backpack and pulled out the map. Blocking the wind was all but impossible. It came at them from all directions, tearing at her hair, whipping his into a dark halo around his head. Keeping his body low and the map close to the ground, Nick anchored one side of the flapping paper with a heavy rock while Melissa flattened her trembling hand over the other.

"Don't let go," he warned her, adding a rock to her side for good measure. "This is what's going to get us out of here."

Rising from his crouch, he planted his feet and swept his glance across the vista she had first seen. He didn't seem at all affected by the altitude, the elements or the fact that there was nothing for 360 degrees but view. With his hands on his lean hips, hair whipping and needing a shave, he looked every bit as untamed and rugged as the wilderness he surveyed.

His broad shoulders almost seemed to relax when he turned full circle. It occurred to her, vaguely, that under other circumstances, he might have enjoyed being exactly where he was. Might even have sought it out on his own.

The impression had barely registered, inconceivable to her as it was, when he looked back toward the nearer mountain.

"The ridge bisects the upper quarter of the map on the right. It'll look like a series of long elliptical lines. Do you see a lake shaped like a horseshoe anywhere around it?"

Focusing on the map was good. It kept her head down. "There are a couple like that," she said after a few moments of searching the shapes and squiggly lines. The map wasn't like any she'd ever seen before. There were tiny sets of numbers everywhere.

"How about one between two mountains? I think there's a road cut through the trees down there, too. Maybe a logging road. Or Forest Service."

By searching for shapes, she thought she found the lake, but with all the lines, she couldn't tell if there were any roads.

Compass in hand, Nick crouched beside her again and checked the map himself.

He couldn't find a road, either. But he did have their bearings. With the scale on the map, he also had their distance.

"If we could travel in a straight line, we'd have about fifteen miles to go. Since we can't, it'll be more like thirty. There's a landslide below us, so we'll traverse this until we get past it, then we can start down."

He might as well have said they had to walk a rope across a canyon. The thought of walking along something only ten feet wide with a definite pitch on one side and a drop-off on the other, robbed her of her last bit of color.

The shaking in her hands made its way to her voice. "Can we go down the way we came and walk around this?"

She had no idea what Nick was thinking while he crouched there studying her face. All she knew for certain was that she couldn't move.

"The ridge goes for miles in either direction. Add another ten or so to get back down and circle around and you're looking at maybe fifty miles just to get where we could be in a couple of hours."

"What does that translate to in days?"

"Nearly a week." Careful to keep the wind from catching it, he folded the map and pushed it into the pack. "Even if we both didn't need to get to a phone, we don't have supplies for that long,"

They barely had enough supplies to last through tomorrow, he thought. He was hungry even now. The granola bars had barely been an hors d'oeuvre.

Ignoring the low growl of his stomach, he rose, pulling on the pack, and held out his hand. "We'll be off this ridge in no time. In the meantime," he said, watching her eyes go wide when he pulled her upright, "you can tell me why you really became a veterinarian."

Her breathing went shallow. Gripping his hands, she focused on the white undershirt visible between slashes of damp and darkening leather. "What?"

"That business about your mom not letting you have a pet. Rebellion isn't really why you did it, is it?"

"Do we have to talk about this now?"

"Why not?" He glanced behind him to see where he was stepping, then tugged her forward. "So why did you really do it?"

Melissa knew exactly what Nick was doing. He was trying to distract her, as he had when they'd crossed the stream. To keep her mind off the freezing water, she had concentrated on the heat she'd felt in his body.

Now she concentrated on the strength in his hands.

"Maybe there was a little rebellion in there." Her grip tightened as she took another cautious step. She would try it his way. If it didn't work, she was sitting down. "I did it because animals are more honest than people. They don't lie to you about where they were or who they were with, and they don't spend the rent on Jack Daniel's."

"Are you talking about the guy you moved to Harbor to get away from?"

Anxiety met confusion as she glanced up. "What guy?"

"The one people in town think you're trying to get away from."

"There is no guy. I'm talking about my mom and my sister."

She had no idea why he frowned at that. Nor did she care. Her concern was with the swaying sensation threatening her balance when she swiped back her hair and glimpsed the perilous view below.

"Oh, geeze," she muttered, and lowered herself to the rocks.

Nick sank with her.

Her response about her family had caught him totally off guard. Now was not the time, however, to have her elaborate. He was more interested at the moment in getting them across the narrow ridge without her totally freezing up on him.

He had never known true fear. Not until yesterday. He'd been in business situations that had scared the hell out of him. He'd been afraid of losing everything he'd worked for. He'd feared for lives his decisions could put at risk. He'd just never feared for his own safety until those moments when he'd realized his plane was going down and there was nothing he could do to stop it. Foreboding had sunk its claws deep and hung on until he'd set foot on solid ground. As blessedly short-lived as those moments of fright and dread had been, he could only imagine how awful such anxiety had to be when faced with a couple hours of it.

He found it telling that she hadn't yet actually said she

was afraid. It was as if the moment she did, she would lose whatever control she had.

"There's another way down," he told her, wondering just how much of that control she had left. She hadn't failed him yet. He prayed she wouldn't now. "It will take a little longer to get where we're going, but we'll get off the top of this sooner. The slide starts behind us, but the worst of it is ahead. If we go the other direction, we can start down once we get past it and skirt it from the base."

With less enthusiasm that he would have hoped for, she looked behind her. The view in that direction looked pretty much the same.

He swore he saw discouragement in the moments before her glance fell to her knees.

He couldn't let her give up now.

Slipping his fingers under her chin, he tilted her face to his. "I need you to do something for me," he insisted, growing more uneasy by the second with her fear. "I need you to tell me the hardest thing you've ever done."

"I...I can't remember."

"Try."

"All I can think about is how far it is to the bottom."

She started to look away. He wouldn't let her. Taking her face between his hands, he held her eyes with the determination in his. "I'm not going to let you fall, Melissa. We'll crawl off here if we have to. Now, tell me. The hardest thing."

The insistence in his tone matched the intensity in his piercing eyes. Mel wouldn't have blamed him had he finally become impatient. Or, if he'd told her she was being foolish and unreasonable and paranoid and all the other logical things she suspected he was thinking just then. Yet, all she saw was certainty. All she heard was the assurance that she didn't have to do this alone.

The hardest thing, she thought, when she could barely think at all.

"The time I had to leave Mom in jail." Her glance faltered. "I couldn't bail her out."

Nick's brow pinched at the admission.

"That would be tough," he agreed, studying the sweep of her dark lashes. He couldn't imagine what would have put her or her mother in such circumstances. "But you survived that. You'll survive this, too.

"I'll make you a promise," he said, urging her eyes back to his. "I got you out of the air without breaking anything essential, and I'll get you off this ridge and back home if you'll just do as I say." His thumb brushed her cheek. With the wind-driven mist dampening her skin, her flesh felt as smooth and cool as marble. "Do you trust me to do that?"

Mel swallowed, hard. He said he promised. That alone should have told her they were doomed. Whenever a man promised her anything, he disappeared on her. But she'd never had to put her life in a man's hands before, either. And so far Nick's hands hadn't let her down.

Grasping that thought, she did something she would never have thought she could do. She'd spent so much time propping up others over the years that she had come to think of leaning on anyone as a sign of weakness. Heaven knew, she didn't want to be weak. But this wasn't something she could handle alone, and Nick was telling her that she didn't have to. So she let go of the idea that she had to be in control. She let go of the idea that she alone was responsible. No one was looking to her to find the way out.

Had she not been so frightened, she would have found enormous relief in that.

"I trust you," she finally whispered.

Her surrender hadn't come without a struggle. He felt certain of that as his hands slid to his thighs.

Thunder rumbled in the distance. Hearing it, he silently swore. Rushing her wouldn't be a good idea, but they had problems enough without trying to dodge lightning bolts, too.

He reached for her hand as he rose. "Stay behind me and hold on to the pack. Just step where I step. Going this way, we only have to be up here for a few hundred yards." His eyes darted to the clouds. "It's better we're not up here any longer, anyway."

Melissa didn't need to look up to know what concerned him. The thunder had slithered along her already-raw nerves, taunting her with an entirely different set of worries. But as good as she was at multitasking under ordinary circumstances, she could only deal with one anxiety at a time for the moment.

Walking exactly where he walked, she focused on the fact that they didn't have to go nearly as far on the crest as they would have going the other way—even if it would take them longer to get to civilization. She didn't care if it took them the rest of the month to get there. All she cared about was that minute. That second.

She couldn't stop the trembling. Even her knees seemed to be doing it as they made their way along the crest to the slanted boulders they crawled down to start their descent. When her eyes weren't on the ground, they were on Nick.

He went first, turning his back to the free-fall view to take the first steps down. She sat, then turned, guided by his hands and his voice and trusting him to set her feet where they needed to go.

With the ridge above her head, she was no longer surrounded by nothing but sky. She could reach out—on one side anyway—and touch something other than air. Knowing that helped. Knowing Nick was watching her every move helped more. It just seemed to take forever for them to work their way from rock to bushes and into a stand of pine. But any relief she might have felt at being able to hold on to trees for balance was pitifully short-lived. Within minutes, pine had given way to a copse of golden aspen—and a four-block-wide slope of dirt and tiny pebbles.

The landslide that appeared below them wasn't nearly as broad as the one they were avoiding. But going around it would add even more time.

Behind them, the first drops of rain ticked against the leaves other rains had beaten from the trees.

With his hands on his hips, Nick glanced to where she stood with her arm around the slender white trunk of a barren tree. "It's going to start pouring any minute."

Watching him check out the terrain parallel to them, she felt a few drops hit her head. The shirt she wore already felt damp from mist. The fat drops making dark circles on her sleeves were going to make it feel plain old wet.

She gave a sober nod. "I hear it does that a lot in the Northwest."

"Only from October to July."

She'd heard that, too.

"So," he said, looking from the sparse crop of timber behind them to the long, relatively smooth-looking slope stretching below their feet. "There isn't any shelter up here. And this," he continued, nodding to what lay below them, "is going to be mud in a matter of minutes."

A faint hint of apprehension slithered through her as she looked from the dark circles springing up on his jacket. She knew exactly what he was thinking. The fact that she could read his mind wasn't nearly as troubling as the fact that she agreed with him. "That's true."

"What do you think?"

The slope looked steep, and there wasn't a thing to hang on to. Thinking of where she had just come from, it just didn't look nearly as steep as it might once have. Certainly, it didn't look as dangerous as the ridge.

He had promised to get her home. She'd promised she wouldn't slow him down. All things considered, they would probably make excellent time taking the more direct route.

She would give anything to be standing on level ground. "Do we go straight to the bottom?"

The light of a smile entered his eyes. "Angle to the right. See that rise in the ground down there with the trees below it? We might be able to make a shelter in front of it."

His last words were drowned by a crack of thunder that nearly shook the ground. The flash came three seconds later.

Melissa had started down on two.

The ground was loose. And traction was a definite problem. Her heels kept slipping from under her, which meant she kept landing on her palms and her backside. But each time she did, she slid a little farther. Since she could slide faster than she could walk, she gave up on the latter and just let the ground carry her while she used her heels for brakes.

From the rocks skimming past her, she knew that Nick wasn't far behind.

If she hadn't been so concerned with flipping over or hitting one of the boulders that hadn't been swept to the bottom, she might have looked around to check. It occurred to her, fleetingly, that she would know exactly what she would see if she did. He was probably loving this. The glint in his eyes when he'd smiled hinted at a taste for adventure. She supposed all pilots possessed that, given the nature of flying. It was just hard to grasp that he actually liked doing what she saw only as an opportunity for character development.

The rain turned to hail, pelting her knees, stinging her face. Hail was good, she told herself. It wasn't as wet as rain. The last thing she wanted was for them to be cold, drenched and covered with mud. Cold and damp would be uncomfortable enough.

The rise Nick had pointed out rapidly approached on the right.

Skidding to a stop, she felt him grab her by the arms from behind and hoist her up. Her feet were barely under her when he snatched her wrist. With his head ducked against hail that rapidly slicked the ground with white, he hauled her toward the wall of rock and pine the landslide had sliced right past.

She thought he would let her go as soon as they were inside the trees. Instead, he pulled her along, leading her deeper into the protection of the woods. The dark rock wall rising beside them blocked the wind. Surprisingly, it also blocked the pellets of ice that were slowly turning back to rain.

She had just realized they were under a natural overhang when Nick turned to face her. Still holding her wrist, he reached for her other hand and turned them both palms up.

The late-afternoon light would have been dim even without the thunderclouds descending on them. With the narrow rock ceiling jutting a few feet overhead and the trees filtering the light further, everything was muted with shades of gray.

Still, it was easy enough to see the dirt on her hands, and the unmasked concern in the shadowed lines of his face.

"You should wash off to see if you scraped yourself," he said, brushing dirt from her wrist. "Some of those rocks up there were pretty sharp. Are you okay now that you're off the top?"

He didn't need to know that she desperately craved the feel of something solid and strong. With him searching her face and his hands so gentle on hers, he especially didn't need to know she was thinking his arms would do just fine.

Caught unprepared for the thought herself, afraid he might already suspect what she had on her mind, she slowly eased her hands away. Anxiety was rapidly fading. All she felt now was embarrassed.

"I'm sorry about that," she murmured, indicating the general direction they'd just come. "About up there, I mean. I've never—"

"Don't worry about it." He reached out, lifting his hand as if he were about to push back a strand of her damp and flattened hair—only to let his hand fall as if he'd just thought better of it. "There are a lot of things I can't handle, too."

He gave her the closest thing she'd seen to a real smile. He just turned his back on her too quickly for her to get the full impact. "What do you say we find some place to ride this out?"

Wishing he hadn't withdrawn his touch, unable to deny how badly she craved it, she came up beside him. She couldn't imagine him fearing anything. "What can't you handle?"

"Whiners. People who pretend to be something they're not. Sleepless nights."

The packed earth beneath their feet never saw the sun and was bare of vegetation. The rough rock wall along their side hung with moss. He absently touched a thick patch as they passed. She'd noticed him doing that before, touching foliage, tree bark, stone. He was a tactile person. A man who appreciated textures and shapes.

What he'd done had just told her more about him than what he'd said. If he had any real fears, he wasn't sharing them with her.

"Then last night must have been a real challenge," she concluded.

"I doubt tonight's going to be much better. This looks about as good as it's going to get."

Ahead of them, the wall of rock they followed swung out slightly, creating what would have almost passed for a cave—had it been deeper and more closed in. But they had something solid on three sides and a roof of rock to protect them from the elements hammering the trees and everything else surrounding them.

Nick watched Melissa tug a strand of damp hair from her cheek as she looked up at him. Curiosity danced in her eyes. "Did you know this was here?"

"Never been here before in my life." He slipped off the pack, swept the moisture from his forehead with his jacket sleeve. They were both dirty and damp. He was also starving—and feeling more than a little curious himself. "I guess it's just time we had a little luck."

He saw her smile. Not much, just enough to let him know she figured they were due, too. There was too much strain in her features to allow the bright energy he'd seen before.

"So now we build a fire?" she asked.

"And we eat." Digging into their supplies, he pulled

out a half-dozen large, slightly crushed pinecones. ''While we're doing that, you can tell me which of your relatives has trouble with the truth and which has the problem with the bottle.''

Chapter Six

He wanted to know about her family.

Melissa stood at the edge of the overhang, holding her hands palms up in the rain. There was never a stream or lake around when a girl needed one.

Behind her she heard the snap and spit of flame catching the pinecones and the sounds of Nick peeling bark from a limb he'd hauled under the overhang to get to drier wood.

He already knew she was difficult. He already knew how she looked after a miserable night, a more miserable day and without a shower, a comb and her mascara all but gone. She had dirt on the cuffs of the shirt he'd loaned her, up its back, ground into the back of her jeans, and from the way he kept glancing at her cheek, probably on her face. What difference could it possibly make if he now knew her life had been as big a mess as she was?

She pulled the handkerchief he'd given her yesterday

from where she'd tucked it in her vest pocket. Using it to dry her hands, she turned back to where he was building a neat little pile of sticks. Wood cracked as he used his knee to break a small branch in two.

"Any scrapes?" he asked.

"Just a couple of little ones."

"There's antibiotic ointment in the pack."

"How about you?"

The wood landed on the stack. Wiping his hands on his pants, he glanced down, murmured, "They're fine," and reached for the canteen.

She promptly intercepted it and set it back on the pack.

"Let me see," she said, reaching for his wrist. "The other one, too."

Picking up his other hand, she turned them both over in hers. Deep lines creasing his broad palms. A callus ridged the skin below the knuckle on his bare ring finger. Wiped free of dirt, she could see that he'd escaped without the minor scrapes she'd earned, but it was the callus that brought the faint hint of consternation. It would have taken years for a ring to have left such a mark.

"You didn't believe me?"

She forced a smile at his accusation. "Just wanted to be sure."

Metal clicked against metal as she handed him back the canteen and the cup. "My sister's the one who tends to bend the truth," she said quietly, ripping open a packet of potato soup mix. "My mom is the one who can't handle liquor."

Nick watched her pour the mix into the container he held, then take the canteen from him to add the water. Leaving the stick she'd saved from that morning in it so he could stir, she turned back to the pack to pull out the little first-aid kit. She wasn't doing anything that didn't need to be done, but she seemed very much to need to be doing it.

"Mom's doing okay, though." She removed the lid from a small tube of ointment, spread a dab on her finger. "It's been hard for her, but she's had the same job for over a year now. And she has a nice older lady for a roommate."

The scrapes on the heel of her hand appeared to have the bulk of her attention as she massaged the ointment into them. Setting the cup on a flat stone he nudged into the flames, Nick waited for her to say something more. When a dozen seconds passed and all he heard was the rain in the trees and the snap of the small fire, he figured that was all she was going to offer.

What she'd told him had answered part of his curiosity. But there was something else he needed to know. Something that had bothered him since they'd been up on the ridge.

"How old were you the night you had to leave her in jail?"

The motion of her finger stopped. Her shoulders rose with the deep breath she drew. "Fifteen," she said, trying to keep her voice light. The cap went back on the ointment and she dropped the tube into the kit. "Almost. The next day was my birthday."

Nice present, he thought. "Where was your dad?"

"My dad left when I was five. It was my sister's dad who'd been around the most. He'd left the year before. That was when Mom started drinking. Or when the drinking got out of hand, anyway." The kit stowed, she pulled out a granola bar. "Can we split one of these?"

They only had a couple left. He thought of the extra hours their little detour had added to their hike. "Sure," he said, because he suspected she wouldn't have asked unless she'd been starving, too.

She broke off a quarter and handed him the rest. "You're bigger," she explained, and sat down on the space blanket he'd tossed by the fire.

Her bite was already gone when he sat down beside her. So was his.

"How old was your sister?"

The heat made her shiver. "When?"

"When her dad left."

"I think she was six. I was thirteen. She's seven years younger than I am."

"So how did your mom wind up in jail?"

With her knees raised, Melissa leaned forward, opening the sides of her damp shirt to capture the heat radiating toward her. She hadn't thought about a lot of these things in years, but she could still remember the sense of shame and powerlessness she'd felt. And helpless. Until today, she had never in her life felt so helpless as she had then.

"She'd spent the rent paying the tab she'd run up at the corner bar and got into a fight with the landlord about being so far behind on the rent. She never would have swung at her if she hadn't been drinking."

"And you had to go get her?"

"She was my mom," she replied, simply. "When she called, she begged me to come and told me they had it all wrong. She was crying and saying how sorry she..."

Mel cut herself off, shaking her head as if to shake off the thought. "I had to try," she quietly explained, "but the bail bond people wouldn't talk to me. Mom didn't have any collateral, and because I was a minor I couldn't be held responsible for the money they put up if she didn't make her court date. Everyone I talked to said the same thing. The neighbor wouldn't help, and Mom had told me not to call Dad or Bill.'' She blinked at the winking sparks, her voice dropping. ''It was a rough time for her.''

Nick rubbed the hollow spot in his growling stomach, frowning for her as he did. She didn't have to say it for him to know she'd spent most of that night trying to navigate a system to which she should never have been exposed. Her mother's actions were irresponsible, immature and negligent. Yet, it obviously hadn't occurred to Melissa to do anything but get her mom out of such a place.

''So what did you do?''

Beneath the baggy denim of his shirt, her slender shoulders lifted in a shrug. ''There wasn't anything I could do. She had to stay until she went before the judge the next day and was released on her own recognizance. After that I started hiding the child-support checks so we wouldn't get evicted.''

''Who was taking care of you and your sister while she was doing all of this?''

''Me. There wasn't anyone else to do it,'' she said, as if the matter were of no consequence at all. ''Not that Cam was a willing participant in that arrangement,'' she added dryly. ''I think she was about twelve when she decided that she didn't have to listen to anyone. Especially me. She made a concerted effort to do the exact opposite of everything I said or suggested,'' she continued easily. ''I swear she started skipping school just because she knew I'd get the call in the morning because Mom would either be at her boyfriend's or sleeping. She knew I wouldn't tell Mom, either. When Mom got upset about anything she'd drink even more.''

Confusion colored Nick's tone. ''Why would your sister act out against you?''

A piece of the bark he had peeled lay near her boot. Picking it up, looking as if she were buying time, Melissa picked off a few pieces and tossed them into the fire. "My counselor at school said Cam was looking for the attention and love she wasn't getting at home." She flicked in another piece, her tone far less casual than it had been only moments ago. "I tried to make home as normal for her as I could because she really didn't have anyone else, but I guess I just didn't know how."

Her counselor had also told her it wasn't her responsibility to make that home, but no one else was bothering and they really were all each other had. Their fathers rarely came around; they had new families. And the men that came and went in their mom's life after Cam's dad left weren't interested in playing male role model to a rebellious teenager and her overprotective older sister— which was just fine with both her and Cam.

That was probably the only thing they'd agreed on in years.

She didn't mention any of that to Nick, though. She couldn't believe she'd just told him all she had.

"You know," she said, trying for a smile, "this was all a really long time ago. Mom *is* doing okay now. And my sister is doing better, too." She had been anyway. "There's really nothing else to tell."

She wanted to change the subject. Watching her lean forward to stir the soup, Nick figured he couldn't honestly blame her.

"Just one more thing."

Reluctance kept her eyes on her task. "What's that?"

"How did you get through vet school?"

"Scholarships," she replied, still stirring. "It took me twice as long as everyone else because I was still at home helping Mom with the rent and trying to help with Cam while Mom when through rehab, but I had a guidance counselor who was as determined as I was to get me through.''

She had told him she was tougher than she looked. As he studied her gentle profile, Nick began to suspect that whatever toughness she possessed hadn't been born willingly—and that beneath the bravado rested a very soft, very abused heart. Her sister hadn't been the only one to suffer their mother's emotional absence from their lives. Yet, Melissa had alluded only to how difficult life had been for the two of them. She hadn't said a word about how hard it must all have been for her.

''So, when did you move out?''

''Last week.''

His eyebrows shot up. He'd been thinking more in terms of a year or two. ''It's no wonder you ran to Harbor.''

Puzzled, she glanced toward him.

''You wanted as much distance as you could get,'' he concluded. ''Not that anyone would blame you. And, by the way, Harbor's a great place to hide.''

Mel's puzzlement turned to an odd sense of suspicion. His last remark hinted heavily at firsthand knowledge. The flatness of his tone. The conviction in it.

He had told her he was going home. Until that moment she hadn't considered that he'd also been escaping it.

''There is no running involved.'' She wondered now if that was why he'd sounded less than thrilled at the prospect of returning. She wondered, too, what would have driven him so far. ''I left because I finally could. I just wanted something different from the life I had there.''

She tipped her head, her expression suddenly cautious. ''Is that what you were doing when you went to Harbor? Running?''

He clearly hadn't expected her perception. From the

way his glance jerked from hers, he didn't seem terribly comfortable with it, either. Or maybe he wasn't comfortable with what he had just revealed.

"I prefer to think I was just taking a break."

"How long a break?"

"Longer than I'd planned." The admission came easily. It took a little longer for him to concede, "Six months."

He had assumed up on the ridge that she was running from a man. The assumption now had Melissa wondering if the wife he no longer had was a significant part of what he was taking a break from—until she remembered that his question had apparently been prompted by local gossip.

The unsettling thought had barely registered when a rumble of thunder ended in an overhead crack that slammed her heart against her ribs and her hand to her chest. Lightning turned dusk to daylight, then snapped them back to dusk again.

Protected as they were, they were spared the wind and the rain that bent the tops of the trees outside their little shelter. The wind made itself heard, though, its moan nearly as loud as the heavy beat of the deluge hammering the forest beyond.

"Man, I'm glad we're not out there," Nick muttered, relieved by nature's timing. Talking about the weather seemed infinitely preferable to where their conversation had headed. Watching out for the woman beside him had occupied him all day, as well as spared him thoughts of his past and his future. Grateful for the reprieve she'd allowed him, he wasn't anxious to consider anything about them now.

He especially didn't want to consider how disturbing it

was for her to have so easily zeroed in on what he'd done. "We'd be soaked."

"Or toast," Melissa concluded, anxiously looking toward the trees. "That sounded awfully close."

So did the next one. And the one that came fifteen seconds after that.

"Maybe this will move through fast."

Hoping he was right, she echoed, "Maybe," and hugged her knees.

Yes, he thought, talking about the weather was infinitely easier. It was something strangers did when they were stuck with each other. And they were definitely stuck right where they were at least until daylight. The problem was that the woman uneasily watching the storm wasn't feeling much like a stranger anymore.

"What?" she asked, catching his frown.

"Nothing. You want to see if that's warm yet?"

Grateful for something to do other than jump at thunder and wish she hadn't been so blunt when she'd asked if he'd been running, Mel checked the soup, declared it too cool yet, and considered the man adding more tinder to their fire.

Nick didn't strike her as a man who gave up easily. Or one who blew off his responsibilities or simply walked away when life got rough. She knew men like that. And they didn't possess an ounce of the nobility or strength she saw in Nick. Yet, he had been pushed to escape—and to stay away for months.

She knew the pain of a relationship ending could be brutal—and was wondering if that was what he'd sought to flee when the sound of the driving rain changed pitch. It beat against the ground, fat drops of muddy water suddenly bouncing toward them, causing the fire to sizzle, dampening the knees of pants that hadn't even begun to dry out.

Dusk was rapidly fading to darkness. Behind her, dark rock danced with their wavering shadows. Moments ago she had barely been able to make out the nearest saplings and firs, much less those deeper into the woods. Now, jerking her glance from her darkening cuffs, she stared beyond the glow of the fire at a wall of water cascading in a solid sheet six feet away.

Smoke rapidly turned to steam as she grabbed the soup and scrambled to her feet.

Nick was already on his.

Now that they were both upright, there didn't seem to be much else to do. They both just stood behind the sputtering fire and stared at the yard-wide waterfall coming over the overhang.

Nick looked totally unperturbed. "I didn't figure on that," he said, his tone utterly dry.

Mel handed him the mug, not feeling nearly so calm.

She was tired of feeling shaky, of having her heart lodge in her throat, of having her nerves tweaked by fate, nature and her own personal paranoias. She was tired. Period. She had been that way when she'd awakened to the sounds of Nick rustling through the bushes. After the physical exertion of walking heaven only knew how far, most of it uphill, and the emotional energy she'd expended being scared and trying not to be, she figured she might even be pushing exhausted. When she'd jumped up just now, the muscles in her legs had warned her of just how sore she was going to be tomorrow. Now that she was on her feet, she realized they hurt, too.

She wanted chocolate.

She wanted their fire to keep burning.

More than anything she wanted Nick's easy acceptance

of little inconveniences like a mile-high ridge or the waterfall that was currently drowning their only source of warmth.

There was no other place to put a fire.

In the dimming light, she saw Nick take a sip of the tepid liquid and hand the mug back to her. "You might as well drink it while it's warm."

Determined to match his calm even if she didn't feel it, she took a sip of the seasoned liquid paste passing for soup and handed it over once more.

Nick dug out a crunchy chunk of potato with the stick. "What would you order for dinner tonight if you could have anything you wanted?"

He was doing the distracting thing again. She was sure of it. Grateful for the diversion, she didn't even hesitate. "Fettuccine with mushrooms. And a huge Caesar salad."

"No protein?"

"Cheese bread. I don't eat anything I could have made eye contact with."

He seemed to consider that as he stabbed another cube. "Since your work is with animals, I guess that makes sense. Sam's wife is a vegetarian, too. So, what about dessert?"

"Chocolate mousse."

He handed over the speared potato. "Pretend it's a crouton."

"What about you?" she asked, refusing to give in to the urge to curl up in a ball by the wall. "What would you order?"

"A thick filet. Medium rare. Au gratin potatoes, heavy on the gruyere. French bread, roasted asparagus and a glass of a good cabernet."

She shouldn't have been able to imagine it so easily, but she had no trouble picturing him at a table with white linen holding a goblet of ruby-colored wine. The image of his big hands cupping the fragile crystal intrigued her. It also caused her to look away when something about it reminded her of how he'd cradled her face between his hands and promised he wouldn't let anything happen to her.

The pull she felt deep inside was unfamiliar. It also felt dangerous. And rather one-sided. Since she'd told him about her family and nudged into his past, he'd seemed intent on keeping the course of their conversation deliberately light, deliberately distracting. The weather and food. Safe, harmless subjects. Since they'd found shelter, he'd also made no attempt to touch her that hadn't somehow been necessary.

Necessary, she thought. Necessity had prompted nearly everything he'd done for her.

Water continued to pour from the overhang as they shared the last of their meal. Using the waterfall like a spigot, she stuck the cup into it to rinse and stuffed it, wet, into the pack. The stuffing part she did by feel. The last of the fire had just sputtered out, and the flashlight didn't work.

Beside her, Nick lowered himself to a patch of ground as far from the growing puddle as they could get and still be under the overhang. She couldn't see him, but she could easily feel his presence as he sat with his back against the rock wall. Damp air swirled around them as thunder continued to rumble. Robbed of the fire, that damp grew increasingly chill.

The blanket rustled as Nick held it out to her.

Lightning flashed.

"Thanks," she murmured, groping for it as they were plunged back into darkness. She bumped his arm, backed away a step. "Sorry."

''No problem.''

She couldn't wrap herself up and leave him to shiver in a jacket and T-shirt. Necessity worked both ways. Easing herself down a foot from his shoulder, she flipped out the fabric so it covered him, too, and pulled a handful up to her neck.

Nick couldn't see her, couldn't even make out her profile. But he had already been aware of how she would jolt with each crack of thunder. Feeling her draw up her knees to her chest and wrap her arms around them beneath the blanket, there was no doubt in his mind of how tightly she was holding herself now.

Ever since they had been on the ridge, she had looked as pale as the opal glass his secretary had collected. With nature on a rampage, he had the feeling that, inside, she was feeling just as fragile.

''Would you feel better with an arm around you?''

''I'm okay,'' she quietly replied.

He didn't believe her for an instant. Nor did he question why he felt compelled to let her know the offer stood. ''Well, it's here if you need it.''

''Thank you,'' she murmured, and rested her head on her raised knees.

She had leaned on him enough. Or so she was telling herself long minutes later when the heat of his body had her edging toward him, anyway.

Nick didn't say a word. He just slipped his arm around her shoulder, snugged her to his side and drew her head to his chest.

Beneath the soft leather of his jacket, she could hear the strong, steady beat of his heart. She didn't care that the leather was damp. His arm around her felt warm, heavy and wonderfully protective.

For the first time in over twenty-four hours, Melissa

felt herself relax. Completely. Every tired muscle. Breathing in the scents of fresh air and warm male, she didn't let herself care that she had only met him yesterday. She had discovered kindness beneath his cynicism. Strength in his character. And he offered her a sense of shelter she was too weary to deny that she craved.

He had said he would get her home, and she believed him.

Nick felt her slender body slowly sink toward his, her fist uncurling to curve against his chest. With his hand on her back, he could feel the rhythmic rise and fall of her breathing.

At that moment she reminded him of his five-year-old niece—the one who protested long and hard about not being tired so she wouldn't have to go to bed, then promptly fell asleep in front of the television. As certain as Melissa had sounded about not needing comfort, she'd wasted no time succumbing to it.

Any resemblance she bore to a headstrong five-year-old ended there.

The faint scent of her shampoo still clung to her wind-tangled hair. It was something clean and light and entirely too innocent to be creating the heat he felt breathing it in. And soft. Like her hair itself. Even damp, those fine strands felt like satin as he smoothed them down to keep them from tickling his chin.

He remembered catching that mass in his hands on the ridge. He wondered now how it would feel to slip away the piece of fabric loosely securing it and sift it through his fingers, spread it over his chest.

Pulling a deep breath, he sank lower and stretched out his legs to get more comfortable. He kept his hands right where they were, one at the side of her face so her head wouldn't slip, the other on her shoulder beneath the blanket covering them both.

She had said on the ridge that she trusted him, but there he figured she'd had little choice. She had a choice now, though, and she trusted him enough to fall asleep in his arms.

The thought had him resting his cheek against the top of her head, holding her a little closer. There was something compelling about knowing that. Something that appealed to a part of him he honestly thought could no longer be touched.

The least he could do was not lie there mentally disrobing her.

The thunder and lightning moved on. The rain did not.

The sound of it pouring across the overhang and beating against the ground entered Mel's consciousness first. Right behind it came the realization that she was practically lying on top of a warm, very solid male.

Opening her eyes to the gray light of morning, she found her hand gripping the blanket beside Nick's strong neck and her head on his chest. She wasn't sure when they'd stretched out flat on the ground, but sometime during the night they had curled around each other as intimately as lovers.

She lay halfway across him, one leg trapped between his. His right arm curved across her back, his hand splayed over her ribs. Obviously they had been seeking each other's warmth.

She let her eyes drift closed again. It was too early to rationalize. Content just to be warm, still foggy with sleep, she fought for the oblivion of unconsciousness.

The battle was miserably short. The instant she snuggled closer, sensations that went beyond creature comforts prodded her more fully awake. Nick's fingers brushed the underside of her breast when he shifted beneath her, drawing her closer. Tingling warmth tightened her nipple. That same sensation gathered in her stomach when his free hand caressed her hip.

Her breath had barely caught at the contact when the warm muscles beneath her turned to stone. Even the lulling rise and fall of his chest ceased in the frozen moment before the hand on her hip slowly inched away.

It didn't take a rocket scientist to figure out that he'd just wakened enough to realize what he was doing. She also thought it a fair bet that, in those first flashes of consciousness, he'd thought she was someone else.

His breath eased out cautiously, feathering the hair at the top of her head. Beneath her ear, his heart seemed to beat less evenly—the way hers did when she was where she didn't want to be.

Her first instinct was to draw back. Her next was to make the awkward situation as easy as possible for both of them by pretending she hadn't noticed a thing.

Drawing her hand from his neck, she let herself slip from his chest.

"It's still raining," she muttered, dead certain he was as anxious for her to move as she was. The man had offered her an arm and she'd practically used him for a bed.

"You're awake."

"It's a relative term."

She pulled herself up, her hair spilling over her shoulder, the pink scrunchie caught in the ends. Tugging the bit of fabric the rest of the way out, she ducked her head to avoid his eyes and turned to sit with her back to him. As she did, the blanket slipped. The cold air rushing between them made her grab for it again.

"Sorry," she said, tucking part of it back over him as she wrapped one end around her shoulders.

Nick raised himself to his elbows. Leaning on one, he drew his hand down his face, then shoved his fingers back through his hair. The woman sitting with her slender back to him was doing the same.

Watching the silky blond tangles fall between her shoulder blades, he took a couple breaths of cold damp air, and thought about the benefits of standing naked in the waterfall.

As icy as that water had to be, the purpose would be twofold. Getting cleaner wasn't his first priority.

He'd awakened wanting her. He still did.

"Thank you," he heard her quietly say.

"For what?"

"For your shoulder." Another pass through her hair with her fingers and she whipped the pink fabric into it again. As she did, she glanced to the soaked ground six feet away. If there hadn't been a downhill slope to the ground beyond them, their little oasis would have been a pond. "We're not going to be able to build a fire, are we?"

He said nothing about having been her pillow. From the way she'd immediately changed the subject, and how she now deliberately avoided eye contact with him, it was painfully apparent she was uncomfortable with how they had awakened. It seemed fairly certain, too, that she wanted only to get beyond it.

Still faced away from him, she smoothed her hands over her cheeks, tucked back a stray strand of hair.

"Don't see how." The strand fell forward again. "I have a comb if you want it."

She tugged the pink fabric right back out, ruffled the tangles. "That would be great."

Sucking in another breath, his jaw clinched.

He needed to stop watching her.

He needed to get up. Get moving.

"I'm going see if it's raining all that hard out there." He frowned at the water splattering against the wet ground. "That could just be runoff."

Mel felt the slight weight of the blanket increase as he draped his half over her. Hearing his groan when he rose, she glanced up to see him jam his fingers through his hair, then reach for his back pocket and pull out a small black comb.

Without another word, he handed it to her, sidestepped the splashing waterfall and headed along the rock wall under the protection of the ledge.

By the time she'd worked the worst of the tangles from her hair and twisted it into a spiky knot at the back of her head, he was back.

"It's pouring," he announced flatly and stuck his hands into the fall to splash water over his face.

She could practically feel his displeasure when he shook his hands, droplets flying, and wiped them off on his dirt-streaked khakis. His shadowed jaw was darker than it had been the day before, making his lean features look even more dangerous somehow. Or maybe it was the odd tension surrounding him that did that.

Feeling that tension radiating toward her, feeling the need for escape herself, she handed him back his comb and the handkerchief she'd used for a towel last night and headed out the way he'd gone. She would never take indoor plumbing for granted again.

She wouldn't take heat for granted, either.

Or simply being comfortably full.

There had been some lean times when she was young. She couldn't recall there ever being enough money for her mom to buy a car—they always took public transportation—or for a stereo, or for new clothes. To the day she'd left L.A., she'd shopped the resale stores around the colleges because she could buy what was in style for a third of the price. But she and her sister had never gone without a roof over their heads or food.

She returned to find Nick crouched by the backpack. He had combed his hair straight back, giving him a look that would have spoken surprisingly well of boardrooms and country clubs, had he not been in such need of a shave.

"We'll give it a while and see if this lets up," he said. "It'll be miserable trying to climb out of here now."

"How much farther down do we have to go?"

"A couple thousand feet. We're heading for sea level."

Rising, he held out the last granola bar.

"You take it," she said, certain that hunger must be contributing to the odd edginess she sensed in him. "I'm on a diet. I'll just have cold coffee."

His glance moved slowly up her body, his eyes darkening. "I don't think so," he replied, and broke the bar in two.

The heated look in his eyes was unexpected, unnerving and gone by the time she'd taken what he offered.

She cleared her throat, shivered a little. She was imagining things. She was sure of it. "How's your shoulder?" she asked, thinking that might be contributing to the problem, too. He was uncomfortable and hungry. It stood to reason he would be a little testy.

He said it was all right, which she figured could have meant just about anything, and walked out under the narrower part of the ledge to watch the trees drip heavily onto the forest floor. She didn't know how long he planned for them to wait, but with each minute that passed, he quietly grew more restive. The more restive he became, the more conscious she grew of the distance he had deliberately put between them.

Last night she hadn't realized just how confining it was in their little space. But with her, Nick and his tension, all jammed between the rock wall and the trees, it was beginning to feel terribly crowded.

Chapter Seven

Melissa had been in uncomfortable situations before. She had once walked in on one of her professors and a student doing the wild thing in the chemistry lab. She had encountered a man who'd broken a date with her for that evening having a cozy little dinner with a gorgeous brunette. She'd been in the awkward position of being the third wheel when a blind date didn't show. She'd just never been in quite as uncomfortable a position as she was now.

Knowing Nick wanted distance from her was unsettling enough. Knowing she had nowhere to go and no idea of how long they were going to be stuck there made the discomfort so much worse.

Sitting down where they'd slept, she pulled the blanket around herself, raised her knees and absently rubbed her sore calves. With nothing else to do but wish she were somewhere else, she thought about going back to sleep.

An hour or two of oblivion held enormous appeal. But the ground was cold and as hard as a concrete slab. Without Nick's body cradling hers, she would hardly have rested at all last night.

The thought of how intimately they had curled around each other made her even more aware of the man she was doing everything short of counting fallen pine needles to avoid thinking about. Nick leaned against the wall of rock, slowly consuming bits of his skimpy breakfast while he pondered the misty view. With his brow drawn low, she couldn't decide if he looked brooding or simply lost in thought. Either way, she figured he was thinking about the things he needed to do, the people he needed to contact and the frustrating fact that there was nothing he could do about either at the moment.

He had to hate that.

She knew she did.

Minutes inched past before he pushed himself from the mossy rock and turned toward her. His glance seemed guarded as it flicked over her huddled form. That was how he looked, too, when he headed for the pack, dropped in his wadded wrapper and pulled out a deck of cards.

She had thought it odd when she'd first noticed the cards that such a thing would be among survival gear. She realized now that that they were there to help a downed pilot pass the time. Or, more likely, to keep him from going stir-crazy.

Nick's voice sounded oddly rough when he asked if she played.

Certain he was only asking to be polite, she told him she didn't.

When he asked if she wanted to learn, she told him that, if he felt like talking, she'd rather have him tell her about Harbor.

"What about it?" he asked, lowering his big frame to sit Indian-style a couple of feet away.

"Anything you can tell me. I've driven around a little and met a few people in town, but I've spent most of the time since I got there cleaning and getting set up."

He dealt seven cards facedown onto the packed dirt.

"You said your stay there was only temporary," she coaxed, watching him deal more cards on top of them. "But you must know something about the place since you worked there."

"I got to know it fairly well," Nick admitted, latching on to the topic. All he wanted was to stop thinking about how incredible her body had felt against his, how perfectly it had fit. He would take any distraction he could get. "It's a busy place in the summer. People come over from the mainland to kayak and camp and take the charters out whale watching. Things slow down a lot after Labor Day."

"It was after Labor Day when I first visited. I never saw it busy."

"It'll get that way," he assured her, head down, eyes on his cards. "They swarm like ants off the ferries. That's how most people get there. Sam and his partner's airline must shuttle a few hundred in and back a week, but most of their flights that time of year are to the more remote islands."

"Is that what you did? Fly people to remote places?"

"Pretty much," he replied, too busy making himself focus on the cards to respond to the interest in her voice. "It's a quiet place once the tourists leave," he continued. "The locals tend to keep to themselves for the most part. But there's still a strong sense of community."

"I'm not sure I understand that."

"I wouldn't have either if I hadn't been there." He

flipped over a couple of cards, placed one on another. "It's a good place to be if you aren't a conformist. Or if you're a loner. Or," he added, thinking of Sam and Zack, "if you're raising a family."

She remained quiet for a moment, studying either him or the cards, he wasn't sure.

"I take it you're not a loner," she concluded.

It had taken him all of a week to get sick of his own company when he'd first headed to the San Juans—which is why he'd gone in search of Sam. "I don't mind my own company," he admitted easily enough, "I just wouldn't want to be my only friend."

He thought her lush lips curved. Though something inside him badly wanted to see that smile, he didn't let himself look up to make certain. He was aware of her enough, even covered neck to boot as she was

"Since you're not staying there," she continued, the blanket shifting as she crossed her arms over her raised knees, "I take it you're not unconventional, either."

"I'm probably about as mainstream as they come."

"I can see why Harbor wouldn't hold that much appeal for you, then."

"I didn't say it didn't appeal to me. It's just not where I need to be."

He needed to be in Denver. She knew that, but she didn't seem interested in stalling the conversation by mentioning it.

"What about raising a family?" she asked, since he'd mentioned that, too. "Is that something you want to do someday?"

Cards snapped against each other as he flipped over three at a time from the stack he still held in his hand.

"A family is one of those things that got put off a little too long," he replied, spotting a play. Distracted by her question, he promptly lost track of it. He would be starting his business over soon. Given all he had to do before he could even get into start-up, it could easily take three or four years to get himself back to where he'd once been. Even if he were interested in finding a woman and starting a relationship, he didn't know if he'd ever consider having a child with her. He couldn't imagine having what Sam and Zack had. He'd never known two men who so thoroughly enjoyed their offspring. Or their wives. "I can't see myself starting one now."

"Why not?"

He placed the card and flipped over three more. "Too old."

"How old are you?"

"Thirty-seven."

She made a faint, scoffing sound. "That's not old. That's just an excuse." The blanket rustled as she worked a hand free and pointed to a card. "Black six plays on red seven."

He didn't bother pointing out that age was only part of the equation.

"I thought you said you didn't know how to play."

"You asked *if* I played," she pointed out reasonably. "I don't. But that doesn't mean I don't know how.

"So," she continued quietly, reaching over to make the move for him, "don't you like children?"

"I like them fine. Other people's especially." The truth was that he didn't particularly want to be a father anymore. That dream belonged to his past. He had a totally different set of priorities now. "They're just a responsibility that doesn't fit in with what I need to do."

He didn't know if she was digesting the information or questioning it as the delicate arches of her eyebrows drew together. Not wanting to give her any more thought than was necessary, he turned his focus back to his game. "I thought you wanted to know about Harbor."

"I do."

"So what else do you want to know?"

She wanted to know what he needed to do that would preclude something as major as having a family of his own. It was that kind of curiosity he could see lighting her eyes in the moments before she quietly said, "You can tell me about the locals. I've met a few of them, but the only one I really feel comfortable with is T.J."

He hadn't realized how much his muscles had tightened with the conversation until he felt his bruised shoulder twinge. Relieved that she'd so easily moved on, he made a conscious effort to let that tension go. "The people are polite enough," he said, getting back into his game. "It just takes a while to get their stamp of approval. I was there for months before they started treating me like one of them. There's a core of people in town who seem to know pretty much everything about everyone. If they don't know it, they make it their business to find out."

"Would one of those be the woman who owns the café by the ferry dock?"

"That would be one of them. Maddy means well," he muttered, thinking of her efforts to set him up with the very woman watching him now. "She's just the kind of person who's not happy unless she's straightening out other people's lives."

Melissa's chin sank to her arms, her expression pensive. He thought she might be considering what he'd said about Maddy. Or about it taking six months before the locals took a newcomer off probation. But in a matter of seconds, Melissa had worked her way light-years beyond the surface and plunged to the heart of what she apparently needed to know.

"Are they mean gossips or just nosy?"

The question was nowhere near as idle as it sounded. Seeing the disquiet in her pretty blue eyes, he sensed genuine concern.

He could never picture Maddy being mean. Since she seemed to be the grande dame of the grapevine, he said, "Just nosy, I think."

"Was she the one who said I was running from a man?"

The lines of worry marring her fragile features pulled his focus from his game. He rarely paid attention to talk. When he'd gone to the Road's End, it had been to fill his belly. He'd eaten at Sam's house one night a week at T.J.'s insistence because she knew the only meal provided at the B&B where he'd stayed was breakfast. The Road's End was the only place with a counter, so that was where he headed when he wasn't in the mood for the pizza place. But Maddy's café always buzzed with talk about something, and even when he wasn't paying any particular attention, he couldn't help picking up bits and pieces of what was being said.

As uneasy as Melissa looked, it seemed important that he get his facts straight now.

"I'm not sure who suggested it," he admitted, because while he'd heard it, he'd pretty much dismissed it. "It was either Maddy or the mayor's wife. It doesn't really matter, does it? It was just speculation."

"Which is another word for rumor," she quickly reminded him, "and rumors have a nasty habit of taking on a life of their own. First, they say I'm running from a man, then the next thing you know they're trying to figure out if I was running because he was abusive or if I caught him with someone or if he kicked me out."

His tone went indulgent. "It hasn't gone anywhere near that far."

"Yet," she qualified. "That stuff gets out there and even when it isn't true, some of it never dies. What else are they saying?"

She couldn't possibly know how vulnerable she looked, Nick thought. And he couldn't believe how protective he felt of her as he watched her search his face. The people in Harbor didn't know her at all. They'd just seen a trendy-looking single woman, heard she'd had something to do with the rich and famous and started forming assumptions.

The fact that he'd done it himself balled a little knot of guilt in his gut. It also compounded the need he felt to help her out now.

"The only other thing I heard was that you'd come looking for a man," he admitted. "But certain people would assume that about any single woman. I wouldn't pay any attention to that one."

"I have to pay attention to it. I want to fit in there. What I don't want to be is a source of gossip."

"It'll blow over."

"Not before a lot of stuff that isn't true gets out there," she countered, truly distressed. "I finally have a chance to get on with my life and I thought a quiet little place like Harbor would be a great place to do it. I can't afford to go anywhere else, and I don't want anything to ruin that chance."

Jerking an arm free, she pushed her hand over her smoothed-back hair and shook her head. The motion seemed as agitated as she looked—until she caught herself and pulled her arms back around her knees.

The impulse to touch her, just to offer reassurance, was far stronger than he would have expected. "Nothing is going to be ruined," he said instead. "You already have friends there. T.J. and Sam. Try not to worry about the talk. You can't do anything about it until you get back, anyway."

He started to lift his hand, only to drop it back to his thigh. "And if you are looking for a man," he continued, surprised at the grudging reluctance he felt to share the information, "it won't be long before Maddy will be trying to fix you up. I think she's on a personal mission to see that no resident of the island stays single."

Their situation already prevented her from taking care of certain responsibilities. Knowing there was yet something else she could do nothing about at the moment, robbed any trace of light from her smile.

"Thanks for the warning," she murmured, "but I'm not looking for a man. I wouldn't mind finding a nice one to marry someday," she qualified, "but I'm okay if that doesn't happen for a while. I'd like to see what it feels like to just be responsible for myself."

Guilt suddenly washed over her face. "I know it sounds selfish," she confessed, not terribly comfortable with the admission, "but I really am looking forward to that. It's not like my luck with men has been all that great, anyway," she added, sounding as if she needed something less self-serving for an excuse. "Maybe time will help me improve my lousy judgment."

Nick figured it was a given that she had lived with chaos of some sort or other most of her life. He could only imagine what she'd had to put up with dealing with her mother and a sister who sounded like pure trouble. And he could hardly blame her for wanting to be responsible only for herself for a while. He didn't know another living soul who would have stuck around as long as she had to make sure everyone else was taken care of before she moved on herself. But it was what she had said about wanting to get on with her life that struck a chord deep within him.

They were seeking to do the very same thing. They were moving on. Yet, where he was starting over, she was really just getting started. It was where she'd chosen to make that start that told him as much about her as anything she'd said herself.

She was free for the first time in her life. Yet, rather than seek excitement or exploit the freedom she craved, she had sought a small, quiet, almost isolated place. Knowing what he did about her, he figured what she really wanted was something she'd probably never had. Some semblance of peace.

He told himself he was just bored with solitaire when he carefully placed the cards he held atop the nearest stack. It was easier than admitting that his curiosity about her had totally stolen his concentration.

"What do you mean by lousy judgment?"

She gave a small shrug. "I tend to pick men that scare off easily," she replied, picking up the cards he'd abandoned.

"I've only had two even semiserious relationships," she admitted. "The first guy dumped me because my family demanded too much of my time. The other one couldn't handle that I had an alcoholic mother." She played the top card, her voice dropping as she flipped over three more from the deck. "Of course, he waited until after we were talking marriage and he finally got me into bed to tell me that."

Nick wasn't fooled for a moment by the offhand way she spoke. Both men had hurt her. The second, fairly badly he imagined. What he couldn't figure out was why she didn't seem more resentful than she did. About everything. The men. Her family.

"There's probably nothing wrong with your judgment. It can take a while for some people to reveal who they really are." An edge crept into his voice. He knew how it felt to discover that someone was less than what they'd seemed, to have trust completely trampled. "Maybe what you need to do is develop better armor."

She lifted her eyes to his. "I'm not sure what you mean."

"Don't let yourself care quite so much," he said with surprising ease. "And don't give anyone anything they can hurt you with." He couldn't believe how open she was with him, how freely she shared herself. She was totally without artifice, which in his mind left her pretty defenseless. "You don't hold much of anything back," he told her, bristling at the thought of the guy who'd probably known all along that he would let her go. "If you'd protect yourself better, it wouldn't be so easy for someone to take advantage of you."

For a moment Melissa said nothing. She just swallowed at the cynicism in his cool, gray eyes. There was no doubt in her mind that he wore emotional chain mail. It wasn't always obvious, but she'd bumped into it often enough already to know it was there.

"I hope I never develop that kind of armor," she said quietly. How weary he had to be, lugging around something so heavy. "I've known too many people who live their lives behind it. They wind up bitter and alone or drowning their sorrows in a bottle. I refuse to do that.

"And by the way," she added, setting the cards back down, "most of the things I've told you, I've never told anyone else. Chalk it up to being stranded."

The confines were definitely getting to her. She

couldn't imagine why else she hadn't kept her mouth shut about her lousy love life. And last night she probably shouldn't have spilled her guts about her family. That was no one's business but hers.

Feeling foolish, hating it, she pulled herself to her feet. Doing something physical suddenly seemed very necessary. Aware of the sore muscles in her legs, she figured movement might even help them, too.

"I think the rain has slowed," she said, methodically folding the blanket. "As much as everyone says it rains here, if we don't go now, we could be stuck until next summer."

She'd just tucked the blanket into the pack when Nick reached in front of her. His arm brushing hers, he dropped in the cards and pulled the blanket right back out.

Crowded by his big body, she immediately backed away. "I really think we should go," she insisted, crossing her arms. As restive as she was now feeling herself, there was no way she wanted to spend heaven only knew how many hours fighting the strain slithering between them. Getting drenched was infinitely preferable. "It doesn't make sense to waste daylight when we have so far to go."

Nick pulled himself to his feet, skimmed her guarded expression. Except for a lock curved by her face, her hair had been twisted through the pink fabric at the back of her head, the ends poking out in unruly spikes. Her makeup was gone. Not that she needed it. The denim shirt hanging on her slender frame was bent at the collar points and wrinkled all the way to the hem.

That was as far as he got before his jaw tightened at her protective stance and he handed the blanket back to her.

"I agree." He felt like a louse. She had done nothing

but honestly answer his questions. He'd had no idea that she wasn't as forthcoming with everyone else. "That's why we're going to need this."

Aware of her sudden confusion, he pushed his hand into the front pocket of his pants and pulled out his pocket-knife. "We need to cut it in half."

"You're going to cut it?"

"We're going to get soaked if we don't."

Nick told himself he should have thought of this before. Considering that he'd probably been too preoccupied, he had her double the long rectangle of silicon-coated fabric so he could cut it in two, then made a slit in the middle of each piece. The confines were getting to him, too. So was the woman quietly watching him. What troubled him more as he handed half the fabric back to her was thinking that she needed to be as disillusioned as he had become.

Material rustled as Melissa lifted it up and poked her head through. The makeshift poncho covered her shoulders and fell over her wrists. Blowing the loose straggle of hair out of the way, she glanced down to see the slightly lopsided hem hanging above the dirty knees of her jeans and her dirt-caked boots.

Things seemed to just keep getting worse.

She was telling herself not to ask how much worse they could get when she saw Nick's head pop through his half of the silvery fabric. He didn't get quite as much coverage as she did, but the way it fell over his broad shoulders made him look like a linebacker.

It also reminded her of how it had been tucked up under their chins when she'd first wakened.

Knowing they wouldn't be sharing the blanket again, ignoring the disturbing twinge of disappointment she felt at that, she reached for the pack.

"I'll take it," he said. Slipping it from her hand, he

saw her glance dart to his injured shoulder. "It's my turn," he explained, marveling at how easy she was to read. "And you're right, this could last all day."

The misty rain they started out in lasted all of ten minutes before it turned to a steady drizzle that soaked anything their new rain gear didn't cover. The sky remained solid gray. Melissa didn't let herself think about the water plastering her hair to her head and slicking her face. As long as they were moving, the disquiet she felt with the big man walking beside her wasn't quite as acute as it could have been. She was just relieved that Nick seemed to agree it was necessary to continue on.

It took four hours to get to the area they would have reached had they come straight across the ridge. It took another three to find what had looked like a road from above but turned out to be an old hiking trail.

The relief Melissa felt seeing the thin strip of earth others had walked on lasted all of five minutes. Because it was so overgrown with bushes, they quickly lost the path, which meant wandering around looking for it before they picked it up again.

She swore they lost the trail at least a dozen times. Nick said it was only five. But then, he'd said the dried vegetable soup mix they ate from their palms for lunch tasted like the crackers some bars served with their drinks, so she figured he was just trying to minimize frustration. For all the walking they were doing, they weren't getting that far. Each step she took reminded her calves and her thighs of the thousands of uphill steps she'd taken yesterday. And every time they had to retrace steps they'd already taken, she'd forced herself to not groan out loud. Or to simply sit down right where she was, pull off her boots and refuse to take another step.

She was sorely tempted to do just that when they worked their way to a flat, marshy-looking meadow and couldn't tell where on the other side the trail picked up again.

Nick pushed back his jacket sleeve to look at his watch. As gray as everything had been all day, it was nearly impossible to tell what time it was.

Rain ticked unnoticed against his poncho.

"We only have another half hour of daylight," he said. "And there could be quicksand out there." He scanned her profile as he spoke, checking her over as he had more times that day than she could count. "We should think about building some kind of shelter and tackle that tomorrow."

They had been beating bushes with their sticks as they'd walked, which meant thoughts of bears and other critters with large teeth had alternated with a longing for liniment. The thought that the earth could disappear from beneath their feet had never occurred to her.

"Quicksand?"

"You find it in places with underground springs. We'll just take the perimeter around. We'll be fine by the trees."

Taking the perimeter meant walking even more. Faced with that prospect, Mel drew a breath that felt surprisingly shaky. "What kind of shelter do you have in mind?"

"That stand of hemlocks over there," he said, nodding to a copse of ancient trees edging the meadow. "We can pile up branches between a couple of them and lay some over the top."

Of course we can, Melissa thought, and followed him without saying a word.

She didn't know exactly what he had in mind. She was visualizing more of a little house with a roof. What they came up with after scouring the area for fallen branches of fir was more of a lean-to with a bit of ceiling, but she honestly didn't care where she put her body at that point or what, if anything, protected it from the constant rain.

She was cold. She was tired and wet and her calves were cramping. She didn't even care that Nick left her alone because he thought he heard a stream and had gone off to find it. Unless something large and furry came charging toward her, she wasn't moving until morning.

Leaning forward, she rested her forehead on her knees and rubbed at the knots in her calves.

That was how Nick found her, huddled under the fir boughs in the fading light. With her head down, her shoulders still, it almost looked as if she'd already fallen asleep. If not for the kneading motions of her hands above her ankles, he would have thought she had.

A twig snapped beneath his boot as he walked toward her. Wearily she lifted her head.

"Did you find it?"

He held up the canteen he'd refilled. "It wasn't that far."

Any distance apparently seem too far to her just then. Dragging her palm from her forehead, she smoothed back her soaked hair. "Thanks for getting the water."

He told her she was welcome and, with a faint groan, sat down beside her. "We're not going to be able to build a fire. There's only one starter left and nothing around here dry enough to burn."

She looked as if she'd pretty much suspected that. "So, rule number one to getting stranded in the woods is to carry your own fuel," she concluded flatly.

"Rule number one is to not get stranded."

"Yeah," she murmured. "There's that."

"You okay?"

"I'm fine."

"Liar."

Her glance met his. "Okay. I'm cold, I ache and I'm miserable." She shrugged, dismissing it all. "Is that better?"

"It's more honest," he conceded.

Her gaze fell to his injured shoulder. "You're a fine one to talk."

"It looks worse than it feels," he admitted, and took her by the knees to swivel her toward him.

Picking up the leg she been working on, he pulled it across his lap and curved his hands around her calf himself.

The cold fabric against her skin felt awful. But any thought of protest died the instant Melissa felt his thumbs dig into the knots.

"How much farther do we have to go?"

In the shadowy light, she saw him shake his head. The rain had turned his hair as dark as ebony. Droplets glistened in the growth shading his jaw. "Don't think about it right now."

That was what he'd said she should do about the talk going around about her. Don't think about it now. She already had a list of things waiting for her in Harbor she was trying not to worry about. Feeling the heat of his hands penetrate her wet jeans and the way his kneading softened her muscles, she decided to add worrying about tomorrow to the list, too.

His motion suddenly slowed. His deep voice turned pensive. "I never would have thought you could do this," he said, sounding as if he was sorry he'd been under that impression. "Most of the women I know would have fallen apart at least once by now."

The quick discomfort she felt at his candid admission was overridden by the apology buried in it. "Maybe you just underestimate most of those women.'' She would forgive him his assumption. He'd proved himself far different from the man she'd first met, too. "It's not as if a person has a lot of choice in a situation like this.''

"Don't underestimate yourself," he countered, determined to make his apology stick. "And I can think of several women who wouldn't have made it this far without some major theatrics.''

"Who?'' she asked, since he'd brought it up.

"My old secretary for one. She was amazing in the office. Could handle anything. But put her car in the shop for a week and you'd think she was the only person who'd ever had to deal with a hassle. Then, there's my ex-partner's wife. Definitely high maintenance." Like my ex, he thought, but didn't say. "And my sisters," he admitted as his hands started moving again. "Don't get me wrong. The two of them are great. It's just that their idea of roughing it is a hotel without room service.''

Curiosity kept Melissa silent. The man was a pilot. He flew people in and out of remote places. She had assumed that flying was what he'd done in Denver. If not for a major airline, then for a corporation or an individual. Yet, he'd just mentioned a secretary and an ex-partner.

Praying he wouldn't stop what he was doing, she decided to ask about his sisters instead. The easy way he spoke of them made the topic seem safe enough. As unhappy as he was about returning home, the last thing she wanted to do was make him withdraw. "I take it your sisters didn't go with you and your dad when you went fishing.''

"Only once. The whole family went. After that Mom and the girls stayed home and went shopping.''

"Smart women," she mused, torn between the heavenly feel of his hands and the curiosity that wouldn't go away.

"So, do their husbands do the outdoor thing?" she asked, trying to push it aside anyway. "With their sons I mean?"

"One of them does. The other is the academic type. He isn't into sports at all."

"That's whose son you've taken camping?"

"Yeah," he murmured, now working the muscles around her knee. "Mike and I have a great time," he said, speaking of his nephew. "And my sister looks forward to it, too. She and Jeff take off for wine country whenever Mike and I head for the mountain. They like getting away together."

"It sounds as if they have a good relationship."

"Both of my sisters do."

His sisters had good marriages. From what he'd said about his father the other night, she had the feeling his parents might have been blessed with a good one, too.

She couldn't feel the callus she'd seen on his ring finger, but she was conscious of its presence in the long moments she sat wondering what had happened to his own marriage. After the way he'd advised her to be less trusting when she'd divulged her personal life to him, however, she thought it highly doubtful he'd be all that generous with his own past.

"What?" he asked, catching her hesitation.

"Nothing," she replied, loath to lose the ease they had managed to find.

Faint exasperation colored his tone. "Don't do that."

"Do what?"

"That," he emphasized. "A woman never says 'nothing' unless there is something."

"That's not always true."

"It is right now."

He had a point. She just hated the thought of him pulling back from her.

"Melissa," he prodded.

"Why don't you ever call me Mel?"

"Because you don't look like a Mel. And don't change the subject."

"I just wondered how long you were married."

She knew it would happen. His hands went still. A breath later, he eased them away.

"You asked," she quietly reminded him, and slid her leg from his lap.

Nick regretted the loss of contact. Still, he did nothing to stop it as Melissa tucked her legs back under her poncho and hugged her knees to her chest. The position was the most efficient way to stay warm, but the practicality of it wasn't what struck him. It was the way it made her look as if she were protecting herself from the way he'd pulled away from her.

When he'd reached for her, he had been thinking only of how much her legs had to be hurting. Having noticed her rubbing them this morning, he figured they'd been killing her all day. Yet, feeling her muscles relax in his hands, drawn by how she responded so trustingly to his touch, had somehow eased him, too.

"Nine years," he finally said. "The divorce became final a couple of months ago.

Her soft voice became even softer. "Did it have anything to do with the ex-partner you mentioned."

The woman didn't miss a thing. He gave a mirthless laugh. "It has a lot to do with that."

"Oh, geeze. She was cheating on you. And he was your best friend."

He couldn't have imagined anything at that moment

that would have made him smile. But the sympathy in her wildly erroneous conclusion managed to do just that. He could see now why she worried about rumors. "That actually might have been easier to handle." He circled her ankle with his fingers. "Give me your other leg. Come on," he coaxed, feeling her reluctance. "I know they hurt."

The gesture wasn't as altruistic as it might have sounded. Touching her calmed him. It made no sense, given that touching her also made him aware of just how slender and supple she was. But at that moment, all he cared about was keeping that oddly soothing contact.

"It was a problem that started in the company," he conceded, planting her foot between his raised knees. "My partner and I had a difference of opinion about how to handle something, and my wife...my ex," he corrected, tugging up wet denim, "sided with him."

The light was all but gone now, leaving Melissa's features obscured except for her shadowed shape and the glitter of her eyes. "What kind of a business do you have?" she asked, shivering a little when he curled his hands over her cold skin. "I thought you were a pilot."

"I fly," he confirmed, letting his heat seep into her, feeling hers start to seep back. "But that's kind of like saying I drive a car. I was just helping out Sam and Zack for a while. The company I owned with Reed designed aviation systems."

"Reed is your partner," she concluded flatly.

"Was," he corrected.

"And you're an aeronautical engineer?"

"That's what my degree is in. That and business."

The sounds of the wilderness surrounded them, some creatures settling in, others beginning their night. Mel barely noticed.

"What was the difference of opinion about?"

"How to handle a design defect in a ground-clearance system. Reed knew about it," he said, slowly working her tight calf, "but he didn't admit it until I asked him about a letter we received from an independent testing company. I hadn't known until then that they'd notified us of a problem the week before we'd gone to production. He'd conveniently forgotten to mention it."

"If there was something wrong, why wouldn't he want to fix it?"

"That," he said after a moment, "was actually the bigger problem."

His hands never ceased their soothing motions as Nick explained how he had insisted that the system be pulled from production while they went back through the designs and schematics and found the flaw. But Reed had insisted that the failure rate was small enough that they could take a calculated risk and market it, anyway. It would cost a fortune to stop production, and the profits they would lose would be enormous.

His wife had sided squarely with his partner.

Nick said nothing about the sense of disloyalty he must have felt, but Mel could practically feel it for him as he methodically massaged her achy muscles and told her that neither his wife nor his partner had seemed to care about what could happen if the system failed, about the potential risk to human life. His partner had pointed out that any claim an airline might have would be covered by insurance. It was how everyone did business. Acceptable risk, they called it.

But it clearly wasn't acceptable to Nick.

"If we knew of a flaw, it was our responsibility to fix it. So I stopped production myself. We had retooled and reprogrammed everything to fill orders from aircraft manufacturers. Since we were a small, specialized company, that effectively shut us down.

"We might have been able to ride it out, get it fixed and get back into production in a month or two," he speculated, "but all Reed could see were the million-dollar orders waiting to be filled, and he wanted the money now. When I wouldn't back down, he lost it in front of a couple of our engineers.

"When word hit the street about what had happened," he said, deep in his thoughts, "the airlines canceled their orders. By then, he was even more furious because his personal reputation was shot. Ellen was angry with me, too." At the mention of his wife, his voice fell. "It killed me to close something I'd worked so hard to build. And we wouldn't have had to close if Reed hadn't demanded his half of the remaining business assets. I tried to explain that to her, but all she cared about was the money we'd lost."

He didn't have to say another word for Melissa to understand that his ex had been far more interested in the immediate effect on their bank account than in Nick or their relationship. What struck her most, though, was that Nick had needed support in his decision. Had deserved it. Yet the woman he should have been able to count on to help him work through the upheaval of such a decision hadn't cared enough to be there for him.

"How long ago was this?"

"It started last year." Probably even before that, he admitted to himself. He and his wife had stopped communicating long before the problems developed with the company. He'd just been so busy earning money and she so busy spending it, that he hadn't noticed how little they had come to have in common. "Six months ago I filed for a divorce and the dissolution of my partnership."

"On the same day?"

"Yeah." He paused, intent on not rubbing too hard. "I look on that as my emancipation. My personal Independence Day."

It was no wonder he wore armor, she thought, sensing the loss beneath his cynicism. He had lost everything he'd worked for. His wife. His business.

"It sounds to me more like the day all your dreams died."

"Dreams are highly overrated."

"We only say that when we've lost them," she quietly countered. "So what are you going to do now. Start another company on your own?"

"That's the plan," he conceded. "But I have to finish buying out Reed's interests and get his name off the patents before I can start up again. I just hope I can do it without a lawsuit."

"What about your ex? Do you have loose ends to clear up there, too?"

"We're finished." There was no hesitation. "She got the house in Denver and the condo in Vail. When her attorney told her she might not even get that much if Reed and I did battle over the patents, she took them and ran."

"It's no wonder you're not anxious to go back," she murmured. "All that unfinished business to take care of."

For once he didn't deny that he wasn't truly looking forward to the experience. It had nothing to do with what awaited him. The phenomenon was due strictly to the woman sitting in front of him. Listening to her quiet voice, absorbing her quiet understanding, he felt none of the burning in his gut that usually accompanied thoughts of all that had happened. Touching her seemed to relieve that effect.

"What would you do if we couldn't get back?"

His unexpected question made her go still. Caught thinking how noble his actions had been, she frowned into the darkness.

''I'm not even going to consider such a possibility. You promised you'd get me home.''

Curious, she couldn't help but ask, ''What would *you* do?''

For a moment he said nothing. Then she felt his hands slip from her leg. An instant of disappointment collided with the feel of his hands cupping her face.

Her utter trust in him was balm for his bitter soul.

''This,'' he murmured, and lowered his mouth to hers.

Chapter Eight

Soft, Nick thought. He had never felt anything so soft as Melissa's mouth when he brushed his lips over hers. Warming her cold face with his hands, he brushed his lips over hers once more, drawn by the velvety feel of her skin.

Her sudden stillness gave way to a sigh. Her body seemed to sink toward his.

She wanted his kiss.

The thought rocked through him, bumping his heart against his ribs. Slowly tilting her head, he sought more, coaxed her closer.

He had caught her unprepared. He knew that. But he wasn't prepared himself for how the taste of her heated his blood when her tongue tentatively touched his, or how her scent filled his lungs and tightened every nerve in his body.

He swallowed her faint moan. A groan of need rumbled deep in his own chest.

That guttural sound drew Mel closer, allowed her to curve her hand at the side of his strong neck. Beneath her palm, she felt the steady beat of his pulse under strong cords and muscle.

The night air felt damp and cold. The rustle of wind-blown trees and the steady tick of rain joined the distant howl of something feral. She was far more conscious of Nick's hands framing her face and his tongue teasing hers, seducing her with gentleness. His beard prickled her skin, his warm breath merged with hers.

It wasn't enough. She wanted to be in his arms. She had wanted him to hold her since they'd come down off the ridge. With him so close, that need felt more necessary by the second.

The desire had no sooner swept through her than he eased back to touch his lips to one corner of her mouth.

When he lifted his head, she felt her breath shudder in.

"You asked," he reminded her, still cradling her face.

Eyes closed, she swallowed hard and slowly nodded.

His thumb brushed the underside of her jaw. The blackness surrounding them made it impossible for her to see his face, his eyes. Except for that slow, almost thoughtful motion, she had no way of knowing what might be going through his mind.

It seemed that he didn't want to let her go.

She didn't want him to let her go, either.

"Nick?"

"Yeah?" he asked, his voice a low rasp.

The heat of his hands shimmered through her, causing her to shiver. "Would you hold me?"

His thumb traced the small curve of her chin. "Cold?"

Just needy, she thought. "Freezing."

The motion on her face stilled, his hands slowly falling away.

The rain had started up in earnest again. The drum of it on the ground underscored the rustle of fabric as he edged her knees from between them. Rather than slip his arms around her, as she'd thought—hoped—he would do, he stretched out, coaxing her down with him and turned her back to his chest.

With one arm under her head, Nick slipped his free hand beneath the fabric covering her. Flattening it over her stomach, he tucked her against him and ruthlessly bit back a groan.

He had thought it wiser to turn her away from him. If he faced her, he knew he would kiss her again and he was in no mood to torture himself. The feel of her tight little backside pressed to the bulge beneath his zipper was agonizing enough. If he had her where he could roll onto her, he would want to be inside her, and that wasn't what she had asked for at all.

He wanted to be inside her, anyway.

Resting his head on the pack, he pulled in a deep breath and felt his body tighten more when he inhaled the faint scent of something herbal still clinging to her wet hair.

He eased his hand toward her waist. As he did, she threaded her cold fingers through his.

"We can't stay like this for very long," he quietly warned her.

"I know. We need to eat."

That, too, he thought. "And I need to stash what's left of the food away from us so we don't get unexpected guests."

"How will you see? The flashlight keeps going off."

Concentrate on that, Nick told himself. Rather than thinking about freeing her hair and tasting the smooth skin of her neck, figure out how you're going to hang the bag in a tree you can't see and find your way back in the dark. ''I'll think of something.''

Mel nodded into the ebony night. She hoped he would take his time coming up with whatever that something was. The tug of disappointment she'd felt when he'd turned her back to him had long since faded. He was doing more than holding her. Spooned together as they were, he was giving her the warmth and protection of his body. From her neck to her calves, she could feel him behind her, his broad, solid chest to her back, his heavy thighs radiating heat into the backs of hers. She craved that warmth, dreaded the moment he would take it away.

Now that he'd moved his hand, it was infinitely easier to relax.

Her breath had gone thin when his fingers had splayed low on her stomach. She'd stopped breathing completely when he'd pressed her back against him. She shouldn't have felt his touch as intimately as she had. Not with all the layers separating them. But with her nerves already humming from his kiss, the bold contact had aroused, taunted and made her stunningly aware of how fiercely attracted she was to him.

The admission lingered in her mind, her last conscious thought. Warmer now, feeling safe in his arms, her achy muscles relaxed, her body slowly caved in to fatigue.

Nick could feel himself giving in to it, too. Cradling her close, he could easily feel the rhythmic rise and fall of her chest and the calming of his own breathing as it fell into sync with hers. Lulled by the rain, he closed his eyes and sank against her softness.

He was surprised she had lasted as long as she had tonight. Admitting now how exhausted he felt, he didn't think he'd last much longer himself. He was comfortable there. Relatively, anyway. His bed was cold, hard ground and his pants were wet from the thighs down. But he would have no trouble finding sleep. His only problem was that the longer he lay holding Melissa, the harder he knew it would be to make himself get up.

The last thing he wanted to do was leave the softness and warmth of the woman in his arms and go out in the rain.

He did it, anyway.

Rather than taunting sleep, he forced himself to ease his arm from under her. He had promised he would get her home. And that meant making sure he took whatever precautions he could to keep from attracting anything wild and hungry to where they slept. As for any kind of meal for the two of them, Melissa was clearly more tired than hungry. Fumbling in the dark for the rope and the plastic bag holding their negligible food supply, he decided fatigue had the greater hold on him, too. All he cared about now was sleep.

There was no moon, no stars, no lightning. Nothing to relieve the pitch-black of the night. Or the rain. Kicking himself for not having taken care of the food sooner, he dug out the flashlight and knocked it against his leg to see if he could get the thing to work.

The beam flickered on, wavered and flickered back out. He tried it again, the beam holding a little longer this time. He only needed to get a few dozen yards away. If light would just hold for a minute, that was all the time he'd need.

The beam held, it just grew progressively dimmer. But it got him where he needed to go. It flickered out twice on the way back, leaving him to whack it again, but the dim beam reappeared, giving him something to follow back to where he found Melissa sitting up, waiting for him.

She looked almost ethereal in that pale glow, her skin luminous. Yet what struck him most as he flicked the light out himself and settled down behind her once more, was her soft smile of relief that he'd come back safe.

Mel became aware of Nick's absence even before she fully awakened. She didn't know long he had been up. Or even where he'd gone. She just knew he was no longer holding her.

Opening her eyes enough to see that it was daylight, she groaned and ducked her head back toward her chest.

"What's the matter?"

Nick's deep voice rumbled from the other side of the branches and fir boughs forming the little cave.

"It's still raining," she said.

"I noticed," he muttered, crouching in the low opening. "But not as hard as it was." Raindrops clung to his dark hair, dotted the silvery fabric covering his wide shoulders. "We have a little problem."

The man had no mercy. He simply didn't get the concept of coffee first, problems later. And food. Even dried soup sounded good to her just then. They'd been too tired to eat last night. As hungry as she felt, Nick had to be starving.

She slowly sat up, pushing back the strands that had come loose from her hair as she did. She didn't know how it was possible, but she ached in between the places that still ached from yesterday. She decided to blame the ground. It had as much give as cement.

Then she saw Nick hold out his hands.

Aches were all but forgotten as she let him pull her from under the boughs and onto her feet. For a moment he just stood there, looking as tall and strong as the enormous trees swaying in the morning breeze. His glance swept her face as he held her hands, but the instant his smoky eyes fell to her mouth, he let his hands slip away.

"I thought you might be feeling a little stiff," he said, as if to excuse why he'd touched her.

He took a step back, the odd unease in his expression putting the same in hers.

"What kind of a problem?" she hesitantly asked.

"Something got to our supply. Do you want the good news first or the bad news?"

She hated it when people did that. "The bad."

"The food's gone."

Her empty stomach sank. "And the good?" she asked, unable to imagine what that could be.

Reaching under his poncho, he pulled three little red packets from his pocket. Except for the tooth marks puncturing one of them, the rest were unharmed. "Whatever got to it doesn't like coffee."

Her first thought was for the now-lost chocolate bar. Her next was that something had been prowling awfully close to where they'd slept.

She hadn't heard a thing last night. Wrapped in his arms, sounds that normally would have jerked her upright hadn't even registered.

Marveling at the phenomenon, a little disconcerted by it, she noted the size of the punctures. "At least it was something small."

"I think those might be from something that came along later." Plastic crinkled as he pulled out what was left of the clear storage bag. The thin white rope still knotted the top. The bag itself had been shredded by something with claws an inch apart. "I couldn't see well enough last night to get the bag toward the far end of a branch. I hung it too close to the trunk.''

Nick had gathered what he could find of the packages of soup and cocoa that had been ripped open and licked clean and stuffed them into the bag. Now, not wanting to leave trash in the forest, he stuffed the shredded bag and wrappers into the pack.

"If you can wait to head for the bushes for a few minutes, we might want to get away from here now. Just in case it's still around.''

With the possibility of a cougar or bear being nearby, Mel had no problem with getting an immediate start. As soon as Nick slung on the pack, they headed for the curved edge of the lush green meadow, picking their way through knee-high grasses and trying to avoid gopher holes that could cause an ankle to twist or break. She barely noticed the constant rain or her protesting muscles, intent as she was on the sounds that came from within the trees they skirted. Beyond what might be lurking in those deep shadows, she was conscious only of the man walking beside her and the fact that he made no attempt whatsoever to repeat what she couldn't get out of her mind.

She couldn't believe how gently he'd kissed her. Or how something so fleeting could elicit such need.

The rational part of her knew it didn't matter what he made her feel. Their futures were going in opposite directions. Their goals had nothing to do with each other. Yet, as the morning wore on, she couldn't shake the wish that he would touch her, just hold her hand.

Nick wanted far more than that.

He had awakened ravenous. If he were to let himself dwell on it, he would have to admit that the feeling had yet to subside.

Melissa spotted a broken Forest Service marker that led

them to the overgrown trail. Focused as he was on not getting them lost, he just wasn't sure which hunger was greater. The gnawing in his belly or the desire he felt for the woman who'd slept so serenely in his arms.

He knew she trusted him. He refused to take advantage of that. That was why he kept his hands to himself when touching her wasn't absolutely necessary, and why he kept his glance from her mouth whenever he would look over to see how she was doing. She was his responsibility and he would protect her—even from himself if he had to.

They made terrible time. Rain alternated between showers and downpours. The temperature, Mel swore, hovered just above freezing. With the rain coming through thready patches of fog, the primordial, moss-hung forest seemed surreal to her, a place time had forgotten to touch. But then, time itself seemed irrelevant there. As they worked their way over lichen-covered rock falls and fallen logs, one hour melding into the next, morning into afternoon, she considered that the differences in her goals and Nick's might well be irrelevant, too.

Her future now had been narrowed to nothing but putting one foot in front of the other. That and simply surviving.

Sloughing through mud added weight to her boots, and fatigue came faster with hunger. Nick suggested she keep her eye out for berries, something recognizable so they didn't wind up poisoning themselves.

"Did your dad teach you how to forage for food?" she asked, fully expecting his hunting-and-gathering skills to greatly exceed hers.

"The only foraging we did was with a fishing pole.

Just don't eat anything you wouldn't see in a supermarket.''

She promised she wouldn't and sloughed on, now searching the foliage for what grew on it as well as what might be lurking behind it. She noticed Nick doing the same. His features seemed to grow more taut as the day wore on, but neither of them found anything they were starving enough to risk putting into their stomachs.

By nightfall, hunger and cold had her shaking inside and out. She said nothing about it to Nick, though. She just helped him pile up boughs the way they had last night and crawled with him inside. But then, she didn't have to tell him how she was feeling. He noticed everything.

"How are you doing?" he asked, stretching out behind her when she went from a crawl to prone in a matter of seconds.

She practically sighed when his arm came around her. "Better."

Nick liked the way she tucked herself closer, hated that she was so cold. Hypothermia was always a possibility when a person was as wet as they were. But at least their torsos were dry. And when they weren't moving, they could share their warmth.

Wearily lifting himself up, he pulled off his poncho. After pushing his half of the bisected blanket under them, he worked hers over her head to cover them with.

Sex should have been the last thing on his mind, but there was no denying how badly he wanted her when he asked her to unbutton her denim shirt and open her vest. She didn't question what he asked. She simply did it, fumbling because her fingers were so cold, then went willing into his arms when he opened his jacket and pulled her to him.

Only when he felt the warmth flowing between them and heard her heavy sigh, did he say, ''I'm better, too.''

She snuggled closer.

He stroked her hair. That was the only touch he allowed himself before he rested his cheek against the top of her head. And slept.

The nights had become far easier than the days to Mel. She wasn't sure what Nick thought of how they'd started to share them, though. He usually woke far more ready to take on the day than she did. But the next morning he seemed quieter, already lost in his thoughts as they made cold coffee, washed up from the canteen and headed out under a solid gray sky that, for the moment, wasn't leaking.

Like the day before, there was still a certain sense of protectiveness about him, along with a certain distance. It was that distance that bothered her. And his silence. She didn't trust it.

Following the orange backpack through the dense forest, she couldn't help but wonder if he was doing it again—if he was thinking about something she needed to know and not telling her about it.

She was about to ask when she literally stumbled onto a patch of something that looked deliciously familiar. A snag caught her foot, turning the question to a gasp and almost sending her to her knees.

Catching herself with her palms in the dirt, she was already scrambling upright when Nick swung around ahead of her.

''Are you okay?'' he asked, reaching to help even as she brushed her hands off on her jeans.

Her only response was an excited, ''Look!''

Bending back down, she shoved aside the leaves of a

bush autumn had turned flame red and exposed the green vine she'd seen growing under it. Following the smaller leaves up, she pointed to where the vines spread through the surrounding vegetation, overtaking some with its profusion of little black fruits.

Nick pushed his fingers through his hair. "Blackberries?"

She grinned, shoving back the silver fabric and denim covering her hands. "Breakfast."

Nick couldn't help returning her smile. Anything edible was manna from heaven right now. But it was her expression that had him grinning back. He had almost forgotten how bright her smile could be. Watching her dive into the bushes to free the shiny black morsels into her palm, she reminded him of a kid who'd just been given free rein in a candy store. It was that kind of delight he saw in her; that kind of pleasure suffusing her pretty face.

Handing him her first handful of fruit, she went back in for more.

"Watch the thorns," he warned, as she popped berries into her mouth.

She already had scratches on the backs of her hands from the stickers spiked along the trailing vines. "What do we have that we can put some of these in?"

She spoke with her back to him, working her way past a barren patch to get to the fruit beyond. He worked behind her, snatching those she missed and popping them like peanuts while he mentally inventoried what was in the pack.

"The cup's about it...unless you want to put some in the outer pocket."

"We'll do both." Bushes rustled as she stretched toward a particularly large clump. Swallowing what she'd just chewed, she picked another handful. "That way we'll have lunch and dinner."

Dirt from her palm had streaked from eyebrow to temple when she'd pushed back the strands hanging limply by her face. The streak of dirt made the gold studs she still wore in her ears look oddly incongruous, especially with her clothes as wrinkled and dirty as his. But at that moment, smiling back at him from the wild thicket, she looked perfectly content to be right where she was.

Drawn by the light in her blue eyes, he wondered how long it had been since he had felt anything remotely resembling contentment. Satisfaction and happiness had slipped away so slowly that he hadn't even noticed they'd been missing until his life had literally fallen apart. But the disturbing thought had barely registered when he mentally pulled himself up short.

Contentment had been what he'd felt last night when he'd held Melissa.

He'd felt twinges of it, too, when she'd fallen asleep against him the night before.

He was telling himself what he felt could have just been exhaustion when movement beyond her caught his attention.

His heart dropped like stone.

Melissa had worked her way ten feet ahead of him. "Don't look behind you. No! Don't," he said, his quiet tone urgent when she started to follow where his glance had gone. "Just keep looking toward me, take it slow, and get over here."

Alarm killed the light in her eyes. "What is it?"

"Come on!" he whispered. "It hasn't seen us yet."

The berries in her hand fell across the ground as she moved toward him, taking it slow, looking as if she wanted to run. "What hasn't?" she whispered back, aiming for the hand he held toward her.

The instant she reached it, he grabbing her by the arm and shoved her behind him. "That."

His gaze remained fixed on the weather-grayed and tangled roots of a fallen hemlock thirty yards away—and the undulating mass of gleaming brown fur lumbering beside it. The bear, all three hundred pounds of it, nosed at the roots, searching for grubs or termites living in the decaying wood.

"Oh, geeze," Melissa whispered as the breeze shifted.

The bear's huge head snapped up.

Nick swore. They were ten feet from a shallow ravine on one side. Thick, thorny vines blocked the other. They would never be able to outrun the huge animal if it decided to charge, and climbing a tree was something it could do a whole lot better than could either of them.

"Get into those trees down there," he whispered, his focus never leaving the shiny black eyes curiously watching him. The head tilted, the nose came up. "They're too close together for him to get into."

"What are you going to do?"

"Nothing. Unless he does something first. Just go, will you? He can't follow both of us."

"Nick."

"Damn it, Mel." He'd been about to tell her to go again. Mel was sure of it. But the bear was already moving toward them, a mass of shifting brown fur with a huge black snout and a head the size of a beach ball.

Noise discouraged bears. So did making yourself large by waving your arms. Or, so Nick had told her when they'd walked away from the plane. The problem was that no one had told this particular animal that he was supposed to run off when people yelled at him. He kept coming, not at a charge, more at a lazy, curious but decidedly intimidating stroll.

Her teeth jarred hard when Nick shoved her toward the ravine. "Get down there!"

From the corner of her eye, she saw Nick jerk off the orange pack. The bear had already gained ten yards when he ripped the maps out of it and heaved it toward the lumbering animal.

Distracted by either the object itself or the scents clinging to the food wrappers inside, the bear's massive head swung down to sniff toward the pack.

Nick didn't wait to see how much time he'd just bought. But he could hear fabric ripping as, clutching the rolled map in his fist, he skidded down the slick, moss-covered ground to where Melissa had stopped, her face ashen, just inside a grove of aspen. A low-hanging branch clipped him in the forehead on the way down. He barely felt it. Ducking beneath another low limb, he grabbed her by the wrist when he reached her and practically hauled her over the slick ground and deeper into the rain-dappled trees. When the trunks started to thin out again, he slowed, then stopped and turned to the rise they had just come down. Still shackled by his grip, Melissa turned, too.

Willing the pulse beating in his ears to slow, he listened for the sounds of something large crashing through bushes, annoyed snorts or any other sign that the animal had followed him. All he heard was the absurdly peaceful whisper of the wind in the treetops.

Adrenaline was still pumping when he let Melissa go and pushed the two-foot-long roll of map under the back of his jacket and into his back pocket to keep it dry. His heart felt as if it were pounding out of his chest. "I vote we go around him."

Melissa gripped his arm. "We're unanimous."

"We lost the flare gun."

"We haven't heard any planes, anyway."

That was true enough. He'd told her as they'd walked yesterday that it was doubtful anyone would go up looking for them. The rain was too heavy. The clouds and fog hung too low.

"Okay, then." He released a breath, blowing off the tension.

Melissa looked up at him. He couldn't honestly say he'd never seen her look quite the way she did just then. He had seen her fearful. He had seen her frightened. He had just never seen her afraid for him before.

Unmasked concern melded with anxiety as she searched his face and slowly lifted her hand to his forehead. Her touch, trembled. "You're bleeding."

He was only now aware of the dull throb where tree bark had scraped off skin. Reaching for her hand, he drew it away, threading his fingers through hers.

"Not much we can do about it. The first-aid kit is up there, and I'm not going after it. Come on," he coaxed, checking out the rise once more. "There's a lake ahead of us. Once we get there, we only have a few more miles to go."

What he didn't say was that the lake was ten miles away. But as she dug his handkerchief out of her vest pocket so he could press it to the raw scrape, and he led her between the trees, he wasn't as comfortable with the omission as he could have been.

When the plane had first gone down, he had regarded her as he would any other passenger he had flown for his friends. The way he saw it, when a passenger paid for a flight, it was the pilot's job to see her safely to her destination. Or at least to safety. How he did his job, and any concern he had about doing it, was his problem, not hers.

The problem now was that he hadn't honestly thought of her as only a responsibility since they'd come off the ridge. And the throbbing in his head, minor as it was, reminded him of why he owed her more than he was giving.

She wasn't just a responsibility. He truly cared about her. He'd been thinking about that even before they'd stumbled on the bear. And because he cared, he couldn't stand the thought of what might have ultimately happened to her if that bear had decided to have him for lunch.

He wanted her safe, and that meant making sure she would be if his luck happened to change. He'd cheated a plane crash and a bear. Before the plane had gone into a dive, he'd pretty much considered himself physically invincible. Though some might say he'd just proven strong leanings in that direction, thinking of Melissa, he was feeling slightly more cautious now.

He didn't bother to question his conclusions as they continued on. He simply decided that he would talk to her about them when they cleared their lumbering friend's turf and turned his focus to the land and what occupied it.

A mile later they reached a sloped clearing that allowed them to see the grassy, rolling hills beyond.

Deer grazed near a stand of tall firs in the distance. A stone's throw away, a small stream tumbled toward a bigger one at the bottom, then wound its way between two hills and disappeared.

He nodded toward the rapidly flowing water. "I bet we can follow that to the lake we're heading for."

"How far is it?"

"My guess is eight, maybe nine miles."

"Nine?"

There was no mistaking the discouragement in Mel's tone. They hadn't been running. It had just felt like it as they'd hurried away from where they'd been, making as much racket as they could with new sticks since theirs had been abandoned along with the pack.

It was getting harder by the minute for her to find an upside to anything. All Mel could come up with now was that at least here, out in the open as they were, they weren't as vulnerable to a surprise attack as they'd been in the trees.

Trying not to think about the berries they hadn't had time to gather, weary of walking and beyond trying not to be, she took the wadded-up handkerchief from Nick's hand and trudged through the mud and the meadow grass to the stream.

Sinking into the ground beside it, she washed the blood out of the handkerchief as best she could in the cold clear water. She didn't care that the grass she knelt on was wet. Her jeans were wet, anyway.

Apparently, Nick didn't care, either. Pulling the map from his back pocket, the compass from another, he sat down beside her.

"Let me see your head," she said, rising beside him to rest on her heels. Cupping one hand to his cheek, she peered at the blood caked around what looked like a floor burn and angry red brush marks. At least he wasn't still bleeding, she thought, and gently touched the wet cloth to the darker blood in his eyebrow.

He'd smeared it to his temple, pushed a streak back toward his hair. There wasn't anything she could do but clean around the wound—and be enormously thankful that he hadn't been injured more severely. She might not have studied the behavior of certain mammals in the wild, but she understood animal aggression and how little it took to provoke a curious animal to attack.

Nick had shoved her out of harm's way. He had thought of her first.

She didn't ask if the abrasion hurt. She didn't want him to feel as if he had to dismiss it if it did, the way he had when she'd first asked about his shoulder. She had the feeling, though, that he, too, was thinking about how horribly wrong things could have gone.

He sat with his feet planted wide, his wrists draped over his raised knees. The hair shadowing the sharp angles of his jaw and above the sensual lines of his mouth now barely allowed skin to show through. That dark growth made his eyes look more silver than gray, more intent, more piercing.

"You need to learn how to read the map," he said, watching the concentration in her face as she cleaned the skin at his temple.

"Why?"

"I just think it would be a good idea. In case I can't."

She frowned at his eyebrow. "Nothing's going to happen to you," she said quietly, carefully dabbing. "We'll make it out of here together."

"I don't plan on anything happening," he told her. "And we *will* make it out of here. But it wouldn't hurt for you—"

"If we stay together, we'll be fine," she insisted. "We have been, so far."

He sighed, as much from the gentleness of her ministrations as her stubbornness. He was hungry, wet, sore and scraped, and her touch felt incredible. "We were together back there."

"And we made it away all right."

He closed his fingers around her wrist, stilling her hand, drawing her eyes to his. "But if we hadn't and if something had happened to me, you could be back there now having no idea where you need to go.''

''Nothing will happen.''

''Mel—''

''Please, Nick. Don't do this.'' For days he had been the hope she had clung to. She refused to let him deny her that hope now. ''I need you to be all right. I need…''

You.

She didn't say the word. Yet, it seemed to hang in the air between them like the puffs of their breath as Nick's eyes held hers.

Never in her life had she allowed herself to count on anyone the way she had him. She suspected he knew that, too. What she prayed he didn't suspect was that she might need him in ways that had nothing to do with physical survival.

He let go of her hand to smooth back the straggling hair from her cheek. His touch was tender. His rugged features held understanding. ''It's just the circumstances,'' he said, slowly tucking the hair behind her ear. ''It will all seem different when we're out of here.''

She swallowed at the inevitable truth in his conclusion. She just couldn't quite believe it was only circumstance drawing her to him as she again touched the handkerchief to the edge of the scrape. Knowing what kind of man he was, she would have started falling for him no matter where they'd met.

Nick closed his eyes as she pressed the cold cloth to his skin.

''All we have left is a compass and the map. We're not leaving here until I know you can use them.''

Her fingers slipped through the hair at his temple, easing it from the wound. ''Okay.''

Nick felt a twinge of relief at her quiet acquiescence.

He knew she was vulnerable to him. He could see it in her face, feel it in her touch. But part of him had become vulnerable to her, too.

He didn't trust the pull he felt toward her as she finished cleaning his head and rinsed the handkerchief out again. He was a logical, rational man. And being logical, it made sense that it was only their situation creating the bond between them.

There was no denying that bond, either, as, long hours and miles later, he curled around her under the sweeping arms of an enormous spruce trying to keep them both warm. There had been no question of how they would sleep. No discussion. Without food, shelter or dry clothes, the only comfort they had was each other.

Chapter Nine

They had reached the lake last evening and left it behind hours ago.

"You said a few miles," Mel reminded Nick. "Maybe you should define *a few*."

"Three or more."

"I think we're into the more part."

"We're going slower than we have been. I don't think we've gone that far yet. Are you still looking for berries?"

"Haven't seen a one."

"Neither have I."

Shivering, she rubbed her arms beneath her makeshift poncho. The water in the chill air was more mist than rain, the kind that settled heavily and dripped off everything. Nick's face would glisten with the moisture until he swiped it away. His hair lay against his forehead, damp with it, too.

Mel worked one arm free and wiped her face with the tail of Nick's shirt. As she did, she sneezed.

She knew a person couldn't catch a cold from being cold, but she didn't doubt for a moment that her resistance was down. Her pace was definitely slower than it had been even yesterday. Nick seemed to be moving slower, too. Whether in deference to her or because he was finally feeling the effects of no fuel and protesting muscles, she didn't know.

His steps grew slower even now.

"Are you all right?" she asked, thinking he might not be feeling all that great, either, when she saw his forehead pleat.

He held out his hand, catching her arm, stopping her. "Listen."

Oh, sweet heaven, she prayed, not another bear.

"Do you hear that?"

She couldn't hear anything that she hadn't heard moments ago. Without the crack of pinecones beneath their feet, all that was left was the wind in the trees and the distant sound of rushing water.

Her brow furrowed, too. The water sounded as if it were getting closer. And they weren't moving.

It wasn't water, either. It just took a moment for her to realize that what she was hearing was the distant rumble of a vehicle engine.

His eyes collided with hers. "It sounds like a truck."

The distant rumble grew marginally louder, rooting them to where they stood in the misty rain. Within seconds the sound faded, carried away by the chill breeze.

"This way," Nick said, grabbing her hand. "I think it came from over there."

The ground beneath their feet was spongy with decades of decaying vegetation, but within minutes natural ground gave way to a wide swath of gravel and muddy potholes. The narrow road disappeared into the trees in both directions, fog shrouding the distance.

There wasn't a vehicle in sight.

The quick surge of elation Mel felt at the thought of rescue plummeted like a rock over a cliff. The road looked as if it could go on for miles.

"Come on," Nick said, tighten his hand around hers. "We're almost there."

She wasn't exactly sure where there was until the shape of a truck appeared ahead of them in the fog.

It was parked in the middle of the road.

"Oh, my gosh," she murmured, when she saw a figure swinging something that looked like a gate across the wide path of gravel.

Nick dropped her hand. "Hang on," he told her, and took off at a jog, pulling the severed blanket over his head as he went.

"Are you sure neither of you need a hospital?"

The man who identified himself as Ranger Adams had a graying brown ponytail, sharp hazel eyes and the long, lanky build of a basketball player. He also revealed a hat dent and a bald spot when he tossed his plastic-covered, Mountie-style hat into the space behind the bench seat in his truck and turned up the heater full blast.

He had heard of their missing plane. It had been an item on the evening news, and Forest Service personnel had been notified by the local sheriff's office to be on the lookout for the plane or survivors in the huge wilderness. He'd just never expected to have the survivors approach him to get a lift into town.

"I know you said you don't, but it's no problem taking

you if you do. There's a hospital in Port Angeles. I can have you there in twenty minutes.''

He spoke as he drove, bouncing them away from the gate that read Road Closed for the Winter. Beneath bushy brown eyebrows, he looked at them with both skepticism and concern.

Most of that concern seemed directed at her—which made her figure she looked worse than she'd thought.

Mel had taken off her half of the blanket, too. It was wadded up with Nick's on the floor. But whatever improvement its removal had made in her appearance was marginal. Her shoulders and most of her shirt was dry, but her wet hair was plastered to her head, the scratches on the backs of her hands stood out brightly against her cold reddened hands, and the glimpse she'd caught of herself in his rearview mirror had prompted a mental groan in the instant before she'd glanced away.

Her nose was a lovely shade of rose, her eyes were rimmed with pink and her skin was as pale as milk. But she was just cold.

''Once I get warm, I'll be fine. Honest,'' she said, greedily absorbing the heat blasting from below the dashboard. ''This feels like heaven.''

''You need ointment for those,'' Nick said, over the slap of the windshield wipers. He touched the back of one hand, frowning a little, then glanced back to the ranger.

''Thanks again,'' he said, ''but I don't think there's anything wrong with either of us that a shower and food won't cure. And a telephone. How far are we from where we can find all that?''

Mel watched the ranger finally pull his attention from where she sat between him and Nick. She couldn't believe how good it felt to sit on something with some give to it, or how conscious she was of Nick's leg pressed to hers.

There seemed something significant about that familiar contact. They were no longer alone. Yet she still felt as if he were protecting her somehow.

"We're about five miles from a ranger station. Port Angeles is about ten."

"How about a hotel in town, then?"

"Anyplace in particular?"

Shifting beside her, Nick glanced at his watch. She could see that it was nearly four-thirty. They would be pushing five o'clock before they got anywhere.

"How about the nicest one?"

The limb must have cracked his head harder than she'd thought.

"The nicest?" Her disbelieving glance cut from his unshaven jaw to the mud caking their boots and the bottoms of their pants. "We look like refugees."

The cold had his skin looking a tad red, too, which made him look rather roguish with his dark beard, but his expression was as reasonable as his tone. "That's why we need a place with decent room and laundry service. And good beds. By the time we get cleaned up and eat it could be eight or nine o'clock. I don't know about you, but I'm not going anywhere else tonight."

The ranger poked his head past Mel to see Nick, hitting a pothole in the process. "There's an inn on the way into town that's probably got what you're looking for. Expensive place. L'Auberge, it's called. I hear they're booked a year ahead for rooms, but that's in the busy season. Things are starting to close down around here now.

"Or there's a place a little farther in," he continued with a significant glance toward their clothes. "It isn't as exclusive, but I heard the rooms are nice. You might be more comfortable there."

The second place sounded fine to her.

"L'Auberge," Nick said, opting for the first. "Do you have a cell phone I can use?"

"Just let me make a call first," the ranger replied, clearly thinking he'd have opted for the other himself. "I need to let the station know I've got you."

In the past five days reality for Mel had narrowed to the forest and Nick. Within minutes of arriving at the rustic but quietly luxurious inn, reality went from the simple to surreal.

Nick had asked for the manager when he'd called ahead. He had explained their situation and their needs, warned the man that they wouldn't look like his usual guests when they arrived and, after reading off the numbers on one of his credit cards, been told that two rooms would be waiting for him.

The manager, apparently like everyone else in the area, had heard of the missing plane, too. Because the media would undoubtedly want to follow up on what had happened to them, Nick's last request had been that he not say anything to anyone about them until he could make some phone calls himself. They really needed food and showers before they could deal with anything else.

There was no doubt that the manager agreed with Nick's assessment when the truck pulled up under the portico with its flagstone pavement and brass coach lamps on its pillars and Ranger Adams dropped them off. The trim, copper-haired gentleman in the dark suit and gold-rimmed glasses met them outside himself. After a cursory once-over, he immediately hid his dismay at their muddy boots, introduced himself as Michael Sheridan, extended his hand to her, then Nick and welcomed them to the inn.

Rather than having them check in at the polished-mahogany reception desk at the back of the intimate little lobby, he led them quickly past a round entry table holding an enormous bouquet of gold mums, cattails and pheasant feathers, past a cozy arrangement of sofas and high-backed chairs grouped in front of a ceiling-high stone fireplace, and escorted them directly into his equally tasteful office.

He didn't say a word about the condition of their boots as they crossed the gleaming hardwood floors and tapestrylike carpets. And he did nothing but smile graciously at the half-dozen guests who looked up from the wine and cheese they were enjoying by a fire in a little side room to stare at what Mel figured must look like the local bag lady and her beau. Mr. Sheridan merely lifted his hand in the direction of the young lady behind the desk and motioned Mel and Nick to the upholstered chairs in front of his desk.

Mel wasn't about to sit on that gorgeous damask. "I think I'll just stand," she said. Although sinking onto something soft again sounded like pure bliss.

"Thanks, but me, too," Nick replied, and handed over his credit card. "Keep both rooms on this."

"Of course, sir. Miss Bailey," he said to the young woman who had followed them in, "if you will give them our menus, please?"

Gracious as their host seemed, Mel swore Mr. Sheridan looked relieved that his upholstery had been spared. Most of her attention, however, was on Nick.

She was getting ready to protest what he'd just said when he arched his eyebrow at her.

She had no means herself to pay. Her purse had gone down with the plane.

"I'll pay you back," she murmured, afraid to even guess at how much her room might cost. The attractive young woman in the trim burgundy suit currently eyeing

Nick had just handed her a menu and stood poised with a pad. Entrees started at twenty bucks and went up from there. Salads started at $8.50. Everything was à la carte.

"If you'd tell Miss Bailey what you'd like, we'll have room service sent to you right away. She will also take care of any sundries you might require." Light reflected off his glasses when he aimed a glance toward Nick's face. "You'll find soaps and lotions in your room, of course," he continued, typing into his computer, "but you might be in need of other items. May I have a home address, Mr. Magruder? I believe the news said you're from the Denver area?"

Nick gave him a street address and telephone number. With the manager clicking away, he then smiled at the lovely Miss Bailey. "I could use a razor, shaving cream and a toothbrush. And a filet, medium rare," he added, looking back to scrawl his signature boldly over the bottom of the form Mr. Sheridan pulled from his printer. "How good is your chef?"

"He's excellent, sir. Our restaurant is five-star."

"Then, I'll take whatever he wants to put with it as long as there's a lot of it. How's your cellar?"

"The finest in the area," Mr. Sheridan immediately assured. "Would you like to see our reserve wine list?"

He said he would as he pushed back the form and stuck the pen in the holder on the man's desk. Even as disreputable as he looked, muddy, with nearly a week's worth of beard and wearing wet, dirty pants and a scarred leather jacket, there was an aura of quiet power about him, a sort of command that didn't demand deference so much as it inspired it.

He had bypassed the worker bees when he'd called and asked immediately for the manager. Now he didn't hesitate to ask for what he wanted, and what he wanted spoke of a man with rather highly evolved tastes.

He's used to this, Mel thought. The reason he'd wanted the better hotel was because the best was what he was accustomed to.

"What about you, Dr. Porter?" Miss Bailey asked. The young woman smiled, trying hard not to stare at her soaked and flattened hair. Her voice dropped discreetly. "We have hair dryers in the rooms, and the conditioner is quite good. If you need makeup or anything, our gift shop has a few items. Just let me know what I can bring you."

Mel already felt like something the cat had dragged in. Standing beside the neat and attractive twenty-something who'd already checked out Nick's ring finger and kept batting her baby browns at him, she felt like something the cat had also tried to bury. "Thank you," she replied, "I will."

"So, what can I get for you now?"

Looking at the menu only made her hunger more acute. Already edgy with it, she handed the padded folder back, immediately hiding her dirty nails.

She asked for a toothbrush and, taking Nick's cue to trust the chef, any kind of pasta without meat in it. As she did, she listened to Nick on the telephone. He'd just called Sam.

"Give me an hour and I'll call you with you details. Yeah," he said after a moment, "she's right here. She's fine, too. Sure," he said, after another pause, "give it to me and I'll give it to her."

He wrote something down on the pad Mr. Sheridan handed him, tore off the page and told Sam he'd talk to him in a while.

"Is that everything?" he asked the man waiting with his hands clasped behind him.

"Unless there is something else we can get for you, I believe it is. I'll have our bellman take you to your rooms. I've already sent up fruit and cheese."

Nick held out his hand. "Your service is impeccable, Mr. Sheridan."

"It is our motto," the manager replied, shaking it.

Mel added her own thanks, feeling more out of place by the minute. Not because of her appearance, but because she had never stayed in a place where the management was so solicitous, where you barely had to wish it and it was so. She was also growing more conscious by the second that—except for the bill, which she would repay— she no longer had to rely on Nick. And he no longer had any reason to keep an eye out for her.

There had been a time when all she had wanted was a hot shower, a hot meal and a soft bed. She was wrong. As she followed the young man in the burgundy uniform up the sweeping staircase, all but gritting her teeth at having to climb yet again, all she really wanted was Nick. She wanted what she'd felt growing between them, the closeness, the ease that had finally erased the awkwardness from their silences.

What she got instead was the piece of paper he'd been holding when they stopped outside a door numbered 216 in curling bronze.

"Sam has talked with your sister," he said, his expression vaguely preoccupied. "She left this number for you to call."

With the bellman waiting behind her, she took what Nick held out. Though reality was jerking harder, she tried to smile. "Thanks. I think."

"Yeah," he muttered dryly. "I know. I have some calls

I need to make myself.'' His glance roamed her face, then quickly fell away. ''It's going to take a while.''

She lifted her chin, gave him a nod. ''Do we have to talk to anyone tonight? The ranger said the sheriff might want to talk to us. And you said you'll have to talk to someone from the FAA.''

''Not tonight. Not if I can help it, anyway,'' he qualified. ''I'll let you know if we do. Otherwise, I'll see you in the morning.''

She gave him another nod before he turned to the man patiently waiting for them to conclude. It seemed there should be something more she should say to Nick in case she didn't see him until then. Thanks for getting her back, seemed appropriate. Would she ever see him after tomorrow? was what she really wanted to know. But Nick seemed pretty intent on getting to his calls. And she had a ranger to track down herself. Ranger Adams had given her Wyckowski's number. She wasn't looking forward to explaining how she lost the coyote pups.

Half of the fruit plate waiting for her in the charmingly furnished country French suite was gone before Mel stripped and stood with her face in the steamy hot water. She lathered with soap and shampoo, twice, then finished the rest of the plate a half an hour later, after she'd wrapped her hair in a thick white towel, herself in the white terry cloth hotel robe someone had laid out on the canopy bed and shoved her clothes, boots included, into the laundry bag she'd found in the closet. Her clothes were picked up just as her dinner arrived.

The waiter set a basket of bread and a steaming bowl of fettuccine quatro formaggi on the blue-and-cream-toile-covered table by the armoire hiding the television set. The canopy bed, king-size, draped in matching fabric and piled with pillows, occupied the wall across from them.

That was where she took her bowl after she signed for her meal. Setting it on the nightstand, she picked up the phone and sat down on the edge of the bed. Between bites, she dialed Ranger Wyckowski, left a message on his answering machine and unfolded the piece of paper Nick had given her.

Her appetite immediately waned, but she dialed the number anyway. After the tenth ring, she hung up, finished her dinner and carried her plate back to the table.

It would be so easy to say she had tried to reach Cam and let it go at that. She didn't recognize the number. The area code was the same as Harbor's, but then so was all of western Washington. She couldn't cop out like that, though. Along with a fear of heights, she'd been cursed with a nagging conscience, and there was always the remote possibility that Cameron might be worried.

She dialed again, feeling guilty for hoping there would still be no answer, and listened to the faint rush of water running through pipes in the walls.

Nick's room was next door.

He was in the shower.

She didn't know which disturbed her more. The thought of how she might never again feel the security of his arms, or the click at the other end of the line when her sister answered.

"Hi, Cam. It's Mel."

Cameron practically squealed her name. "I don't believe it! I was afraid they weren't going to find you. Oh, Mel, I'm so glad you're okay. I was going to have to leave here and I really didn't know what I was going to do. Are you back on that island? I really need to see you."

The enthusiasm was good to hear, or so it seemed for

about three seconds. Cameron hadn't missed her. Not in the sense that she'd cared that her life might just possibly have been in danger when the plane she'd been in had gone down in the middle of a lake in the middle of a forest in the middle of nowhere.

She'd missed her because she needed help.

She just wasn't forthcoming about with what when Mel asked why seeing her was so important.

"It's something I have to see you to talk about. So when can I? And you'll be there this time?" Cam asked, going on to hint that it hadn't been terribly convenient having to find a place to stay when Mel hadn't shown up before. She stopped short of sounding put-out, though. When she wanted something, she knew better than to tick someone off. She also tended to get chatty about nothing in particular, which was why it took twenty minutes to get two minutes worth of information out of her—none of which hinted at what she wanted this time.

Mel had just hung up and was rubbing the dull ache in her forehead when a knock sounded on the adjoining door of her room.

Padding barefoot across the carpet, she flipped the latch and opened it.

Nick stood on the other side, freshly shaved, his dark hair combed back and wearing the same hotel-issue white terry cloth. The robe hit her at the ankles. His hit midcalf.

In one hand he held a crystal goblet of red wine.

She remembered picturing that image before, his strong fingers curved around fragile glass. She remembered, too, wondering how his hands would feel on her skin.

Now she knew.

"Do we have to talk to someone?" she asked, quickly trading the thought for relief. There was a bruise on his forehead that dried blood had covered, but the scrape on his forehead from the tree limb didn't look so angry now that it was clean.

He shook his head, his steel-gray glance carefully sweeping her face. "I just wanted to see if you want this," he said, holding out the goblet, "and to make sure you have everything you need." His eyes narrowed on the unease in hers. "What's wrong?"

Mel eyed the wine. He wasn't holding a glass for himself, his she could see still sitting on a table behind him.

She rarely drank, but because he was being so thoughtful, she took what he offered with a quiet "Thank you."

Leaving him free to walk in if he wanted to, she headed back across the expanse of thick carpet, set the goblet on the nightstand and sank back down on the edge of her huge bed. "I just got off the phone with my sister."

"What did she say?"

"Nothing specific. But I have a bad feeling about whatever's going on with her."

She watched him move into the room. He looked different without the hair shadowing his face. Sexier, she thought, but then she'd thought he'd looked pretty incredible with the beard, too.

Deciding she was simply prejudiced where he was concerned, she pulled her glance from the strip of dark chest hair visible between the sides of the robe. It seemed wiser to focus on her ragged cuticles instead.

The bed sank beneath his weight when he sat down an arm's length away. "So you still have no idea what she wants?"

"No," she quietly replied. "But I imagine it either involves money or a place to stay." To keep her eyes from straying back to his chest, she picked up the little bottle of lotion she'd brought in from the bathroom and started rubbing it into her hands. They were a mess. Nails chipped. Scratches.

Nick crossed his arms, watching.

"How about you?" she asked. "Did you get your calls made?"

"Most of them. I couldn't reach a couple of people I had appointments with. The time difference," he explained, an edge surfacing the way it always did when he talked about Denver. "But I talked with Sam and the FAA and a guy from the sheriff's office who coordinates search and rescue. It's what we thought. We didn't hear any planes because the weather was in too low. Sam reported us missing the morning after we went down. That day was the only clear weather we had."

"Is he upset about his plane?"

"He's just relieved we're okay." He paused, noticing the red pressure marks from her boots on the tops of her slender feet. A little bruise colored her ankle. Another marred the smooth skin of her calf where her robe fell open.

Had they still been in the forest, he might have turned her around and taken a closer look at sore spots. Knowing she had to be naked under that robe made him keep his hands tucked right where they were.

"I think he's afraid that you'll sue, though."

Her glance moved to his. The rims of her eyes were no longer so pink, but the faint worry he'd first noticed still shadowed the deep blue. "I'm not going to do that. I'll never be accepted if the first thing I do is sue someone. He gave me the flight for free."

"He did?"

"He said he owed his wife flights for rescued animals for all the times she took care of his kids before they were married. Or something like that," she murmured, sounding too preoccupied to remember exactly what Sam's rationale had been. "Aside from that, a lawsuit would mean involving you, and you…"

"I what?" he coaxed when she paused.

She set the lotion aside, rubbing the last of it into the heel of her hand. "You kept me safe."

She had the towel wrapped high around her head. Her face had been scrubbed clean. There was nothing to cover what she might perceive as a flaw, nothing to hide or enhance. Weariness sucked the energy from her tone and the bubbly brightness he'd first noticed about her had been drained by the demanding, exhausting days, and nights on ground that added more aches than rest soothed.

Still, he couldn't help but think of how truly lovely she was.

"I just did what I had to do," he quietly replied. "We both did."

It seemed there was more she wanted to say. Maybe more she needed him to know. All she did was give a little nod.

"What?" he asked when she'd yet to look up from where she still absently rubbed her hand.

She kept rubbing, a faint frown furrowing her brow. "You are glad we're back, aren't you?"

The question threw him. So did the troubled way she looked when she finally glanced up.

He opened his mouth, fully prepared to say of course he was. Only to catch himself when he realized what had her looking so subdued.

Reconsidering, he had to admit that he wasn't as happy as everyone else would expect him to be. Everyone but Melissa, anyway. The relief he felt to not be sleeping on the ground tonight was tainted by what awaited him when he arrived home. It was that kind of honesty she forced in him.

"I'm glad we're where we are, but I'm not crazy about some of what I have to do now that we're back."

"Neither am I."

"You're talking about your sister," he concluded.

"Her. And my screw-up with the ranger. And straightening out the talk about me."

Nick knew he could tell her that the loss of the pups had hardly been her fault. He could tell her that the talk would die, that she should wait to see what her sister wanted before she worried about it. But she knew her sister better than anyone, and Melissa would worry about all of it, anyway.

Her slender shoulders sank beneath the white fabric. "I wish I was back in that forest."

There was no mistaking the defeat in her voice, and defeat was so unlike her. But it was just fatigue talking. As strong as he knew she was, it had to be.

The end of her robe's belt trailed onto the bedspread between them. Because he didn't trust himself to touch her, he unfolded his arms to touch it instead.

"Back in the forest, huh?" he asked, certain she would be more rational after a decent night's sleep. Tonight she had a mattress, clean sheets and warm blankets. She'd been fed. Tomorrow she would be a new woman. "And what would you do if you were stuck back out there?"

He had asked her much the same question before. Only, he'd wanted to know what she would do if they had no hope of finding their way out. She had told him then that she wouldn't even consider the possibility. Now there was no doubt in her mind what she would do.

Already missing him, wishing she could hold reality at bay just a little longer, she touched her hand to his jaw.

His freshly shaved skin felt impossibly smooth. The corner of his mouth where her thumb brushed it felt far softer than it looked.

"This," she said, and leaned closer.

She heard his slow intake of breath when she touched her mouth to the warmth of his. He smelled of soap and shaving cream. He tasted faintly of rich, heady wine. Where her fingertips brushed his temple, she felt the clean dampness of his soft hair, and the edge of the scrape where he'd encountered the limb.

Thinking again of how he'd pushed her out of harm's way, she wanted to touch her lips there, too. And she would have, had he not slipped his hands to her shoulders.

He edged back, raised one hand to her face.

With his thumb he brushed the corner of her mouth, following the movement with his eyes. "That's what you'd do, huh?"

"Yes."

His glance slowly swept up. His eyes glittering on hers, he traced the fullness of her lower lip.

"What else would you do?"

"If we were stuck there forever?"

"Yeah."

"Probably this," she whispered. Leaning closer, she kissed the underside of his lean jaw and the warm skin behind his ear.

When she kissed the scrape at his temple, she felt him tug the towel from her hair.

His hands slipped into the wet silk tumbling over her shoulders. "Me, too," he murmured, and angled his mouth over hers.

He kissed her long and deep, altering her heart rate along with her breathing, altering his own in the process. Nick had sworn to himself before he'd walked into her room that he wouldn't make any moves on her. He had not, however, considered what he would do if she did.

He tried to consider it now, but all he could think of was the satiny feel of her skin, the honeyed taste of her and the soft way she sighed into his mouth.

He had wanted her long before he had seen her standing there with nothing but a robe separating her from his hands. Every time he had looked at her during the long days they'd spent together, every time he'd held her during the longer nights, he had wondered how she would feel naked in his arms. With her in his arms now, her mouth soft and willing beneath his, all he had to do was pull the tie on the terry cloth and he would know.

The thought had him groaning.

He should let her go, he told himself. He should, he repeated, and was struggling to recall why when he drank her answering moan. With her tongue softly tangling with his, he gave up trying to remember why it mattered at all.

Mel felt his hand at the knot of her robe. Her heart nearly stopped beating when he slowly eased the belt free, then it bumped hard in her chest when he carried his kiss to the underside of her chin and down the line of her throat. He didn't stop until he reached the cleft between her breasts. Then he eased back just far enough to meet her eyes.

She saw hunger glinting in those smoky-gray depths. ''I would do more than this,'' he said, his voice a low rasp of warning. ''Much more.''

She lifted her hand to the collar of his robe, her breath trembling out. Edging back one side, she exposed the hard chest she'd snuggled against, the bruise now blackening his shoulder. She didn't know exactly when she'd fallen in love with him. It could have been on the ridge. Or lying in his arms. Or simply talking with him, learning what kind of man he was. She just knew that she had and that she had never felt anything so strong or so fierce in her life. ''So would I.''

The hunger turned feral. Holding her with nothing more than the heat in his eyes, he tugged back the sides of her robe, then let his glance drift to the gentle swells of her breasts. The cooler air pebbled her nipples. The touch of his mouth and his hands drew them to hard points in the moments before he eased her flat onto the bed and started trailing a path of moist heat the length of her sore, tired body.

The aches were forgotten. So was the weariness. She had always thought his hands were wonderful. Now she thought them magic. He enlivened nerves everywhere he touched. And his hands touched her everywhere.

He skimmed them over her body, the curves of her breasts, her hips, the long length of her thighs. With amazing gentleness, he kissed the slashing bruises on her hips where the seat belt had bitten into her when they'd crashed. He brushed his lips over the bruises on her legs that could have come from limbs or rocks or any combination thereof. He soothed the scrapes on the back of her hands, then locked her arms around his neck to kiss her breathless before edging down again to tease with teeth and tongue.

The taste of her intoxicated him.

The touch of her hands inflamed him.

Nick's blood threatened to turn to steam. He couldn't believe how beautifully Melissa responded to him, the artless way she touched and stroked him in return. She held nothing from him, giving him as good as she got as she trailed her lips from his battered shoulder to the bruises that matched hers on his hips.

That intimate game of follow-the-leader spiked pure

fire through him. The sweet taste of her when he pulled her up his body and rolled her onto her back, turned fire to craving.

The robes they had tugged open tangled between them. Pushing hers aside, he threw his off and claimed her mouth once more. With his hand beneath her hip, he nestled himself between her legs—and gritted his teeth against the raw need ripping through him when he entered her welcoming warmth.

She whispered his name, the sound a soft plea.

He whispered hers back, tightening his hold.

Then there was nothing but the feel of her arching to meet him and the sweet oblivion he found in her arms.

The digital clock on Melissa's nightstand indicated it was near midnight when Nick roused enough to realize they'd fallen asleep. He remembered turning out the light and pulling her against him after they'd crawled beneath the covers. Now he lay curled up to her back, as he had when they'd slept on the ground.

For long moments he simply listened to her breathing, enjoying the softness and warmth of the bed and her body. He could easily remember how he'd curled against her like this in the forest, warming her, himself, and wanting her so badly he ached.

He wanted her now. Again.

He slipped his hand over her bare stomach, caught himself a heartbeat later. She was exhausted. She needed sleep. So did he. Or so the rational part of him insisted in the moments before he felt her stir against him.

Those other nights, he had contented himself with just holding her. As she turned in his arms, her mouth seeking his, he wondered now how he'd ever exercised that restraint.

Chapter Ten

Reality returned long before Mel wanted to face it.

The phone in Nick's room rang at 8:00 a.m. With the door adjoining his room to hers still open, the electronic summons drifted toward where they curled around each other in the middle of the huge canopy bed.

Her head rested comfortably on his shoulder. Her hand splayed over his bare chest. At the insistent sound, she stifled a groan at the intrusion, and felt Nick's arm tighten around her.

"Ignore it," he muttered, his deep voice heavy with sleep.

She would have been happy to. For the past hour, she had lain awake in his arms, trying diligently to stave off the little ache waiting to be felt. In a few hours they would be staying goodbye. With all that waited for her on Harbor, the thought of no longer seeing him, of no longer having him to share with, was more than she wanted to consider just yet.

His phone silenced.

Moments later the phone beside her bed began to ring.

Nick drew back his arm, stretched against her. "I wonder if that's Sam."

"Why would he be calling me?"

"To get you back to Harbor. He said he'd call this morning to get us where we need to go. He'll fly us himself."

The thought of getting on another plane was something else she didn't care to consider at the moment. With Nick clearly expecting her to pick up the receiver, it seemed she had little choice but to consider it as she answered the phone.

It wasn't Sam. The caller on the other end of the line was a reporter from a Seattle newspaper. The very professional, very efficient-sounding woman started by saying she'd tried to reach Mr. Magruder, but had been unable to do so, and that she would like to interview them both, starting with her. Specifically, she wanted to know why and where the plane had gone down, who or what she felt was at fault and how she and Mr. Magruder had survived.

Mel wouldn't have had a problem talking to the woman, even though she was tad pushy. She would be more than happy to tell her that she wasn't placing blame anywhere. She just didn't want to do it right now. She didn't want anything to intrude on what little time she had left with Nick.

Thinking she would also sound more coherent after coffee, too, she glanced to where he lay with his hands behind his head, lazily watching her. With his eyes drifting to where she held the sheet to her chest, she asked the reporter if she could call her back—just as a knock sounded on the outer door in Nick's room.

The male voice coming from hall said he had Nick's clothes.

He probably had hers, too, which meant he would be knocking on her door next.

Mel thought she saw disappointment tighten the hard line of Nick's jaw a moment before he pushed back her wildly tangled hair and brushed his lips over the back of her neck. "You might as well talk to her now," he whispered. Gloriously, unashamedly naked, he slipped from the bed and grabbed his robe on the way to the door. "I'll see you in a while."

The morning passed in a blur. The questions the reporter from the Seattle paper asked were repeated at a press conference attended by the ranger who had given them the ride, his supervisor and the captain of the search and rescue team who expressed as much frustration at not being able to help them as he did relief that they had survived.

Melissa answered the questions posed to her with simple honesty. So did Nick. Yet, neither mentioned the difficulty of having to cross the ridge, the encounter with the bear or how they had managed to stay warm.

Nick's response to a query about the latter was that they'd had survival gear from the plane with them, though he didn't mention how spare it was or that they'd lost most of it. As she listened to his calm, easy recitation of how the plane had gone down and how they'd used his aerial map to get out, she couldn't help but notice how he kept his focus carefully away from her. It was as if all that had happened to them and how they'd face it together was personal somehow. Something that didn't need to be shared with anyone else.

That was how she felt, anyway. As everyone was leaving and they were waiting for the lodge's courtesy van to pick them up, she couldn't help wonder if the real reason Nick had omitted the details was because he was already distancing himself.

After he had left her bed, she hadn't seen him until he'd called from downstairs to tell her that reporters were already there. Now watching him turn from the reception desk of the lodge's elegant yet rustic lobby, she couldn't help but notice that he had the same distracted look about him that she'd seen so often before. The one that told her his thoughts were miles from what was going on at that moment.

He had just settled the bill and thanked the manager and his assistant for accommodating them. Mel had already expressed her own gratitude. It didn't matter that impeccable service was included in the exorbitant price of the rooms. She truly appreciated having clean clothes again. Even her boots had been dried out and brushed free of dirt. And Miss Bailey had come up herself with the mascara and lip gloss Melissa called the gift shop for when she'd heard that the reporters had converged.

Watching Nick approach her now, she rose from the high-backed wing chair by the fireplace. His leather jacket had acquired a couple more scars. Beneath it, the open collar of his pressed denim shirt exposed the bleached white neckband of his undershirt. His khakis sported a couple of stains that apparently refused to be removed, but had a knife-edge crease.

"So," she said, forcing a smile as she glanced back to the shaving nick on his cleanly shaven jaw. "When is Sam coming?"

"We're meeting him at the airport in twenty minutes. Are you okay with flying?"

Considering what had happened the last time she'd been on a plane, she would have most definitely rather taken a ferry. The problem was that there were none from Port Angeles and getting to where she could take one would involve a hundred or so miles of driving in a car she didn't have and no credit card to rent one with. She wasn't about to ask Nick to front her more money. It would also take the rest of the day, which she didn't have either. Her sister would be there from wherever she'd been staying in a matter of hours.

"I guess I have to be," she replied gamely.

A couple of hours ago her first thought would have been that she couldn't do it. Yet, as distressing as the thought was of getting into another airplane, she knew now that she could do even what she thought impossible. The big man giving her a slow smile had proved that to her himself.

She gave him a small smile back, too aware of what was coming to put any real feeling behind it. She had an hour left with him. If that.

Nick caught the subtle play of emotions in her fragile features, the caution, the smile that didn't quite work. Her wheat-colored hair was brushed back from her face, the straight, blunt-cut tresses shimmering in a satiny fall behind her shoulders. What little makeup she wore made her blue eyes look huge. Her lips glistened, full and inviting.

The memory of how eagerly her mouth had moved beneath his had him pulling his glance, forcing his thoughts back on track. He'd been fully prepared to offer whatever encouragement was needed had she balked at the flight. But he should have known she wouldn't. She always did whatever she had to do.

"Okay, then," he said, casually slipping the hotel receipt into the inside pocket of his jacket. "Let's get going. The hotel van will take us there. We'll be on Harbor by noon."

She didn't budge. But the faint anxiety in her eyes turned to confusion.

"We?"

"I'm going with you," he said simply. "I promised I'd get you home. I figure that means I should at least see you to your door."

Confusion eased to a smile that finally held nothing back. She tipped her head, eyes shining. "Such service."

"I aim to please," he said, glad the anxiety was gone, and turned her toward the door.

He could swear what he saw in Melissa's expression was relief. He wasn't sure, though, if it was relief because they could postpone parting a little longer or because she didn't have to face getting on a plane alone. As they walked out into the misty rain and climbed into the waiting van, he didn't bother trying to figure it out. He was having enough trouble figuring out why he couldn't walk away from her just yet.

Part of him believed he was simply keeping his word. Another part wondered if he was just putting off going back to Denver for a little while longer. He couldn't begin to deny that he cared about the lovely woman beside him. But as they reached the six-passenger aircraft where Sam Edwards waited for them with a heartfelt slap on the back for him and a handshake for her, he strongly suspected the latter.

Still, he was constantly aware of her as she took the seat behind their brawny pilot and he took the one up front beside him. The disquiet he'd sensed in her when he'd last seen her buckle up didn't seem nearly as noticeable this time, though. Either she was getting better at masking it or everything she'd been through had numbed her to anxiety.

Less than an hour later he decided she must be perfecting the numbing technique.

There hadn't been much time for conversation on the short flight back. When Sam had asked why Nick was returning to Harbor instead of having him take him to Seattle to catch a flight to Denver, Nick simply told him he wanted to see his passenger safely home. He'd promised her that he would.

If Sam read anything into his blunt response, Nick couldn't tell. Sam asked only if he would be available later to help him answer some questions for his insurance claim for his drowned plane—then dropped off both him and Melissa at her place after they'd landed. He told her again how happy he and T.J. both were that she was okay, and drove off in the ever-present rain because he had another flight.

Melissa's new home was the last building on Pine Street just off Main Road. Low, white and sprawling, the Harbor Veterinary Clinic and Animal Hospital had an office in front, living quarters in back and was badly in need of paint. The back porch roof could use some work, too, Mel realized, when a drip landed between her and the man checking out the peeling sign that read For Veterinary Services Please Use Front Entrance.

"Oh my gosh," she muttered, turning back to see Sam's taillights disappear past the florist shop at the end of the street. "We can't get in. My key…"

"…is at the bottom of a lake," Nick concluded flatly.

She was about to ask how he was at breaking and entering when the door opened on its own.

It wasn't alarm that made Mel's heart sink. It was the unexpected sight of her sister. Cam had obviously caught an earlier ferry. She'd just as obviously picked the lock.

"I heard the truck. Hard not to. This street is totally dead. Come on in," her sister said, casually flipping her blond hair over her shoulder as she invited Mel into her own place. With a blink of her violet eyes, she checked out the big, decidedly attractive man standing stock-still behind her, gave Mel an accusing look for not showing up alone, then turned into the sparsely furnished living room.

Cameron had thrown her long black raincoat and purse over the taupe sofa Mel had bought on sale and paid a fortune to ship. Above it hung travel posters for places Mel had never been. On the pine coffee table, books on Harbor's wildlife and home decorating magazines were stacked neatly beside a collection of brass animals and a bowl of cinnamon potpourri. A copy of *Elle,* which belonged to Cam, lay on the end table by an urn-shaped lamp.

Melissa stepped inside, conscious of Nick's solid presence behind her as he came in and she closed the door.

Cam picked up her magazine and pushed it into her large black purse. "Your television doesn't work."

"It works fine. I just need a satellite dish to get reception."

Cameron wore black boots that added another two inches to her willowy five-foot, eight-inch frame, jeans that clung all the way up to where they rode her narrow hips and a black turtleneck that molded breasts that seemed a lot fuller than the last time Mel had seen her. She had the face of an angel, flawless skin and with her thick blond hair and those violet eyes, she had the potential to be drop-dead gorgeous.

She always had. It was the difference in their heights

that had always seemed to put Mel at a disadvantage, though. That and the defensive stance Cameron always took with her.

Mel felt Nick brush her shoulder, killing the smile she tried to put on anyway. "Maybe I better go."

Her uneasy glance collided with his. "It's raining."

"Like I haven't walked in the rain before?"

She didn't mean to look so pleading. She didn't want him to leave. She didn't want to deal with whatever it was that had made Cameron desperate enough to come all the way to Harbor, either. Desperate enough to make the trip twice—and to pick the lock on her door.

"You don't have to go anywhere," Cameron said to Nick. "I'm not going to be here that long." She picked up her coat, folded it over her arm. "There's a ferry leaving in fifteen minutes. I need to be on it."

Melissa blinked in confusion. "Why did you come all this way if you're leaving so soon?"

"Because I have a job in New York." True excitement brimmed beneath a mask of pure defense. The defense had the greater hold. "And I can't let anything stand in the way. I brought you something."

Crossing her arms over the pine-green vest she wore over her tan sweater and jeans, not feeling nearly as stylish as her sister looked, Melissa started to ask what she was talking about. She was totally lost. Not an unusual occurrence where her sister was concerned. But the sound coming from her bedroom stopped her cold.

The little mewl was unmistakable. So was the hiccupping cry that followed a moment later.

Mel's eyes collided with the guilt in her sister's. Without another word Mel headed into the short hallway, pushing past the boxes she hadn't finished unpacking and stopped cold in the doorway of her bedroom.

A little pink bundle was moving in the middle of the taupe-and-cream comforter covering her bed. Visible above the satin-edged baby blanket was a little round head covered with light brown fuzz, a button nose and a rosebud mouth seeking a tiny, perfect fist.

Mel edged closer. "Cameron?" she called quietly.

"I'm right here."

Cam stood in the bedroom doorway, her coat hanging over her protectively crossed arms.

Questions piled up like a train wreck in Mel's disbelieving mind. She hadn't even known her sister had been pregnant. But then Cam had chosen to stay out of touch for well over a year.

"Does Mom know?" Mel asked, carefully slipping her hands under the fussing child's little back. She didn't know why it relieved her to feel the child's weight, the solidness of the little body as she eased her to her shoulder. Little knees were drawn up, leaving her to cup a tiny padded bottom.

An unladylike snort accompanied a look that clearly said, *get real.* "Are you kidding? What's she going to do besides get drunk? I don't want her raised the way we were."

The tiny bundle in her arms grew more active, screwing up her face, rubbing her nose against Mel's shoulder. Mel, however, felt as if she'd just stopped breathing. "What do you mean?"

"I can't keep her. I told you, I have a job."

"Where's her father?"

"Who knows?"

"Cam," Mel said flatly. "Who *is* the father?"

A faint hint of crimson bloomed across perfectly made-up skin. Whether embarrassment or anger, Mel couldn't tell.

"It doesn't matter."

"Of course it matters. The two of you need to work this out. You have a responsibility to a child. Both of you do. I don't know what kind of job you have, but people work all the time with—"

"I don't know who the father is," Cam snapped, her voice a low hiss. "All right? Even if I did, I wouldn't want anything to do with him. A guy from the gym has an agency and he said he can get me runway work and maybe some catalogs. I have a chance to model, Melissa. I've wanted this since I was sixteen. And don't lecture me on responsibility. Everything's always come easy for you. This is my chance, and I'm not going to lose it."

She whirled on her heel, blond hair flying.

"Cameron. Wait. What gym?"

"Where I worked. I have to go."

"At least tell me how old she is."

Mel swept out behind her, following her past boxes and into the living room.

Nick was nowhere in sight.

"She was born a month yesterday."

"What's her name?" He hadn't waited. The thought had the knots in Mel's stomach doubling. "What does she eat? Is she healthy?"

"The women who baby-sat her at the gym say she's growing like a weed. And her name is Morgan. Her stuff is in the bag in your bedroom. There's a car seat thing in there, too."

Cam hadn't just been working at the gym. Knowing her, knowing how she'd always obsessed about her body, she'd been working out, too. Probably hours a day. That couldn't possibly have been healthy for her, but it would explain how she'd gotten her figure back so quickly.

It also sounded as if her baby's care had been left to everyone else.

"This guy," Mel said, watching her sister stuff her arms into her coat, snatch up her purse. "Is he legit? Have you checked the agency out?"

"Give me a little credit, will you? I know what I'm doing."

Giving her credit wasn't something Mel felt she could manage at the moment. "The number I have for you, can I reach you there?"

"That was a friend in Seattle."

"Will you call? Just let me know you're okay?"

Cam's expression closed, the way it always did when she was no longer listening.

"Cam? Please?"

"Don't do that," she muttered on her way to the door.

"Do what?"

"Don't try to make me feel guilty," she bit back. "I thought I could be a mom and I can't."

Cam didn't turn when she pulled open the door. She didn't so much as glance toward the child Mel held a little tighter in her arms. She just slammed the door as if slamming out everything she no longer wanted and took off, practically running down the gravel drive to the street and the ferry dock four short blocks away.

Mel lost sight of her sister as Cam turned in the mist by the florist shop. Only then did she release a disbelieving breath and stare down at the child drooling on her vest.

Feeling a definite need to sit down, she turned from the window by the door.

Nick stood in the doorway to the kitchen. He'd taken off his jacket. The denim shirt tucked into his neatly pressed khakis made his shoulders look a yard wide, his hard chest impossibly broad.

The need to be held in his arms felt far too strong.

"Thirsty," he said, holding up a glass of water he'd helped himself to. "I thought it might be better if I was out of the way."

He walked in, eyed her, eyed the baby and set the ice-blue tumbler on the pine coffee table. "I'd say your gut instincts about her were right," he conceded, speaking of the bad feeling Mel had had last night. His brow pinched. "But you didn't say you expected anything like this."

Mel sank, stunned, to the sofa. Carefully drawing the baby from her shoulder, she eased the child onto her lap, her little head at the knees of her jeans.

"Nothing like this," she admitted, feeling slightly shell-shocked as she stared at the squirming infant. The little blue-eyed angel waved her tiny fist, popped herself in the cheek. Squinting her eyes, she let out a small, half beat cry.

"I hadn't a clue," Mel said, gently catching the little hand so she wouldn't sock herself again. She knew how to care for newborn pups and kittens. She could handle just about any newborn, for that matter, as long as it had fur. She loved doing it, too. Holding baby anythings had always been the best part of her job. But the thought of caring for a child, of being totally responsible for its welfare, filled her with insecurities she hadn't even known she possessed.

More disconcerting still was the assessing way Nick watched her. He stood on the other side of the coffee table, three square feet of tastefully distressed wood deliberately separating them.

"Why did you just let her go like that? You didn't even try to talk her out of leaving her here."

"I couldn't have stopped her."

"You didn't even try," he repeated, sounding baffled by that. "You just let her take off without saying a word about how any of this would affect you."

Mel steeled herself against his quiet reproach. Touching her finger to the infant's soft cheek, she felt her heart catch when the little head turned to seek that touch with her mouth. "It would have been a waste of breath," she defended. "Nothing can change Cam's mind once it's made up. She'll find a way to do what she wants no matter what. And she won't care who it inconveniences or who gets hurt along the way."

"Even you and her child?"

"Obviously." It didn't matter that she thought her sister was making the biggest mistake of her life. The fact that Cam had come so far twice to leave her child indicated just how serious she was. "I just know this baby is better off with someone who will care for her than wherever else she might wind up."

Nick planted his hands on his hips, his expression somewhere between thoughtful and brooding as he watched her. "I know kids need to be cared for," he agreed. "But you're just getting started here. You told me yourself how important it is that you make this job work. How are you going to manage a veterinary practice with a baby?"

Mel closed her eyes, drew a breath. It was possible that Nick was only playing devil's advocate. It seemed like something he would do. But there was an edge to his arguments that sounded more personal, more as if he was questioning how he felt about this little turn of events himself.

Her sister had just cast off her child as if motherhood were some failed experiment she had tried in order to find herself, much like she'd walked away from the beauty school Mel had anted up the tuition for, and the secretarial program she'd quit after two weeks. Mel didn't know what she could do to help her sister. She was beyond trying. But she could help her precious new niece.

She was already drawn to this child, its helplessness, its innocence. That pull was also a little frightening. But then, so was what she felt when she glanced up to find Nick warily looking from the baby to her and pushing his hands into his pockets.

As she met his eyes, she swore she could feel the fragile bond between them start to crack.

"I'm not sure at the moment," she finally replied. "But I'll figure it out somehow."

"So, you're keeping her."

She didn't know what to make of the note of finality in his voice. Or of the considering way he watched the baby stretch her pink terry-cloth-covered arms then flail them back to her chest. She didn't get a chance, either, to ask what he would do if the tables were turned.

The long, low blast of a marine whistle drifted on the breeze. It was the ferry's signal that it would leave the dock at the town's only pier in two minutes. There was something terribly final about that sound, but Mel had no time to consider just how final it was.

A big red Suburban had just pulled into her drive. Someone who had arrived in a white SUV was already knocking at her door.

Nick turned toward it, a muscle in his jaw jerking. "It looks like Maddy with the mayor's wife," he said, glancing out the window on his way. "The Suburban belongs to T.J."

Mel's first thoughts were that T.J.'s timing wasn't the greatest, and that the local gossips were the last people on earth she wanted to see just then. Her next was that she didn't have a thing to offer company.

She needn't have bothered to worry. Nick no sooner opened the door than a cake box and a casserole were followed in by the redheaded Maddy from the café and the polished and decidedly curious Winona Sykes, the thirty-something mayor's wife and owner of the local real estate office. T.J. was fast on their heels, her wildly curly auburn hair flying as she blew through the door with the damp air and a tofu-and-garbanzo-bean pâté.

The women were all talking as they came in, telling Nick how frantic everyone had been and how glad they were that they were all right when Winona, who everyone knew as Winnie, noticed Mel moving from behind the coffee table. Specifically she noticed what she was holding. T.J. and Maddy were a split second behind.

As if a bell had rung, all the women turned from where Nick stood with his hand on the open door and headed, arms out, for the suddenly fussy baby.

T.J.'s green Save the Whales sweatshirt nearly matched the moss green of her eyes. "Who is this?" she asked, those gentle eyes smiling.

"Oh, I know you," Winnie cooed, stroking a little arm.

Maddy, grandmother of four, handed her coat to Nick and slipped a hand over the little back. "Can I hold her?"

Mel felt her niece leave her arms even as she opened her mouth to respond.

"There, there," Maddy soothed, bouncing the baby lightly as she settled her against the shoulder of her white blouse. "What's the matter, sweetheart?"

Shrugging off her coat, too, Winnie moved behind Maddy to get a better look. Winnie had three children of her own, all in high school. "She sounds hungry."

"I think she sounds wet," Maddy replied

"How old is she?" T.J. asked.

"A month."

T.J. looked from Mel to Maddy. "No one said who she is."

Glancing from the women cooing over the baby, Mel took a deep breath and looked back to Sam Edwards's willowy, rather bohemian wife. T.J. Edwards had a huge heart, a kind heart. It was she who had approached her within hours of her arrival to welcome her and to tell her about the animals she rescued and the pups she had found. The pups Mel had lost.

Thinking about how those pups weren't where they were supposed to be made Mel's heart sink even further. "She's my niece," she said, hoping T.J. wouldn't ask about them now. "She's going to be living with me."

Winnie was pushing up the jacket sleeves of her navy-blue pantsuit when her head popped up.

"Living with you?"

Mel could practically see the woman's antennae rise through her stylish wedge of glossy brown hair. She was more concerned, however, with Nick. He had pulled the door open again. But instead of walking out as she'd had the horrible thought he might do, she saw Sam walk in, saying that his partner had just taken his flight for him, then warned that the reporter from the *Harbor News* was about a block behind.

Nick clearly looked relieved to no longer be the only male. Beyond that, Mel could only guess what was going through his mind as the women waited patiently for her response.

"Is your sister going to live here, too?" Winnie asked when no answer was immediately forthcoming. "Maddy and I met her when she was here last week," she said to T.J. "Her and the baby. Striking girl," she hurried on to say to Melissa. "That was the day your plane went missing. She was in the café asking if anyone knew you and when you'd be back. I guess she'd been waiting on you for hours."

"She told me she left a phone number on your door for you to call," Maddy offered, since it was her café her friend was talking about. "She left it with me, too, in case I saw you. Last I saw of her that night, she was getting on the last ferry to Seattle. I gave the number to Sam when we heard your plane had gone down so he could call her. But she never said a thing about coming back to stay."

"So where is she?" Winnie asked, looking around as if she expected Cam to walk in from another room. "Will she be working for you in your office? You know, Hannah Baker used to work for Doc Jackson," she continued before Mel could even open her mouth. "She's working part-time at the market, but I'm sure if you need her to get your sister familiar with the files or whatever, she'd be glad to come in for a while."

"Hannah is very efficient," Maddy said helpfully.

Mel glanced toward Nick, who stood beside Sam, who was eyeing the food the women had dropped off on the coffee table. The look he gave her had a hint of understanding in it, as if he now got what she meant about how talk could quickly get out of hand. The women, pleasant and helpful as they were trying to be, were light-years off in their assumptions.

The reality of what was going on had Mel shaking her head before the assumptions could go any further.

"My sister isn't staying here. She…has other plans," she decided to say. "It'll just be Morgan. But if she wants to help in the office in a few years," she added, skimming her finger over the baby's soft head, "I have no problem with that.'' She smiled, hoping they could leave it at that. ''Would any of you like coffee? I can—''

Winnie's jaw had dropped. ''You mean, she just…left her?''

Mel hated how that sounded. ''It's complicated,'' she murmured, though it truly wasn't. Her sister had done exactly what the mayor's wife just said.

''What will you do if she wants her back?''

The thought hadn't occurred to Mel. As well as she knew her sister, the prospects of Cam wanting something she'd cast off were roughly the same as a snowball's chance in Hades. Still, Winnie's question made Mel realize that the possibility that Cam would one day come to her senses and want her child did exist.

Because Mel could see nothing encouraging in Nick's carved features, she focused on the concern in Maddy's. ''I'll do whatever is best for Morgan.'' She couldn't deal with how she would feel under such circumstances. Not now. Not with everything else that was going on. ''She's who counts here.''

An odd sort of consideration crossed Winnie's face. She was a pleasant-looking woman, neat, polished. But there was a judgmental look about her that made Mel rather nervous.

That judgment seemed directed at Cam, however, not at her.

''That explains why she was acting the way she was,'' the woman announced, accusation heavy in her tone. ''She never let on why she was here, but she was sure upset that you weren't.'' She shook her head in disgust, the neat ends of her hair swinging. ''And to think I felt sorry for her,'' she muttered.

''I do feel sorry for her,'' Mel defended softly.

Winnie had the grace to look uncomfortable. ''Well, of

course you do," she replied. "She's your sister. And blood's blood. But my feelings toward her have nothing to do with you. As far as I'm concerned, this little one is lucky to have you. It's not everyone who'd take on a newborn," she pronounced, cocking an ear at the sound of another vehicle pulling into the drive. "Lord knows I wouldn't know what to do with another one.

"Now," she continued, lowering her voice as she gave a meaningful nod toward the door. "That'll be a reporter from the *News*," she confided, obviously having caught what Sam had said. "Mike Tilley is okay, but if it's Josie Heber, don't say anything around her you don't want to see in print."

"Oh, she's not that bad," Maddy countered. "She just can't seem to get a quote straight is all."

"Well if you're getting paid to repeat something, you ought to at least get it right."

T.J. gave Mel a sympathetic smile. She was obviously accustomed to everyone knowing everything about everyone else. "Would you like me to put the food in the kitchen and set out some plates?" She nodded toward Sam, who was eyeing the bakery box Maddy had brought. "Maddy's pies are famous. And my husband is starting to salivate."

"Would you?" she asked as Nick opened the door again.

The reporter was obviously Mike. The short, balding guy in the lumberjack plaid shirt was apparently also the paper's photographer. He had a camera bag over his shoulder, and the first thing he did after shaking hands with Nick and Sam and thrusting his hand toward her was look around the room for the best light.

Still holding the crying baby, Maddy stated the problem was definitely the diaper.

Mel glanced back toward Nick. Any chance of getting him alone now seemed as remote as their forest. "Go ahead," he said, "I'll take care of this."

"So," Maddy whispered to her as she nudged her into the hall. "What do you think of Nick?"

That was easy. "He saved my life. I think he's great."

Maddy's eyes glittered. "Of course you would. But I mean, if he hadn't, what would you think of him then?"

"She wanted to fix you up with him," the chatty Winnie confided, looking at the white wicker twin bed Mel had slept in since she was twelve. The comforter Maddy laid the baby on was considerably newer. "You better put something else under that baby," she suggested to Maddy. "Something rubber. Where are her things?"

Desperately grateful for the change of subject, Mel picked up the cartoon-animal-print diaper bag beside the decidedly secondhand infant carrier. The clothes inside were clean, as were those the baby wore, but there were few of them. There wasn't much of anything else, either. Six disposable diapers, a couple of plastic bottles and a few cans of baby formula.

"This baby could use some diaper cream," Maddy announced.

"There isn't any in the bag," Mel said, heading into her little bathroom for a clean washcloth. "What can we use until I get some?"

"Cornstarch."

"I don't have any."

"She's going to need powder and baby soap, too," Winona announced, looking into the bottom of the empty bag. "And shampoo. And some more sleepers." The bag landed by the carrier. "I'll be right back. The drugstore closes in half an hour. What else do we need?"

"Baby wipes," Maddy said.

"Got it. I'll stop by Candace Johnson's house, too. She has all those baby clothes her little girl has outgrown. She told me the other day she doesn't know why she's even keeping them."

"As long as you're there, run by my daughter's and ask if we can borrow her old bassinet."

"Give me an hour."

The mayor's wife on a mission was a sight to behold: color bloomed in her cheeks; her eyes brightened. It was no wonder she chaired so many local committees. Energy fairly leaked from her pores.

"Wait!" called Mel from where she was observing the diapering process. Except for a hint of diaper rash, her niece had beautifully unblemished skin and healthy little fat rolls at the tops of her thighs. Whoever had cared for her had cared for her well. "Let me give you some money for the drugstore."

Looking totally affronted, Winnie whirled around in the doorway. "Don't you dare. This is my treat," she informed her. "We help each other out around here. Just like you're doing with your niece," she concluded, and with that she slipped right past T.J. and was gone.

"Don't mind Winona," Maddy calmly said, snapping up the pink terry cloth sleeper. "She's as opinionated as they come. But she's always there when you need her. Here you go."

She held up a much happier little girl, but her own eyes were serious as she handed Harbor's newest resident over to her aunt. "I am inclined to agree with her, though."

"My sister's not a bad person," Mel quietly said. "She's just had it kind of rough."

Maddy shook her head. "I'm not going to attack your sister. I was talking about the baby being lucky to have you. But as far as your sister goes, just because a woman can give birth doesn't mean she has the instincts. It looks like you have them, though. What do you think, T.J?''

"Sure looks like it to me," she said, smiling at the way Mel held the baby back slightly, cupping her head so she could see her face.

Blue eyes blinked up at her aunt, the tiny mouth opened in a huge yawn. From the sleepy way her eyes drifted closed, it seemed a safe bet that her mom had fed her sometime before Mel had arrived.

T.J. held up her hands. "My turn to hold her. They need you in the other room. Mike wants a picture of you with Nick."

"I'll go cut my pie," Maddy said, scooting past them.

"There's not much left to cut," T.J. called over the ring of the phone, which competed with the ring of the doorbell.

"Then, I'll get the phone," Maddy called back. "You go take care of what you need to, Melissa."

Nick had assigned himself door duty. As Mel entered her crowded living room, she saw him opening it yet again. It struck her that he looked very much as if he belonged right where he was, dominating the room with his quietly powerful presence, talking to people he knew far better than she did.

The woman at the door was the florist from the end of the street. She'd closed her shop early to come by with her teenage daughter, a lovely bouquet and a plate of cookies. Right behind her, came one of the clients she'd stood up, bearing a bean dish, and the chief of police, who had heard from his dispatcher that Nick and the new veterinarian had arrived safely.

"Melissa?" she heard Maddy call from her kitchen. "It's a Ranger Wyckowski."

Standing beside Nick, her hand outstretched to welcome her guests, Mel felt her smile falter. The chief, a man whose gruff voice belied his easygoing manner, just wanted to say welcome back, glad everything turned out all right and to introduce himself to her, since he hadn't met her yet.

He, like everyone else, wanted to know what had happened, how they had survived.

Nick must have caught her consternation as she called to Maddy that she would be right there, then turned back to ask the sheriff if he would excuse her for a moment. She felt the familiar touch of Nick's hand on her arm, drawing her eyes to his.

He knew how worried she had been about the little coyotes. He knew she'd worried, too, about the effect losing them would have on her relationship with those running the relocation program.

"It wasn't your fault," he quietly said. "I'll talk to him myself if you need me to."

Touched by his offer, she whispered a quiet, "Thanks," a faint smile curving her mouth. Until she had met him, the concept of sharing a problem with someone actually involved in it had been totally foreign to her. That kind of sharing was definitely something she could grow accustomed to. Yet, as reassuring as it was to know she had backup for this particular problem, she had the awful feeling she would soon be left to fight her battles on her own once more.

She headed for her cheery little kitchen with a knot the size of a fist in her stomach. Behind her she could hear Nick answering the chief's questions, telling him and everyone else the same things they had told the reporters that morning and omitting everything they had omitted before.

There was only one change to the story that had started

with Nick noticing engine problems and ended with them approaching a ranger closing a road for the winter. She made that change herself within moments of hanging up from the ranger, who had admitted being so annoyed at being stood up that he'd fired off an angry e-mail to the head of the program the next morning—only to retract it when he learned hours later that her plane had gone down.

"They know where the pups are."

Conversation stopped, all heads turning to where she stood in the kitchen doorway, trying not to grin like an idiot. "They picked up the signal from the tracking devices they had me implant. The ranger said both pups are still together and that they've worked their way to a lower elevation." The smile grew, anyway. "They have as good a chance of making it through the winter there as they would anywhere else."

T.J.'s expression mirrored her own. From across the room the reporter immediately wanted to know who she'd just spoken with and how to spell his name. But it was Nick who held her glance. A smile moved into the depths of his smoke-gray eyes.

He felt truly pleased for her. She could feel it as surely as she did the quick and urgent need to throw her arms around his neck because she was so pleased and relieved herself. But his encouraging expression lasted only long enough for her to wonder what he would do if she did. In the space of seconds the warmth faded.

His glance had just shifted to the baby nestled against T.J.'s shoulder.

The crack in the bond felt as if it grew a little wider. Though he spoke with her as easily as he did everyone else when conversation picked up again, Nick seemed to consciously keep his eyes from lingering on hers too long, and to keep from touching her. Even when Mike asked them to stand in front of the bookcase in her living room for the picture that would appear on the front page of next week's edition of the *Harbor News,* Nick kept his hands in his pockets.

No one watching seemed to pick up on the tension she could feel snaking between them. Conversation flowed, right along with the curiosity, the concern and the coffee someone had made and started serving. But Mel felt that tension toy with the nerves in her stomach every time their eyes would meet, and he would slowly look away.

That unease underscored a faintly overwhelmed sensation at all that was happening. She couldn't believe how everyone had pitched in, taken over, helped. Winnie returned and immediately enlisted the aid of the nearest men to bring in boxes of baby clothes and a lovely white wicker bassinet. The clothes needed to be washed since they'd been stored for a while, so Maddy started a load before she apologized for having to run before the dinner crowd arrived at her café. T.J. had to go, too, since she had children to pick up at her mom's, so she laid the sleeping baby on a fresh pillowcase Mel put in the bassinet and left with Sam. Winnie left twenty minutes later, after promising to pop by tomorrow. Behind her went the florist and her daughter, the latter of whom offered to baby-sit any night but Friday. That was movie night at Harbor's only cinema.

Within the hour everyone else was gone. Everyone but Nick and her and the baby Mel could hear stirring in the bassinet now in her bedroom.

Nick had just closed the door behind the chief. Turning, he plowed his fingers through his hair and looked to where she stood by the hall.

Torn between whatever he was going to say and the

need to pick up the baby, who undoubtedly now wanted to be fed, she glanced from him to the door of her room.

"Go ahead," he said, as he had so many times that evening when the need for her presence had been divided. He nodded toward the kitchen. "I need to make a call, anyway. Mind if I use the phone?"

Chapter Eleven

"I know. I thought I'd stay until tomorrow, but I just checked and there's a 9:40 flight out of Seattle. If you can take me tonight, that might be easier for you than taking me ahead of your other flights at four in the morning. Yeah," Nick said, pausing. "If you wouldn't mind, I'd really appreciate it. Just fax me the stuff you need for the insurance claim. And tell T.J. thanks for letting me borrow you tonight, too. Sure. I'll be ready."

Mel glanced at the digital clock on her nightstand. It was 6:43.

For the past few minutes she had sat on the edge of her bed, changing her niece's diaper and smoothing on some of the cream and powder the slightly overpowering Winnie had brought. While she had, she'd listened to the low, deep tones of Nick's voice as he'd called first an airline, then Sam and made his arrangements to leave.

She had always been a practical person. She had never

believed in fairy tales, her fantasy life was nonexistent, and the only miracle she'd ever experienced was animals giving birth. That was why she didn't know how she'd allowed herself to hope that he might have wanted to use the phone to tell someone he was staying for a while.

It had occurred to her the instant it registered that the thought was utterly foolish. He had started withdrawing from her the moment her sister left. Maybe even before that, she considered, but she'd been too thrown by what Cam had done to notice nuances.

She had known all along that he had obligations and plans away from Harbor. But her heart hadn't listened to her head. And now that he'd tripped over some of the baggage that came with her family, it seemed he couldn't wait to say goodbye.

He didn't even want to wait until morning.

He was near the sink when she entered the kitchen, his back to her as he added a glass to those someone had thoughtfully put in the dishwasher. From the utility room beyond her whitewashed table and chairs, came the soft drone of the dryer.

She hoped her smile looked natural enough as she set a bottle and can of formula on the counter and, hoisting the baby a little higher on her shoulder, reached into a cabinet for a bowl. Maddy had said just to heat the bottle in warm water.

"I usually wait a little longer to spring my family on a guy," she said, hoping her tone sounded natural, too. There was something to be said for baptism by fire for a man, though. It weeded out the faint of heart. "But you can't hold me responsible for half the town showing up. I never expected that."

Nick caught her smile, uneasy as it was, as she ran hot water into the bright-yellow bowl. She'd hung yellow curtains on her kitchen windows. A row of blue and yellow canisters sat near a ceramic coaster of a sunflower. It was dark beyond the windows, but inside her home she'd brought sunshine.

"That's just the way people are around here," he replied, thinking of how graciously she'd welcomed her unexpected visitors. Sunshine suited her. "I don't think you have to worry anymore about being accepted. I'd say you've been adopted right along with your niece." Picking up the can of formula, he gave it a couple of shakes and popped the tab on the lid. "How much?"

"Maddy said a couple of ounces but to give her more if she still seems hungry."

He checked the marks on the bottle, started to pour. "I guess they don't eat much at first, do they? It's been a while since my nephews were that small." Precisely hitting the two ounce mark, he set the can aside, twisted the nipple into place and set the bottle inside to heat. "How warm is this supposed to get?"

"Maddy said body temperature. If I can't feel it when I drop some on my wrist, that should be about right."

"So Maddy's your resource, huh?"

"Thank heaven." She wished he didn't look so natural doing what he was doing. He seemed just as comfortable with a baby bottle as he did a crystal goblet or the controls of an airplane. "I'd be okay if Morgan was a little Labrador, but we're sort of flying by the seat of our pants here."

"I have a feeling you two will be fine."

"As long as we have all of her surrogate aunts to fall back on," she concluded, glancing down to where the infant rested against her shoulder. The baby had Mel's finger tight in her little fist. Hungry, she sucked madly on the end of it.

From beside her, Nick reached over and skimmed his finger along the busy little cheek. "You would be fine even without them, Mel. I'm beginning to think there isn't anything you can't handle."

She watched him pull back, wondering at the thoughtful way he'd touched the baby, and at how sorely he over-estimated her abilities. But she had the feeling he wasn't talking so much about what she was capable of, as he was telling her what he couldn't help her with himself.

He had promised her nothing, except that he would get her safely home.

The need for a little self-protection nudged hard. "So," she said, keeping her tone deliberately light, "Sam is on his way?"

Nick's glance immediately faltered.

"Yeah," he said, scratching his eyebrow below the abrasion. Looking uncomfortable, or maybe it was restless, he turned to lift his jacket from the back of a kitchen chair. "I thought it might be better if I headed out tonight. You have a lot going on here, and I really need to get home."

She lifted her chin, felt her heart start to sting. "I know you do. And I know you have a lot waiting for you, too." She tipped her head, studying his handsome profile as he shrugged on the soft leather. He had never really favored his injured shoulder, but he still winced a little when he moved it wrong. "Just get it done so you can be happy, okay?"

Nick wasn't quite sure how to respond to that. His plans would take years. And it wasn't as if he were totally miserable. But the sound of a vehicle rumbling into the drive spared him any further concern about how very well she had come to know him.

"Sam's here," he said, at the quick honk of a horn.

Mel had known the time would come when they would

say goodbye. Known and dreaded it. Now that the time was here, it seemed there were a dozen things she needed to say to him. With him seeming so restless to go as they moved to the door, she focused only on the necessary.

"Don't forget to send me the bill for my room."

"Forget it. That was on me."

"Nick," she said flatly. "I told you I would pay you back."

"And I'm saying you don't have to. Do you really want to argue about this now?"

Maybe, she thought, if it would keep him here a little longer. "No," she replied, because if he wanted so badly to go, then that was what he should do.

"Good. I don't, either." He pulled a deep breath, blew it out as he glanced toward the door beside him.

"I know you don't want to keep him waiting," she said, hoping to make things easy for both of them. "So, thank you, Nick. Thank you for saving me. I don't know what I would have done without you."

Her smile looked soft and maybe a little sad. He hated that the sadness was there. He had the vague feeling that she might have saved him somehow, too. He just wasn't sure at the moment why that was. All he knew for certain was that he couldn't justify staying. Mel did what she had to do. She was doing it even now by taking on a responsibility he'd known she wouldn't refuse. He needed to do the same.

The need to get on with all that he'd put off merged with a strong and compelling need for a little distance. Her life was as complicated as his. Once he was away from her, he would have the perspective he needed. And he felt sure that once he was away, none of what he had gone through with her would even seem real.

"If it hadn't been for me, you might not have lost the

pups,'' he countered, wanting the sadness to go away. Reaching over, he skimmed the smooth skin of her cheek with his knuckles. "If I'd given it another minute, I might have been able to figure out how to pack them out with us."

"Another minute and we might all have drowned."

"There is that," he agreed, smiling. "I'm glad they've tracked them."

"Thanks." She smiled back. "Me, too."

The horn sounded again.

A heartbeat later she felt Nick's hands cup her face. Tipping up her head, he lowered his and pressed a kiss to her forehead. The feel of his lips was soft, bittersweet and far too brief before he drew back and stepped away.

"I have to go," he said.

"I know."

"I'll call," he said, because, right now, she was still very real

"That would be good." But it's what they all say, she thought.

"Take care."

Afraid her voice would crack, she swallowed. Hard. "You, too."

Nick's gray eyes were totally unreadable when he touched the baby's shoulder as if saying goodbye to her, too, then turned to the door.

He hesitated, his broad back to her, but before she could wonder what had given him pause, he turned the knob and stepped out into the cold autumn night.

Mel watched the door close behind him, heard the hurried beat of his boots on the steps. As the slam of a truck door echoed like a gunshot, she hugged the little girl who'd come to live with her just a little tighter.

* * *

Nick never called.

Mel thought little of his silence when the first few days came and went without her hearing from him. Though he was almost constantly on her mind, she knew how preoccupied he could get. Having been away for so long, he undoubtedly had more to catch up on than just the business he'd told her about.

By the fourth day, though, she missed him more than she could have imagined and began rushing for the phone every time it rang. The only time she didn't snatch it up was when she had company or was with a patient and its owner, but those latter occasions were rare since everyone seemed to think she needed time to recover from what Winnie called her ''ordeal'' before scheduling appointments.

It actually proved to be a blessing that business was slow. Between caring for Morgan, who wanted to be fed nearly every other hour and who fussed far less when she was held, and coming down with the cold she had tried desperately not to get, Mel had little time and less energy.

Her break from work ended abruptly the next week. The morning of her fateful flight, she had placed an ad in the local paper announcing that the clinic was again open and offering discount checkups to get clients in. Now she had at least five appointments a day, including surgical procedures of three canine teeth cleanings and two neuterings. It seemed that the Jennings puppies had matured and the little-boy dogs were marking everything they could lift a leg on, including the shoes of Mrs. Jennings's luncheon guests.

By the end of that week, however, anticipation no longer surged at the ring of the phone. What rushed through her at the sound was more a sense of disappointment waiting to be felt because each ring was a reminder that it might not be Nick. She knew he called Sam, because T.J. mentioned it in passing when she came over with her children to see the baby and get her cat its yearly vaccination. But T.J. never said that he asked about her, or in any way suggested he even remembered she was there. As much as that hurt, she tried to concentrate on the good things that were happening. Her cold was almost gone, and Morgan had started smiling at her.

By the time another week passed, the cold was history, Morgan had started cooing, and it had become painfully obvious that what she and Nick had shared in each other's arms had meant far more to her than it had to him.

The knowledge didn't make his silence hurt any less. It just made a good argument for why she should stop missing him when she would lie awake between ten- and two-o'clock feedings. After all, if he'd cared, he could have found five minutes somewhere to let her know how things were going for him. Since he hadn't, she supposed she should stop worrying about him. It wasn't as if she didn't have anything else to do. Yet, as rational as that conclusion was, he seemed to be constantly on her mind.

"You're drifting again."

"I'm sorry, Hannah." Mel shook her head, clearing it as she stuffed her hands into the pockets of her white labcoat and looked up from the appointment calendar on the clinic's reception desk. What she'd seen on the calendar hadn't registered any more than what her assistant had apparently just said. She'd heard that morning that Nick had come to see Sam. Knowing he was so near and that he hadn't even called, she hadn't been able to think of much else. "What did you say?"

"I said, don't forget that I'll be a little late tomorrow. I have to run cupcakes by the school."

Hannah Baker crossed her arms over the red and teal paw prints on her white scrub top. Straight golden-brown hair framed her freckled face. Tiny laugh lines radiated from the corners of her kind brown eyes. She never wore makeup, but managed to look sun-kissed even though Harbor hadn't seen sun in well over a month. "Did Morgan keep you up again last night?"

"She was great, actually. She went six hours between feedings."

"Good for her. Maybe she'll start sleeping through the night?"

Mel could only hope that would soon be the case, although she had definitely hit the floor in a panic that morning when she'd wakened realizing that Morgan still hadn't.

There had been nothing wrong. The child had simply still been blissfully sleeping. Mel had scooped her up, anyway, breathing in the sweet powdery scent of her and relieved beyond belief that her precious little niece was okay. She couldn't believe how quickly she'd become attached to the little bundle of energy. But, then, her heart seemed to know who it was supposed to love, so it took no time at all for certain bonds to form.

With Nick, it had only taken days, too.

"Is your cold coming back?"

"No. No," she repeated, shaking off the thought, forcing a smile. "I'm fine. Just a little preoccupied."

"As long as everything's okay…"

Mel magnified her smile, gave her a nod. Everything was okay, except that not thinking about Nick was next to impossible with him so near. "It is. You go on and I'll lock up. I want to get some paperwork done while the baby is still sleeping. And thank you, Hannah,'' she said, meaning it. ''I'm so glad you're working here.''

''Thanks. After ten years with Doc Jackson, this sort of feels like my second home. Now, don't forget—''

''That you'll be late in the morning,'' she completed. ''By the way, what kind of cupcakes are you making?''

''Chocolate. With sprinkles.''

''Chocolate?''

As Mel's eyebrow arched with longing, a knowing look flitted through Hannah's eyes.

''I'll bring you one,'' she told her. ''Better yet, the kids can have the cupcakes. Now that I know we share the same vice, I'll bring fudge.''

The way she was feeling with Nick so close, Mel figured she could eat the whole plate by herself. ''You're an angel.''

''I'll remind you that you said that when we're both trying to work it off our thighs.'' Patting a rather ample one, she gave a mock sigh and headed for the coatrack behind the filing cabinet.

From behind the waist-high counter of the clinic's tidy little reception area, Mel watched her assistant head for the door, straightening magazines on her way.

She had hired Dr. Jackson's old assistant within days of returning from the forest. Hiring her had been on her list of things to do even before Winnie's recommendation, since Dr. Jackson had recommended her himself. She would forever be grateful for what the woman added to her practice. Maddy had been right. Hannah was very efficient. She was also an excellent technician. The fact that she knew everyone and their pet helped enormously, too. But it was the way she'd automatically pitched in with Morgan that she appreciated most.

Mel couldn't afford to hire anyone to take care of her

niece during the day. She knew she would have to eventually, but for now, especially with Morgan sleeping so much during the day, she took advantage of the door separating the clinic from her living quarters.

Since the door to the clinic's infirmary opened into her hallway, she simply moved the bassinet into the hall during the day and left the door open so she could hear the tiny mewling squeaks and less delicate squalls Morgan produced when she awakened. When the baby was up, Mel kept her in her carrier in her office.

The arrangement worked fine for now. And for now was all Mel allowed herself to consider as she looked down at the calendar for tomorrow. With one ear tuned to the open doors behind her, she ran through what she needed to do in the next twenty-four hours.

Her first appointment was a follow-up on the Obermeyer cat that had been hit by a car and used at least three of its nine lives. Her next was a six-weeks check on a dalmatian litter, followed by a lethargic hamster and a speech on responsible pet care for Candace Criswell's third-graders at the elementary. Hannah was baby-sitting.

She also had a to-do list a mile long. But rather than think about repairs or errands, all she really wanted to do was get rid of the anxious feeling she'd had ever since Winnie had called to remind her of a chamber of commerce meeting and mentioned that she'd heard Nick was around.

Blowing out a deep breath, she crossed her arms and leaned against the sky-blue wall she would someday paint pale sage. She was considering banging her head against it to get thoughts of him out of her mind when the tinkle of the bell over the front door announced that someone had just opened it.

Thinking Hannah had forgotten something, she smoothed

the hair she'd woven into a neat French braid and straightened her white labcoat over her sweater and jeans. Her assistant didn't need to know she was losing it.

"Can we make that a double order of fudge?" she asked, turning around.

The smile that had started to form died on the way. Nick stood framed in the doorway, his hand on the knob.

She barely heard the cheerful tinkle of the bell when he stepped inside and the door closed out the cold air behind him. His tall, powerful frame seemed to fill the entire space, taking all the oxygen, making it suddenly difficult to breathe. The heavy black sweater he wore with his khakis turned his guarded eyes the color of polished pewter. His dark hair was neatly trimmed. The abrasions on his forehead gone.

"Hi," was all she could think to say.

"Hi," he returned, pushing his hands into his pockets.

"I heard you were here," she said, because silence threatened to be awkward. "Winnie said you'd come to see Sam."

"It's good to know the grapevine is still intact."

"It'll never die." She crossed her arms, tilted her head. The nerves in her stomach jumped. "I didn't think I'd see you again."

She saw his glance sweep her face. He seemed to be searching for something. Welcome, probably.

Afraid he'd just come by to say hello on his way back home, she couldn't quite manage it. Seeing him turned the anxiety she'd felt into an ache. So many things had happened that she'd wanted to share, but he hadn't been there, hadn't cared to call to hear. She'd lain awake at night thinking of how he'd held her, longing for him to hold her again. And now, with the longing fresh in her heart, she would have to start getting over him all over again.

"Is this a bad time?" he asked.

For what? she couldn't help but think. "I'm...no. I'm just getting ready to close. Is Sam waiting for you?"

"I drove over. I'm staying at the B&B a few blocks up." He took a couple of steps closer, stopping short of the counter separating them. "How's the baby?" he asked, apparently encouraged by the way her arms seemed to loosen.

"She's good. She almost slept through the night last night."

"You're managing all right with her?"

"We're doing okay."

Nick knew he should have called. He had started to. More times than he could count over the past week. But he had never quite known what he could say to her that would make sense, when he was struggling to make sense of everything himself.

He had thought when he'd left that what they had shared would recede into the background of days filled with legal hassles and meetings with accountants, mediators and investors. He'd known he would be spending whatever hours were left in those days with real estate people looking for a condo for himself and office space for his new venture.

The days had proved to be exactly what he'd expected, but the nights found him missing her spirit, her smile, her touch.

He'd simply missed...her.

"I'm not," he said flatly.

The concern that flashed in her eyes was familiar, and blessedly quick. It didn't matter that little changed about her protective stance. He couldn't blame her for being guarded with him. But if that concern was there, then there was hope that she'd hear him out.

"What's wrong? Are there more problems with your partner?"

"Actually, things are pretty much straightened out there."

"You got his name off your patents?"

"We compromised with some of them. But I'm okay with the agreement."

"There's a problem with your ex, then?"

"Haven't heard a word from her."

"Your mom is okay? Your sisters and their families?"

"Everyone's great."

"Then why aren't you okay?"

He rubbed his eyebrow, gathering courage when courage wasn't a trait he normally considered at all. "I'm not sure where to go from here."

The overhead light caught the shades of platinum and gold in her smooth, shining hair. Tiny silver butterflies glinted on her dainty earlobes. The first time he'd seen her, she'd looked like a bubbly teenager with her ball cap and ponytail bouncing behind her. Now, with her beautiful hair restrained in its intricate braid and the labcoat covering her small, slender body, she looked polished, professional.

In between he'd discovered a woman he admired and respected. A woman who had driven him crazy their one all-too-brief night in bed, who understood family, loyalty and responsibility, and who had taken all of his well-considered plans and turned them to dust.

The woman looking at him now simply looked confused.

"I'm afraid I don't understand."

A neatly organized desk occupied the long space below

the counter. Moving to the end of it, he looked from the secretarial chair that had been pulled away from the desk to where Melissa remained behind it. The need to touch her was like a living thing inside him. But the last thing he wanted was for her to pull away in case his touch was no longer wanted.

"I've taken care of everything in Denver," he said, keeping his hands tucked in his pockets. "I'm just not sure what I'm doing next."

"I thought you were going to start your new company."

"I was. But that's not what I want. I thought it was," he admitted, encouraged by the way her concern drew her closer. She was even with the chair now. Not much of an advance, but at least the barrier was no longer between them. "When I went back, all I wanted to do was get everything tied up as fast as possible so I could start getting those plans in motion. I didn't let a day go by that I didn't accomplish something toward getting it all done. But I kept thinking of you while I was doing it. The way you don't put anything off. How you don't walk away from anything." His brow furrowed, his tone dropped. "How you don't close yourself off."

"You make thinking of me sound like a bad thing."

"I don't mean to." He hesitated, the furrows growing deeper. "Thinking about you has just changed things."

It didn't seem to matter what life handed her. She simply dealt with it and moved on. So that was what he had done, too. Yet, as he'd immersed himself day and night in cleaning up the loose ends he had once so diligently avoided, he'd found thoughts of her overriding the end result he'd aimed for. In the space of weeks, she had become the reason he wanted it all behind him.

"Do you remember telling me that you knew people

who wound up bitter and alone because they shut themselves down?''

The guardedness he sensed about her seemed to slip a little more. ''We were talking about emotional armor.''

''Yeah.'' What he'd been thinking at the time was that she had needed more. He hadn't realized it was he who needed less. ''I have the feeling that's where I was headed before we got lost out there together. I thought I knew what I wanted. Only I hadn't realized what I really wanted until I saw you holding that baby.''

He saw her go still, but she didn't say a word. She did nothing as he took a step closer.

''That's what I mean by not knowing where to go from here. I've gone as far as I can to get my life in order without talking to you.''

He was stating himself badly. He was sure of it. ''Do you ever think about what we went through? All those long days?''

''Of course I do.''

The admission drew him closer. ''And the nights?''

Nick swore he saw longing in the delicate lines of her face before her glance dropped to his chest. ''Them, too.''

Her arms remained crossed. Now close enough to touch her, needing that contact, he stroked his fingers down her arm. ''Then I guess what I need to know is where I stand with you.''

Mel had felt her hurting heart halt when he mentioned the baby. Now it seemed to be beating double time. The small bubble of hope in her chest emerged before she could even begin to quash it.

''I think that would depend on what you have in mind.''

He must have found her response encouraging. Or at

least positive enough to slowly run his fingers down her arm again. The touch was light, tentative, testing.

"Sam asked me a couple months ago to buy into the airline with him and Zack. The offer is still open," he said, which seemed to explain why he'd been talking with him today. "If you think we have a chance together, I'll sell my patents and buy into it.

"I know you said you weren't looking for a relationship right now," he reminded her, needing to state his case before his courage ran out. "You said you were looking forward to being responsible just for yourself for a while. But now that you have Morgan, maybe the idea of having someone to share the responsibility with will rub off on you. I'm not trying to rush you into anything. I just think we owe it to ourselves to see where this goes. And by the way," he said, because he knew how she'd been hurt before, "I really don't care how much baggage comes with you. I figure if we can survive that forest, we can survive anything."

Mel sat down.

Looking worried, Nick crouched in front of her. "Have I read you wrong? Would you rather I just go away?"

The bubble of hope in her chest had worked its way to her throat. She'd thought he'd come just to say hello. Feeling a tad overwhelmed, unable to speak, she quickly shook her head.

"Then it's okay to tell Sam it's a deal?"

She swallowed, nodded.

"Good," he murmured, relieved, and threaded his fingers through hers.

Reaching with his other hand, he cupped her face, sighing inside when she moved toward his touch. "I really won't rush you. I promise. But you should probably know that I have a plan."

He always had a plan. The thought made her smile. One of those plans of his had saved them. "Of course you do," she said, finally finding her voice.

She touched his cheek. It felt smooth. As if he might have shaved just before he'd come to see her.

The thought made her heart feel terribly full. "And that plan is what?"

"Well," he said, tracing his thumb from her cheekbone to her ear, "We know we work well together. We know we can depend on each other. And we know we're good in bed." The motion of his thumb halted. "I was thinking that combination might make a pretty decent marriage."

A teasing light entered her eyes. "I thought you said no rush."

"I did."

"So the idea is to wait to see if we fall in love, is that it?"

"That's where the no rush part comes in. I figured you might need a while," he said, slipping his hand to the back of her head. He drew her closer, leaned forward to meet her. "I'll be ready whenever you are. I already love you."

The words were a whisper of warm breath on her skin a moment before his lips touched hers. The kiss was gentle, designed to let her know how very patient he would be. But the feel of her arms going around his neck and the way she sagged against him when he rose with her in his arms, turned gentleness to hunger and a faintly desperate need to make up for lost time.

Nick's heart was pounding like a racehorse when he finally carried his kiss to the corner of her mouth, her cheek, her temple.

Mel's heart echoed that thrilling beat. "Maybe we won't need the no-rush clause."

Holding her close, he touched his lips to her ear. "Why's that?"

"Because I love you, too."

At her admission, he raised his dark head. His gray eyes held hers. She could see more than hunger in the beautifully carved lines of his face. More than need. There was something in him now that looked very much like happiness.

The smile curving his mouth made her knees feel even weaker than they already were.

"You mean that?"

"Did you?" she asked, smiling back.

"Absolutely."

"Me, too."

He drew his fingers down her cheek. "Then, that just leaves one thing to decide."

"What's that?"

"Where do you want to go for a honeymoon?"

Catching him by the back of the neck, she rose on tiptoe, her smile scant inches from his mouth.

"Anywhere but camping."

* * * * *

If you enjoyed what you just read,
then we've got an offer you can't resist!

Take 2 bestselling
love stories FREE!
Plus get a FREE surprise gift!

Clip this page and mail it to Silhouette Reader Service™

IN U.S.A.	IN CANADA
3010 Walden Ave.	P.O. Box 609
P.O. Box 1867	Fort Erie, Ontario
Buffalo, N.Y. 14240-1867	L2A 5X3

YES! Please send me 2 free Silhouette Special Edition® novels and my free surprise gift. After receiving them, if I don't wish to receive anymore, I can return the shipping statement marked cancel. If I don't cancel, I will receive 6 brand-new novels every month, before they're available in stores! In the U.S.A., bill me at the bargain price of $3.99 plus 25¢ shipping and handling per book and applicable sales tax, if any*. In Canada, bill me at the bargain price of $4.74 plus 25¢ shipping and handling per book and applicable taxes**. That's the complete price and a savings of at least 10% off the cover prices—what a great deal! I understand that accepting the 2 free books and gift places me under no obligation ever to buy any books. I can always return a shipment and cancel at any time. Even if I never buy another book from Silhouette, the 2 free books and gift are mine to keep forever.

235 SDN DNUR
335 SDN DNUS

Name _____ (PLEASE PRINT)

Address _____ Apt.#

City _____ State/Prov. _____ Zip/Postal Code

* Terms and prices subject to change without notice. Sales tax applicable in N.Y.
** Canadian residents will be charged applicable provincial taxes and GST.
    All orders subject to approval. Offer limited to one per household and not valid to
    current Silhouette Special Edition® subscribers.
    ® are registered trademarks of Harlequin Books S.A., used under license.

SPED02   ©1998 Harlequin Enterprises Limited

Your opinion is important to us! Please take a few moments to share your thoughts with us about your experiences with Harlequin and Silhouette books. Your comments will be very useful in ensuring that we deliver books you love to read. *Please take a few minutes to complete the questionnaire, then send it to us at the address below.*

Send your completed questionnaires to:
Harlequin/Silhouette Reader Survey, P.O. Box 9046, Buffalo, NY 14269-9046

1. As you may know, there are many different lines under the Harlequin and Silhouette brands. Each of the lines is listed below. Please check the box that most represents your reading habit for each line.

Line	Currently read this line	Do not read this line	Not sure if I read this line
Harlequin American Romance	❑	❑	❑
Harlequin Duets	❑	❑	❑
Harlequin Romance	❑	❑	❑
Harlequin Historicals	❑	❑	❑
Harlequin Superromance	❑	❑	❑
Harlequin Intrigue	❑	❑	❑
Harlequin Presents	❑	❑	❑
Harlequin Temptation	❑	❑	❑
Harlequin Blaze	❑	❑	❑
Silhouette Special Edition	❑	❑	❑
Silhouette Romance	❑	❑	❑
Silhouette Intimate Moments	❑	❑	❑
Silhouette Desire	❑	❑	❑

2. Which of the following best describes why you bought *this book?* One answer only, please.

the picture on the cover	❑	the title	❑
the author	❑	the line is one I read often	❑
part of a miniseries	❑	saw an ad in another book	❑
saw an ad in a magazine/newsletter	❑	a friend told me about it	❑
I borrowed/was given this book	❑	other: _____	❑

3. Where did you buy *this book?* One answer only, please.

at Barnes & Noble	❑	at a grocery store	❑
at Waldenbooks	❑	at a drugstore	❑
at Borders	❑	on eHarlequin.com Web site	❑
at another bookstore	❑	from another Web site	❑
at Wal-Mart	❑	Harlequin/Silhouette Reader	❑
at Target	❑	Service/through the mail	
at Kmart	❑	used books from anywhere	❑
at another department store or mass merchandiser	❑	I borrowed/was given this book	❑

4. On average, how many Harlequin and Silhouette books do you buy at one time?

I buy _____ books at one time ❑
I rarely buy a book ❑

MRQ403SSE-1A

5. How many times per month do you shop for any *Harlequin and/or Silhouette* books?
One answer only, please.

1 or more times a week	❏	a few times per year	❏
1 to 3 times per month	❏	less often than once a year	❏
1 to 2 times every 3 months	❏	never	❏

6. When you think of your ideal heroine, which *one* statement describes her the best?
One answer only, please.

She's a woman who is strong-willed	❏	She's a desirable woman	❏
She's a woman who is needed by others	❏	She's a powerful woman	❏
She's a woman who is taken care of	❏	She's a passionate woman	❏
She's an adventurous woman	❏	She's a sensitive woman	❏

7. The following statements describe types or genres of books that you may be
interested in reading. Pick *up to 2 types* of books that you are most interested in.

I like to read about truly romantic relationships ❏
I like to read stories that are sexy romances ❏
I like to read romantic comedies ❏
I like to read a romantic mystery/suspense ❏
I like to read about romantic adventures ❏
I like to read romance stories that involve family ❏
I like to read about a romance in times or places that I have never seen ❏
Other: _____ ❏

*The following questions help us to group your answers with those readers who are
similar to you. Your answers will remain confidential.*

8. Please record your year of birth below.
19 ____

9. What is your marital status?
single ❏ married ❏ common-law ❏ widowed ❏
divorced/separated ❏

10. Do you have children 18 years of age or younger currently living at home?
yes ❏ no ❏

11. Which of the following best describes your employment status?
employed full-time or part-time ❏ homemaker ❏ student ❏
retired ❏ unemployed ❏

12. Do you have access to the Internet from either home or work?
yes ❏ no ❏

13. Have you ever visited eHarlequin.com?
yes ❏ no ❏

14. What state do you live in?
_____

15. Are you a member of Harlequin/Silhouette Reader Service?
yes ❏ Account # _____ no ❏ MRQ403SSE-1B

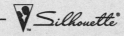

COMING NEXT MONTH